Disposable Lives

LESLIE KOHLER

Aquitaine Ltd
Phoenix, Arizona

This is a work of fiction. Names, characters, businesses, places, events and incidents are either the products of the author's imagination or used in a fictitious manner. Any resemblance to actual persons, living or dead, or actual events is purely coincidental.

Edited by Sally J Smith
Cover design by JD Smith Designs

Copyright © 2014 Leslie Kohler

ISBN-13: 978-0-9914843-7-9
ISBN-10: 0-9914843-7-1

www.aquitaineltd.com

DEDICATION

This book is dedicated to my parents, who always supported my artistic endeavors.

ACKNOWLEDGMENTS

I want to thank my friends and family who have supported my writing and given me endless encouragement—Cathy, Deanna, Auburn, Chayo, Barb, Chris, Heather and Nancy.
And I'd like to give a big shout-out to all my fellow Sisters in Crime-Desert Sleuths who have inspired me along my journey.

CHAPTER ONE

I AM NOT A PLASTIC BAG. A transparent piece of cellulose that can be wadded up and thrown away when no longer useful. I'm a college-educated woman who spearheaded a successful marketing career before retiring to the unwaged workforce of wife and mother.

I had scrawled those words onto an environmental shopping bag retailing for eight hundred ninety nine dollars. Why? I'd uncovered evidence this tote was a gift for my husband's lover. A childish act? Perhaps. But it felt damn good. Until my graffiti landed me smack dab in the middle of murder.

My fifteen-year old son, Ethan, stormed into the laundry room, which my two teens called my office. Relishing the tenth-story workspace with a panoramic view of California's Newport Beach I'd occupied at the height of my marketing career, I didn't find their humor particularly funny. But I'd made my choices.

"Mom, I can't find my golfing shoes. I have team practice today. Where are they?"

Knowing my usual, "Where you left them," had worn thin, I said, "I think I saw your shoes, or what was left of them, in Mazy's slobbering mouth. Now if you'd put them away like…"

Ethan darted out the door faster than his swing off the tee. I knew the dog hadn't chewed his golden spikes. Mazy was a thirteen-year-old boxer, too spoiled by years of pampering to even sniff at anything not labeled USDA Prime. But after

1

umpteen years of chiding my kids to put away their things, I sometimes resorted to dubious means to get my clan organized.

My son huffed back into my office.

"Mazy doesn't have them. I've looked everywhere. I've got to have them. You know how Coach is."

"Yes, I know he's a stickler for proper attire and being on time." I wanted to add, "Which is why you should have looked for the shoes earlier, particularly since school starts in ten minutes." But the nervous look on Ethan's face told me to stop. "Why don't you borrow your father's?"

"Sure. Where are they?"

I wanted to scream, "Where he usually keeps them! Haven't you two golfed every Sunday since you could stand?" But being a mom, again I held my tongue.

Tromping into the garage, I rummaged through Grant's golf bag in search of his shoes. They weren't in the zippered side pouches where he normally placed them after our rounds on the links. Thinking he may have stuffed them in with his clubs, I dug deep into the bottom of the bag.

I felt something stiff, prodded it, and heard a sharp crackling sound. Pulling this anything but golf-like thing out of the bag, I found myself holding a package wrapped in pink tissue paper. Attached to it, a card marked Bridget. And it was sealed with a kiss. Literally. The flap of the envelope sported a puckered print of red lips, the shade of lipstick looking suspiciously like my Candy Apple Red.

I tore open the envelope, not bothering to read the sappy pre-printed verse. My eyes blazed at the all too familiar handwriting at the bottom.

Bridget, you're the hottest woman I've ever met. As hot as the red lipstick I smacked on the envelope. Corny, but that's what I'd like to be doing to your sexy lips right now.

Your love…

Your love? Grant was my love. And I believed he loved me. I couldn't fathom… Ripping open the package, desperate to find what present was attached to this romantic card, I pulled out a clear, plastic shopping bag, adorned by the tiny designer label, Gitan. A plastic tote may not seem like a romantic gift. But with going green being all the rage, designers were cashing in by creating obscenely expensive satchels. These were being swept off store racks by wealthy environmentalists to store their fruits and veggies while they, or most likely their personal assistants, did their marketing.

During my last shopping spree, I'd spotted this particular Gitan at Saks Fifth Avenue. It sold for eight hundred ninety nine dollars. Either Bridget was out to single-handedly save the world from global warming, or she was warming my husband hot.

I held the Gitan to my face. My eyes grazed the plastic bag. A hazy image of porcelain skin framed by sable locks reflected off its mirror-like surface. I felt I was looking through a fishbowl. My world, which I believed had defined rules and boundaries, had suddenly become clouded—like fish swimming through their tiny castle in clear water until a closer look reveals the water is actually murky. Inhaling, I took in the synthetic smell of polymer, contrasting with a hint of my husband's sandalwood-scented Escada cologne. The aroma aroused memories…happy memories that now felt bittersweet. How could Grant discard those memories and do such a thing?

Shredding the wrapping paper and card in a fury, I tore at the overpriced Gitan, desperate to reduce it to useless shards of vinyl. But the artificial material, ironically proposing to save the earth, proved to be non-biodegradable—and indestructible as well.

I raced into the kitchen and grabbed a butcher knife from my granite counter. I raised the weapon, ready to slice into the bag. Ethan shouted, "Mom, what are you doing?"

My eyes locked with my son's. My shaking hand lowered the knife as I forced myself to slow my breathing. "I, um, was cutting off the price tag?"

"With a butcher knife? Looks like you're trying out for the next slasher movie. Let me know how the audition goes." Slipping past me, he opened the refrigerator and pulled out a carton of milk.

"I am not a plastic bag!"

"What?"

"I'm not some piece of shriveled-up plastic that can be tossed in the trash when deemed no longer useful."

"I never said you were." He poured himself a bowl of cereal and mumbled through the flakes, "Hey, Mom, what about the shoes?"

I stormed back into the garage, found them in the golf bag's back pocket, and handed them to Ethan.

I tried to expel the words, I am not a plastic bag, from my head, but they reverberated over and over until they seared into my brain.

I picked up the phone and speed-dialed Grant's office. Carmen, the blowsy secretary, who I thought had a snooty attitude and recommended he shouldn't hire, picked up.

"Leman Land Development."

"Hi, Carmen. It's Maggie. I'd like to speak to Grant."

"He's in a meeting."

"Can you please tell him I need to talk to him?"

"He gave me an explicit order not to be disturbed."

"I need—"

"Mrs. Leman, I'd love to put you through. But your husband gave me specific instructions. He said this appointment is critical to the company's future. Perhaps you could call back later."

I vowed to have a stern talk with Grant about his office staff the next time I spoke to him. Then I scanned the kitchen for an alternative weapon to execute the bag in a way that wouldn't traumatize my son. I snatched a black, permanent marker. Clutching the pen in my fist like a child learning to write, I scrawled these words in big, black, capital letters, I AM NOT A PLASTIC BAG!

Ethan looked at the marked-up tote and said, "I guess that

4

means you're not going to get a phony facelift like Mason Butler's mom. He said his mom looked like a plastic bag afterwards."

"No, I'd never get a phony facelift. But I'm going to find out what a certain phony is up to."

CHAPTER TWO

Unable to reach my cheating husband by phone, I decided to do the next best thing—call my best friend, Regina. Cool, calm, efficient. That was Regina. Not to mention sultry, stunning, with flaming-red hair that made men feel they were on fire, or so I've heard. And with brilliance to match her looks, she had the uncanny ability to blindside males quicker than a sailing boom. This talent proved handy when conducting her duties as a divorce attorney on behalf of scorned wives. Regina had heard every lie, excuse, and angle of opportunity in the book, and she could chew up a man and spit him out before he even knew he was on the menu.

I dialed Regina's private office line. "Mags, darling, what's up?"

What's up? How could I explain my horrific discovery? That my husband, whom I thought loved and cherished me even after my fortieth birthday, was cheating. Sure, with Regina's choice of career, she was privy to these types of stories daily. Somehow, I couldn't squeeze the shocking words from my mouth.

"I thought I'd call and say hi."

Regina, the proverbial multitasker, I could hear nails clicking lightning-quick across her keyboard.

"You didn't call just to say hi, Maggie. You're withholding. What's going on?" Besides being an expert typist, Regina possessed a sixth sense that told her when people were lying. Another trait that deemed her one of the highest-paid attorneys in our upper income, oceanfront town.

Picking up the marker, I traced over my words scribbled

across the Gitan, ominously darkening them. Particularly heavy on the word not. "Can't I call my best friend for the past ten years to say hi? The pal I've counseled and coddled through three divorces and more broken relationships than either of us care to count?"

In rhythm to her computer clicking, she tsked, "My, aren't we testy this morning? I was simply making the point that you're usually so busy. Whether playing golf, perfecting yoga stretches, or mom stuff, you never simply call to say 'hi.' And please don't tell me your New Age muscle elasticity has sent your sex life through the heavens. Because if it has, I'm jealous."

"Regina. Grant's having an affair."

The clicking stopped. "What?"

"I said, Grant's having an affair."

"Maggie, you've heard one too many of my war stories."

"Personal or professional?"

"Take your pick. But, Maggie, Grant couldn't be having an affair. He loves you. I'm not talking about after the trust fund, trophy-wife—although you're lovely enough to be one—faked love. I'm talking about old school, honest love."

I gasped. "Who is this? And what did they do with my friend, Regina?"

"Too funny. I believe Grant loves you. And there was a time I believed in love. Although I fear that memory has now been reduced to a mere flicker. I'd give it another two months, or my next four boyfriends, before my vision of romance is permanently extinguished."

The distant buzz of an intercom voice came over the line.

"I'm sorry, Hon. My next appointment is here. Poor thing, right after she agreed to cancel the prenuptial, she learned her newlywed husband was a transsexual transvestite. Gotta go."

A trans what? Regina's client tales never failed to astound me. And now I felt I was living one.

But Regina's words, flicker, permanently dimming, with their reference to fire, sparked an idea. I rummaged through the kitchen drawer and pulled out a candle lighter. Thumbing the switch, I ignited the flame, and held it under the bottom of the over-priced lover's bag. A thin stream of blue, topped with burning orange wavered, curling the plastic, causing it to crumple in upon itself. I stared at the small spot of permanently destroyed vinyl with morbid satisfaction.

A sudden shriek tore me from my thoughts. "Put that lighter down now. What do you think you're doing? That's a Gitan!"

I thought I'd been busted by the fashion police or in-home arson patrol. But it was my daughter, Avery, staring at me as if I'd just committed a capital crime. I guess to a fourteen-year-old who could only name twenty-five of the forty-eight contiguous states, but could identify fashion designers with one-hundred percent accuracy, setting fire to a Gitan was cause for execution.

Rushing across the room with a zeal I prayed she would one day apply to her studies, she snatched the bag from my hands and stuck it under the kitchen faucet. A sizzle of steam wafted. "Mother, what's come over you? Do you know what these bags retail for?"

I mouthed a sarcastic, "Eight hundred ninety nine dollars."

"Yes. And they're on back-order. You can't even get them off the Internet. Look at its design. It's personalized!" she said, pointing to my childish scrawl. "I've never seen one like it."

"If you like it so much—"

Throwing her arms around me, she squealed, "Thanks, Mom. I love it. And this burnt spot. Ooh, talk about urban authenticity." And she raced from the room, water dripping from the pathetic-looking bag like a dead body seeping blood.

I'd made my daughter happy. But I hadn't meant to give her the satchel. I wanted to finish it off for good. What I started to say to Avery was, "If you like the bag so much, you can channel your energy into getting a job and buying one for yourself." But the teen-aged years are fleeting, and she flitted out of the room with my intended victim quicker than I could react.

I wouldn't be so slow with my next move.

CHAPTER THREE

I dressed in my usual golfing garb. Collared polo shirt, top buttons naughtily open. Silk Bermuda shorts rising high on my thighs. Cotton sweater draped across my shoulders, strategically hugging my bosom.

My choosing to stretch the rules of what was considered acceptable dress at my country club might sound shallow, perhaps vain. But if I dressed as a model member every time I hit the links, baggy shorts hanging past my knees and shirt buttoned to my throat, I'd feel like a middle-aged woman who had a husband catting around. By spicing up my golfing get-up, I felt like a desirable female with a mean swing. My birth certificate stated my age to be forty-one, but people usually said I looked closer to mid-thirties. Although I don't know what good this did me. I still had a husband who was cheating on her. But at least I looked damned good worrying about it.

I drove my silver Mercedes 350 through the guard gate of Newport Hills Country Club. Swinging around the circular entrance, I stopped next to the Adonis valet. Opening my door, he greeted me, "Good day, Mrs. Leman. Do you need me to remove clubs from your trunk?"

"No thank you, Coleman. I'm not playing today. Just lunching."

"Very well. Have a nice meal."

I strolled past the waterfall trickling down the stone wall leading to the entrance. The water sounded like a serenity tape from yoga class. I tried to concentrate on the soothing sound of its waters. But my pulse refused to slow its pace to the slow-moving rhythm. I looked dressed for a casual golfing lunch, but my purpose being here was of a much more pressing nature—to find information on Bridget.

I whisked through the entry lounge, its over-stuffed furnishings accented in shades of ocean blues. A massive limestone fireplace, rarely lit, dominated the room. Southern California's balmy climate didn't warrant many nights of burning a fire.

Entering the dining area, again I was warmly greeted by the staff. "Mrs. Leman, how nice to see you. And you will be dining with…?"

Dining with? Oh my God. I forgot to call somebody to meet me for lunch. I hated eating at a restaurant alone.

I cleared my throat. "I'm meeting Regina Evans. At least I hope I am. Her cell cut out just as we were confirming. With her busy law practice..."

"I'll keep an eye out for her."

"Please do. I'm certain she can make it."

With a shallow bow, he murmured, "Please follow me."

After being seated, I pretended to study the menu. Between lunching with girlfriends, meeting Grant for dinner, or downing cocktails *après* golf, I had the selections committed to memory. But I wanted to look like I was doing something. I needed time to think.

I'd spent my professional years in marketing. Gathering statistics, trolling for information, weaving together every detail needed to garner strategies to raise the bottom line. Newport Hills cost two hundred fifty grand to join, plus seven hundred fifty in monthly membership dues. That wasn't chump change, even in this costly coastal town. And with more private clubs in the area than public schools, there was stiff competition for available clients.

This meant the club had to continually find new prospects while massaging the current members to keep them happy. God knew this establishment doted on my family like we were close-knit relatives. The club went so far as to send us a sympathy card when our cat kicked the bucket.

Because Grant hid the Bridget gift in his golf bag, my guess was this person belonged to Newport Hills. I needed to maneuver my way into the marketing office and get the scoop on this woman who drove my husband to steal my lipstick, apply it to his macho lips, and smack it onto an envelope. And, I knew the perfect person to help me.

CHAPTER FOUR

I set aside the club's lunch menu, about to begin my mission, when a goldenrod specimen of manly muscle sat down across from me. "Maggie, my darling Magpie. What are you doing, sitting here all on your own?"

I stared across the table at Todd Williams. The goldie-locked wonder boy with a bronzed tan who'd made a fortune manufacturing products designed to keep one's motorized vehicles pampered and clean. Purchase his car shampoo and conditioners, and you were guaranteed no dirt, smudges, or dried-out cracks in the cushioned leather of your seats. When Todd introduced his products a couple of decades ago, the public acted like they were the most important inventions of the twentieth century.

At that time I was a marketing intern at Todd's company. Though everybody raved about the revolutionary effectiveness of Todd's leather-care line, I attributed his success to the shirtless infomercials his company aired day and night promoting the product—and him. These spots featured twenty-something Todd sensually rubbing down the upholstery of a Ferrari in a pair of tight white tennis shorts, exuding the sexual appeal of a *Playgirl* model giving a high-dollar massage. Our marketing statistics showed every time one of these commercials aired, sales spiked seventy-five percent.

Todd smiled. "You look great, Magpie."

I leaned across the table to Todd, trying to ignore the musky scent when one's manliness slightly overpowers his deodorant. "Todd, we've been friends for how many years?"

"Long enough to have some sexy rolls on the beach in my

old sleeping bag."

"Ancient history."

He winked. "I love history. I read history books all the time. Well, when I *have* time."

Patting his hand, I murmured, "That's nice. It's good to hear you're doing something other than slathering oil."

"Nothing wrong with that. I like smooth surfaces. Whether it's the upholstery of one of my Porsches, or the beautiful body of a—"

"I get the picture. But Todd, how many times have I asked you not to call me Magpie? It reminds me of an ugly black bird sitting on a dirty statue in a bum-infested park. And I happen to know that Magpies disgustingly hold their food with their feet while they peck at it. Yuck!"

"Magpie, that degree of yuck may very well depend on the scenario. Now with your luscious black hair and milky skin, some California avocados squeezed between your toes…"

"Todd, get a grip."

He shook his head as if he were coming out of a daydream. "Oh. Sorry. A bit fixated. Another heart-wrenching breakup."

"Todd, your idea of heart-wrenching is your girlfriend learning your definition of monogamy is dating only one woman per night."

"Maggie, that was years ago. I've settled down."

"That's not what I've heard twittered about our club's spa."

"In the steam bath or jet pool?"

"Does it matter?"

"No. Just trying to focus my fantasy. So, these women are naked when—"

"Yes, Todd. They're naked. Lathered in sweat, breasts heaving, moaning your name."

"Maggie, stop. Not here." He swallowed hard.

I cocked my head. "What? I was just going to tell you their words."

"What…did they…say?

"That S.O.B. Todd Williams is such a player."

Beaming a wide grin, Todd quizzed, "They said that? About

me?"

"Todd, it's not a compliment."

"It is to me." Todd looked down. "But it doesn't ease the ache of my breakup."

"Even if the ache isn't in your heart?"

Todd laid his eyes on me like he was aching now. "For your information, there have been times in my life when I have been exclusive. Like when we were dating. God knows, the way we went at it, I didn't have the energy or the desire to be with anybody else. Whatever happened to us?"

"Todd, that was years ago. A lot of water under the bridge. Or should I say a flood of women through your bed?"

"I'll admit I've had my share of experiences. But to be honest, the numbers are inflated—no pun intended."

I rolled my eyes.

Todd laid his hands over mine. "Magpie, I'll let you in on a secret. The rumors were good for business. They added to my mystique. Hot guy, hot product. But the two of us—*we* were a sizzling team. Remember the time we experimented with my new line of oil in the back seat of the Rolls? God, Maggie, where did we go wrong?"

I pulled back my hands. "Todd. We've moved on. I'm married."

"Yes, right, uh…" Clearing his throat, he glanced in the direction of the waiter. "I think I could use a crisp Sauvignon Blanc. Care to join me?"

"No thanks. I have some business to take care of."

Todd lowered his eyes. "Business like megabucks? Or funny business?"

A loud clamor across the room stopped me from answering his ridiculous question. I looked over to see my husband entering the dining area accompanied by two men donning shirts that squeezed their midriffs a size too tight—flashing a bit of white stomach between gaping buttons. They sported dark, faux flannel slacks, too heavy for our tepid weather. Judging by their fashion mishaps, I assumed they were non-locals with poor fashion sense. But what really caught my attention were their raucous Scottish burrs resonating across the room. They not only looked like they hadn't signed the guest register, but also sounded like they'd just checked in at Ellis Island.

Strange, Grant never mentioned he'd be entertaining clients from overseas today. We didn't talk about all his business associates but often discussed the interesting or oddball ones. Like the man who couldn't commit to one of Grant's projects before consulting his psychic. While the medium was lulling the potential investor into a meditational trance, she was guiding his hand not across what he believed to be a Ouija board, but transferring his multi-million dollar assets. Between the psychic and greedy ex-wife, the poor guy ended up with nothing.

As Grant's lunch group passed by my table, my husband glared at me sitting with Todd. My first thought was, Oh no, I'm lunching with an incredibly gorgeous man that Grant knows is not only an ex-boyfriend, but also the first man I ever slept with. Damn.

Then picturing the puckered lipstick-stained envelope with its romantic salutation, I smiled. This is perfect. I'm schmoozing with one of the most sought after men in Newport Beach. I can't believe my, uh, Todd's timing. How does it feel, my cheating husband, to see me dining with the first love of my life? Let's face it, sweetheart, once you've had wild sex on the beach, it's hard to top it. Unless you have some Sex-On-The-Beach cocktails to go with it. But I was underage at the time, and my revved up hormones didn't need alcohol to enhance the experience.

Grant's voice jolted me out of my reverie. "Maggie, honey, I didn't know you were coming here today."

I gave a Candy Apple Red smooch to my pouty lips. "Why should you? You're not privy to everywhere I go." Then gritting my teeth, I said, "As I'm not always aware of your schedule, either."

Grant looked at Todd, then back to me. Stammering, he managed to say, "Well, enjoy lunch."

"Oh, Grant," I murmured, "the lobster's *luscious* today. I highly recommend it."

After Grant moved on, Todd raised his eyes. "I don't know what that was all about but say 'luscious' one more time, and I'm going to have to pull you under this table."

"Todd, my husband's less than ten feet away. How can you say such a thing?"

He leaned in close so I could feel his hot breath. "Very softly."

As I slid out of the dining room, I glanced over my shoulder toward Grant's table. The trio engaged in a hushed, yet animated conversation. Faces taut, shoulders hunched. The three looked like they were struggling to control their emotions in this hush-hush country club setting. Whatever the business deal, it was either a grand catch or one that had hit a major snag.

I headed in the direction of the club's marketing office. A former colleague Diana Hutchinson worked as one of the department VP's. I knew if Bridget registered as a club member, Diana would have access to her personal data. Address, phone number, probably even Bridget's dress size. I bestowed evil thoughts this wanton woman wore a size eight, compared to my five foot seven size four.

Glancing at a mirror hanging in the back hallway, I noticed my lipstick had faded. Wanting to appear put-together when I met with Diana, I slipped into the restroom to apply a touch-up. I traced my lips with Candy Apple Red and then twisted a wayward lock into the layers of dark hair that framed my porcelain skin.

When I was young, my mother would say I had skin white as snow and hair black as ebony—just like Snow White. She loved to read me the fairy tale. As I grew into my teens, I hated that look. I wanted to shine like the other southern California beach girls, with golden hair and bronzed tans. But my fair complexion didn't take to the warm rays, so I gave up trying. I'm glad I did. My skin showed none of the premature tanning wrinkles so many women in this area wore.

Looking at my reflection, I remembered the fairytale's words, "Mirror, mirror, on the wall. Who's the...?" Was Bridget the fairest? Or was I still Grant's Snow Queen? Had too many years of kids and marriage turned our love life frosty? Our sexual encounters always seemed satisfying. But maybe the fairy tale had faded for Grant. Was he tired of Snow White and now looking for something hot?

I pushed through the bathroom door and continued down the club's back corridor. My mind racing with lurid thoughts of my husband cheating, I scarcely noticed the man advancing my way. Our paths almost collided, and we experienced that awkward moment when two people move in the same direction, making it difficult to bypass the other.

"Excuse me," I muttered, stepping to my right.

Scooting in the same direction, he blocked my path. I tried to maneuver around him, but with each step, he inched closer.

He sneered down at me, exposing sickly brown teeth, fronted by a tarnished gold crown. He leaned his body into mine, hard. I could feel the sweat from his bristle-haired chest wipe across my face.

Sickened, I pushed back, sidestepped left, and scurried away. I could hear his jeering laugh follow me down the hall. Wiping my face with the back of my hand, a sour smell invaded my senses. Like a dirty bathroom that's been swabbed with a dirty sponge. I pulled out a tissue and tried to rid any evidence of this wretched man from my body.

The encounter lasted only a brief moment, but the effect was jarring. I felt violated—an open invitation to be taken advantage of. If this was his typical behavior in a public arena, I'd hate to see what would happen if trapped alone with this man.

I stopped. Wait! This creep wasn't an arbitrary stranger. He was one of Grant's lunch partners. What was my husband doing cavorting with this disgusting man? Grant always surrounded himself with people of integrity. I'd attended numerous business gatherings where the liquor flowed free as the ink on a newly signed contract. None of Grant's associates ever crossed the line. But this guy personified scum. What was going on with my husband? First, the love bag to Bridget. Now this low-life. Had Grant poisoned our fairytale life?

CHAPTER FIVE

I hoped Diana Hutchinson could help shed some light on what was happening with my husband. Diana and I had been marketing cohorts, or to be more exact, throughout the years, rivals. We worked together at Todd's company. Unfortunately, Diana had a crush on Todd, and was steeped in jealousy because I was dating the boss. I knew, because my coworkers didn't mince words when reporting how she seemed to take pleasure in backstabbing me. Now that I needed Diana, I hoped she no longer harbored ill feelings.

I stepped into the marketing office, finding a room buzzing with frenetic activity. Workers scurried between cubicles, trailing pages of tattered newspaper, barking into portable headsets. I'd been so distracted by Bridget that morning, I hadn't read the morning paper. What could be so important to push the marketing arm of our posh club into such a frenzy?

Diana rushed out of her private office, long legs pumping, and her mousy brown hair straggling in her wake. She burst into one of the workstations. I could hear her voice rising above the privacy partition. "Miles. You're my go-to undercover guy. I told you to kill this story. You said it was handled. Now this!" I heard the crumple, no crush, of what I suspected was a newspaper. My hypothesis was quickly confirmed as a ball of newsprint flew over the cubicle.

Diana then stormed back into her office. I inched through her door hoping her urge to throw things had passed. This probably wasn't the best time to approach Diana, but I had no choice.

I forced a smile. "Wow, looks like you're having a

nightmare of a day. Bet you could use some relaxation therapy from the club's spa."

"Boy, you aren't kidding. A massage would feel great right now."

"Hmm…something big must be going on."

"You wouldn't believe it. And Corporate. They think because you're a marketing exec, you're some magician that can fix everything and," Diana snapped her fingers, "make it go away."

I raised my eyebrows. "What do you mean?"

Dropping her voice, Diana confided, "I mean the suits expect me to cover up every dirty detail of their rich and spoiled members."

"Oh, geez, tell me about it. Remember the rocker who relapsed on his sobriety and paraded around the club naked when the press was all over this place doing national coverage on a golf tournament?"

"Ugh. Do I ever. Have you seen his reality T.V. show? The asshole's reincarnated himself. Now he's Mister Family Man, with a new wife a fraction of his age and kids young enough to be his grandkids. No, make those great-grandkids."

I sighed, easing into one of the leather chairs before her desk. "Now he was wild. It's unbelievable he's still alive."

"Yeah. But that guy was smart. He knew how to play the game and go for the money. But some of these members…are so…stupid!" Diana pounded her fist on the desk. "They don't have the brains to think before they screw up."

I nodded. "These people think because they bleed green they have a license to do whatever they please. What happened? Did a male member pinch a waitress's butt?"

"Worse."

"Carve golf cart brodies across the eighteenth green?"

"I wish. A member got himself murdered."

My breath caught in my chest. "Murder. I can see why you're so upset."

Diana clasped her hands. Laid her elbows on the table. "And this was not a nice scenario. Married, three young kids, found in a dingy motel room with his pants halfway down." She sighed. "A marketing nightmare. And now that the story's been leaked, the club's gossip fodder for the Newport Beach News."

"Tragic. Who was it?"

"Andrew Richmond. He's on a Platinum Membership. Been here about a year. Cute guy. I wouldn't have minded seeing him with his pants down."

My jaw must have dropped, because Diana waved me off. "Oh, don't be such a prude. You certainly weren't with Todd."

I thought, Jesus, is she still hung up on Todd?

"And I bet you're no prim princess with Grant, either." She lowered her eyes. "Not bad for your second choice."

I folded my arms. "First choice. So if you're not grieving the dead, why are you so upset? Mr. Richmond isn't the first member to behave badly."

"Yeah, but this one is bad, real bad." Her eyes grew wide. "The murder took place in Santo Reno."

"Santo Reno? What would he be doing there?"

"Getting laid, for one."

"But he could check into a five star hotel here. A three star. Anything would be better than Santo Reno. Talk about a mood killer."

"Apparently it didn't kill his mood. A maid happened upon the scene. Hysterical, she jabbered on about finding Richmond with two glasses of wine poured, his shirt off, and halfway there with his pants. And bam! A hole blown in the back of his head."

"My God, this is all in today's paper?"

Diana leaned forward, lowered her voice. A crooked smile crossed her face. "No. Just the major facts of the case. I have an inside source."

"You do? Who?"

"I'll let you in on this, but you have to keep it under wraps. Being former colleagues, we share a form of sisterhood. It'll only cost you a Ben Franklin."

"What?"

"Okay. Fifty."

I dug into my Michael Kors but came up empty. "You'll have to put it on my club tab."

"Will do." Then Diana glanced around, as if somebody might have sneaked into the room and was listening. "It's my cousin, Johnnie. Sometimes he's privy to juicy police info. Sells it to me for some extra bucks. He's helped me quash more than one delicate situation before it hit the papers."

"Your cousin's a police officer? And he's leaking privileged information?"

"He's not a policeman. He's what you'd call, uh, an extra pair of eyes and ears for the cops."

"A snitch?"

"One with friends in prominent places. Johnnie convinced the NB News to leave the pants out, er, up. Told them they'd be looking at an Obstruction of Justice Charge if they printed material the cops want withheld from the public. Miles was supposed to make sure Johnnie kept the entire story out of the paper, but he screwed up. And now thanks to him, the paper's also leaving in the fact they found an eco-friendly tote bag next to the body."

My eyes popped. "Tote bag? Did your cousin describe it?"

"Said it looked real cheesy. Made out of plastic. He couldn't believe how some female cop went on about it costing serious bucks. Go figure."

I swallowed hard. Then pressing ahead to try to learn more about Grant's alleged affair, I asked, "So it appears the motive for the murder was revenge on the cheating husband?"

Diana winked. "Possibly. But another fact you won't find in the paper is that motel went into escrow the afternoon of the murder. Odd timing, don't you think? And who'd want to buy a dilapidated building in that seedy town?"

"The murderer?"

"If so, why?"

CHAPTER SIX

My mind reeled with the sordid news of Andrew Richmond's murder. But I had to keep focused in order to bait Diana for information about my husband's mistress.

"All this excitement. What a far cry from my mundane life as a mother. You know, I've been thinking about reentering the job market."

"Oh, Maggie, you've been out so long."

I straightened my spine. "I realize that. That's why I could use your help. I heard there's a member here," I said, testing the waters of a white lie, "probably new to the club, who owns an executive head-hunting firm." Thinking of the kiss-stained envelope and the salacious card inscription, I wrung my hands, straining to get the words out, "Single, good-looking...I believe her name's Bridget."

Thankfully, with Diana's lack of people skills, she seemed oblivious to my stress. "Last name?"

"Last name. Oh. I can't remember."

"It's just as good, Maggie. You've been in my shoes. Or should I say heels?" Diana languidly stretched her legs across the expansive desk, revealing a spiky pair of Jimmy Choo's. "You know company policy—no divulging of personal marketing information."

"But you just told me the gruesome details of a murder."

"Hey, that's my cousin Johnnie's butt on the line. Not mine."

"But, I need to find this Bridget."

"Really?"

"Well, yes. I need a job."

"Oh, I see. The fairy tale trip down the altar heading south? You *need* a job?" Diana gave me a thin smile. "In that case, I can bend the rule—just a little."

Diana ruffled through a file drawer and pulled out several papers. She scanned the sheets and then set them down on her desk. Looking at me, she said, "Sorry, doll. No Bridget."

"Come on, Diana, how many new single female members can there be? Most people joined as a family. She couldn't be that hard to pinpoint."

"Well, there's nothing more I can do to help." Diana picked up a pencil and began tapping it on the table, as if to tell me she had more important things to do.

I held my ground.

"So, Maggie, you look dressed for golf. Did you play a round today?"

"No, just lunch. Funny, as I was leaving the dining area, you'll never guess who was being seated. Todd Williams. Poor thing, sitting all by himself. And looking very lonely."

"Todd? I can't believe it. I heard he had a girlfriend."

"Poor baby. Must have had a break-up."

Diana shot out of her chair. "I've been meaning to talk to him about upgrading his membership. Sorry. Gotta go." And she flew out the door.

I reached across the desk and grabbed Diana's papers. Scrolling down, I searched for members paired with the salutation "Miss" or "Ms." I found two. Snatching my cell from the pouch of my Michael Kors, I snapped photos of their names and corresponding data.

As I took my last shot, I heard the clicking of fast moving heels coming up the hallway. The tapping grew louder by the second. Frantically placing the list back to its original position, I knocked another stack of papers to the floor. I swung around the desk, swept them into my arms, and returned them to what I hoped was their correct placement. My heart raced faster with each staccato step.

Diana pounded through the door. I looked up and smiled. She scowled back.

"So, how'd it go?"

"It didn't. Todd was leaving. No time to talk." Pointing at me like an angry schoolmarm, she hissed, "I thought you said he was having lunch."

I shrugged my shoulders. "Maybe he's so heart-broken he lost his appetite."

Diana plopped into her chair. "I have a good mind to start docking him for the drinks I've been comping him." She sighed. "This morning's been a mess. I've got a lot of work to do." She stared at the papers laid out before her. Her eyes grazed over the papers I'd knocked off her desk, and then she stared up at me. "What the——?"

I bolted out the door. And into Todd's arms.

I hadn't seen him striding down the hall, and we crashed together like two heat seeking missiles searching for their target. A momentary entanglement of arms and legs ensued before I realized what hit me. It took another moment to drown the fire raging through my body, and the torrid images exploding in my brain. By the time I came to my senses and pushed away from his mountain of muscle, I felt I'd died, and my life flashed before me. Only these flashes were hot, and had nothing to do with death.

I'd seen Todd numerous times over the years and never felt such a thermal reaction. Even with all his merciless flirting. Was Grant's affair pushing me toward a dangerous path of fire?

A snide voice echoed in the hall. "Well. Isn't this cozy?"

I turned and saw Diana staring at the two of us, hands on hips, lips pursed tight. She spun around, disappeared back into her office, and slammed the door.

"Maggie, God, I'm sorry. I didn't see you."

"It's ugh…it's okay. I think you landed on my ankle." I gingerly pressed my foot down and started to hobble toward the lobby.

"Here, let me help you," Todd murmured, as he swept his arm around my waist. "Better?"

"Hmm. Todd, you know how you could really help me?"

"Name it, Magpie."

"There's a certain person I'm trying to locate. I have reason to believe she's a member of this club. A single member."

"Shouldn't be too difficult. There are only a few unattached women at this club. I know. I've checked them all out."

"I bet you have."

Todd hugged me closer. "Now, Maggie. I've been a good boy lately. I haven't even been to the club's monthly social mixer in ages. But now with my break-up…"

I stopped and stared up at Todd. "I didn't know they had monthly socials."

"Sure. First Thursday of every month. They're listed in the newsletter."

The first Thursday of every month! Recently Grant had business meetings he swore he couldn't squirm out of. And they were always at the beginning of the month. Did they fall on Thursday? If so, why was he attending social mixers at *our* club without me? Did Bridget attend these events? Grant used the club as a write-off, so the newsletter was delivered to his office. I never thought anything about it. Until now.

Todd and I limped our way through the club and exited the heavy front doors. He signaled the valets to retrieve our cars, eased me onto a cushioned bench, and sat down next to me.

"How's the ankle?"

"A little sore, but it'll be fine."

Todd lifted my leg onto his lap and began caressing my ankle in a slow, circular motion. I started to pull my foot back, but Todd's magic touch proved too inviting. Must be all those years rubbing down leather upholstery with exotic oil.

"So, Maggie, you said you wanted me to find someone."

"Uh, yeah, that's right." With Todd's pampering, I'd almost forgotten my purpose for being here. I pulled out my cell phone, and showed him the pictures I'd taken in Diana's office. "The names on this list are new, single members. I need you to check them out, see what they're like. You said the next mixer is coming up. Sounds like the perfect place to do it." Smiling, I added, "Help out an old pal?"

Before Todd could answer, an angry voice rang out. "Maggie. What are you doing?"

My head snapped. Grant hovered before us breathing hard, fists clenched, looking ready to throw a punch. In my shock, I forgot to remove my errant leg from Todd's thigh, and Grant's knuckles tightened as he stared at it.

Glaring back at Grant, I said, "What am I doing? Therapy. I twisted my ankle, and Todd was kind enough to apply first aid."

Grant stepped in closer, addressing me with clipped words. "Well, it doesn't look proper. Especially here."

"Don't lecture me about proper behavior."

Thankfully, Grant's business associates sidled up and corralled my husband away. The group exchanged enthusiastic handshakes and some requisite back slapping, and then traipsed off in the direction of the self-parked cars.

Todd resumed his therapy. "I guess I don't have to ask why you want me to do some snooping. Consider it done."

"Hey, Todd, if your business ever has a downturn and you're looking for work, I know the perfect occupation for you."

"What's that?"

"Massage therapist."

"Hmm, that could be fun. But only if you promise to be my first client."

Then I heard the powerful hum of Todd's Porsche as a valet swung his car around the drive. He rose from the bench, and in perfect rhythm to his masculine machine, Todd strode to his coach, California sunshine glistening upon his Golden Boy body.

CHAPTER SEVEN

I drove along the green-shrouded lane leading from the club. My mind reeled with the events of the day—my cheating husband, his environmentally conscious mistress, a dead golfer who was also a cheater, and a too-close encounter with the love of my past. My life normally ran smoothly, like an easy golf swing off the tee, sending my golf ball sailing straight down the fairway. But today I felt my life had taken a sharp slice, and I had no idea in which direction it was headed. I needed to sort through these sordid details and get myself back on course.

Grabbing my iPhone, I speed dialed Regina. "Thank God you're in."

"Maggie, you sound awful. I'm so sorry I left you in the lurch earlier. Are you okay?"

"Yes. No. We have to talk. You wouldn't believe what's going on."

"You said that Grant—"

"There's more."

"Oh, dear. Sounds like one of my days."

"Exactly."

A silent pause hung on Regina's end of the line. I knew she was checking her schedule.

"Maggie, I have a four-thirty this afternoon, but I should be able to wrap up by five. Why don't we meet for happy hour at The Shores?"

"Perfect."

Picturing The Shores, an ultra-swank oceanfront restaurant, which had been purchased by a group who'd started in South

Beach, I knew this would be an entertaining setting to meet my friend. The new owners had gutted the place, turning it into an open-air happening spot with a constant background salsa beat and wrap-around bar that served drinks more colorful than the blazing ocean sunset.

Glancing at my golfing attire, I decided I needed something more appropriate to show up at this restaurant. There were two types that frequented The Shores—business people wrapping up their day, and those looking for risky business to wrap themselves up in. Neither group dressed in shorts and t-shirts.

I could stop by my house and change into any number of designer outfits. But visualizing the price tag for the plastic Gitan bag Grant recently purchased for his Bridget, I decided charging an over-priced garb would prove more satisfying. Especially since my husband paid the credit card bills.

I swung onto the drive that fronted a strand of upscale boutiques, which sat along the bluff overlooking Newport Beach. I parked my car and stepped into my favorite shop, Kika's. The owner hailed as the scorned ex-wife of an aging box office star. When Kika's recently divorced husband married his barely legal-aged co-star, many people pitied her. But I knew Kika's ex had an ugly side. He was a raging alcoholic, and she was glad to be rid of the bum.

When I entered the store, Kika came to greet me and bestow me with hugs. "Maggie, it's been ages. How can I help you?"

I was tempted to ask for advice on cheating husbands and divorce decrees, but I checked my chatter. I still didn't know one hundred percent Grant entertained a mistress. My lamenting would have to wait.

"Kika, I'm meeting my friend Regina at The Shores."

Kika opened her arms, bright fabric swirling like a kaleidoscope. "Regina! Such a lovely woman." Kika gave a mock wink. "And a damned good lawyer. She saved my ass, if you know what I mean."

Aware of Kika's generous financial settlement Regina

battled for, I knew exactly what she meant.

"I'll give Regina your best."

After much prissing and primping from Kika, I settled upon a Carolina Herrera. Kika hung the ensemble on biodegradable hangers and draped it in cotton cloth. No rusting metal or landfill polluting plastic bags at this store.

"Oh, Maggie, I almost forgot. I have something fun you might be interested in." Kika directed me to a display in the corner of her shop. "With Grant's high profile in the eco-development business, a reusable tote would be perfect for you."

I stopped, no longer hearing Kika's words, paralyzed by a display sign that read: *Save Our Planet—One Less Bag At A Time.* Beneath it sat a variety of tote bags, some crude hemp, others awash in flowered patterns, along with ugly ones fashioned from clear, plain plastic. On top of the pile was a simple bag, distinguishable only by a tiny Gitan label. Seething, I swung at the tote, crashing it to the floor, along with several over-priced cousins.

I turned to Kika, horrified at my irrational behavior. "Oh my God, I'm so sorry."

"It's okay, Maggie. Are you all right?"

"I'm fine. I just have to…" Grabbing my purchase, I raced out of the store.

I ripped out of my parking stall, almost colliding with a recycling container placed along the curb. I roared down the road that hugged the bluff and then pulled onto the coastal frontage road. Spying the glinting sign of The Shores, I glanced at the time, and then slammed my palm hard upon the steering wheel. Damn. Four o'clock. Too early to meet Regina. I couldn't sit in a bar by myself, tap dancing my fingertips for an hour.

I wheeled past The Shores and headed to the one place I knew would center me. A place of beauty and peace. A place I had stayed away from too long.

I strolled barefoot along the shoreline, feeling the cool, packed sand slightly give way with each footstep. Every few steps a wave impeded my path, its chilly water lapping about my ankles. The seawater, filled with salt and tiny grains of sand, tickled my skin as the particles swirled about.

The late afternoon air hung thick with moisture like an old, familiar blanket. My mind danced with memories of family making the hour-plus drive to come to this beach and frolic along its ocean playground. Almost as soon as my dad pulled into a parking space, my siblings and I would spring from the car and sprint into the surf.

My family treasured those days in Newport Beach. We always wished we could live here, but my father's job didn't provide the kind of money needed to purchase a home in this pricey town.

I turned and made my way down the shore. As I neared the pier, I spotted a feeding hole named Chow Down's. Chow's had reigned as a late night locals' hangout since I could remember. I'd worked there during my college years, tossing chili onto greasy hamburgers and sallow omelets. Until I began my internship with Todd.

I snatched my new outfit from my car, ducked into Chow's cramped bathroom, and quick-changed my clothing. With my nouveau look complete, I exited my old haunt a formidable woman—ready to meet Regina, or whoever crossed our barstool paths.

All eyes riveted to the blazon-haired beauty as she sauntered through the pulsating bar. Regina's dress hugged the contours of her body like a silk stocking. With catlike prowess, she slinked past the congestion of patrons to my table tucked in the back.

A young man, late twenties, his suit bulging with biceps, followed behind. He pulled out a chair for Regina, and she slipped beside me. He took a seat next to her.

Regina clutched my hands as she gave me air kisses. The strength of her grasp surged with reassurance. "Maggie, my sweet. I can't believe Grant acted like such an S.O.B. Sorry to be so blunt. But I find it unfathomable that my dearest friend is suffering. You know I'm here for you."

"I know, Regina. You've always been there when I needed you. I feel better just seeing you. But," I raised my eyebrows in the hunk's direction, "who's your friend?"

Regina cleared her throat. "Oh, I'm sorry. Maggie. How rude of me. I'd like you to meet Jax, my new," her eyes darted to the muscled specimen, "legal assistant. Jax is going to be shadowing me to, uh, learn all aspects of my legal business." She lowered her eyes, letting her glance trace the contours of his body.

Jax, whose chiseled features looked carved from granite, sat unfazed by Regina's politically incorrect stare. But my friend could say, or do, whatever she wanted to a man and get away with it. Men were too mesmerized trying to get to her to realize they were being harassed. Or enjoying it too much.

Regina raised her hand with a slight twirl, and a male waiter appeared from seemingly nowhere. "Donovan, we'd like a bottle of Cristal. And please make it a seventy-four."

"Excellent choice. I'll pull it from the Proprietor's Reserve."

"Regina, I know you have expensive tastes, but reserve champagne? We're here to commiserate my marriage, not celebrate."

My friend sat up, thrust out her chest, tresses flowing over her shoulders. "Maggie, whatever is going on in your marriage, and, as a divorce lawyer I do want to hear the details, we are here to toast your indelible strength. A strength that's never before failed you, and I am confident will pull you through this mess. Commiserating is for the weak. And you, my dear, are not weak."

As if on cue, our bubbly arrived.

We clinked our glasses together. "To women."

"To *power* women," Regina added.

I raised my flute high. "And if we run out of "I Am Woman" toasts, we can drink to the evil fantasies we'd like to bestow upon Grant and his mistress."

We sat in silence for a moment. Breaking into laughter, we chimed our champagne flutes again.

CHAPTER EIGHT

Sitting amongst the moneyed crowd at The Shores oceanfront restaurant, I conveyed the dramatic events of my day to Regina. As the shocking and gruesome details poured from my mouth, I couldn't believe this was my life we were discussing.

When I got to the part about my run-in with Todd, Regina shrieked, "Todd Williams. Oh, God. Grant must have been fuming. Would be lovely to have seen that."

"Yes, it was very…satisfying. Especially the ankle massage."

"Oh, Maggie, please spill."

"There's nothing much to say, except it felt damned good. And of course, Todd always looks good. But you should have seen Grant's lunch partners." I shuddered. "Talk about tacky, and gross." I relayed their appearance, strange Scottish accents, and how one practically molested me in the hall.

Regina's smile faded. Her eyes sliced to Jax. He returned a subtle nod.

"Hey, what's wrong? So, they weren't Grant's usual business associates. It could be worse."

"It is. Maggie, I told you a lie. Jax is not my legal assistant."

"No kidding. So, you've found a new boy toy. Big deal." Wincing, I mumbled to Jax, "Uh, no offense, big guy."

Regina leaned closer, clasping her hand over mine. "It's not that. Jax is my bodyguard."

"Bodyguard!" I almost shouted. Catching myself, I lowered my voice. "What do you need a bodyguard for?"

"Protection. From Scottish Travellers. And it sounds like Grant's associates may be part of their clan."

"What on earth is a Traveller?"

"They're a bit like modern day gypsies, hence the name. But they're much more cunning. They used to run home improvement scams like shoddy roofing repairs. They'd con unsuspecting customers then flee town before the authorities could track them down."

"I have heard of them. But that was some time ago. What does this have to do with Grant?"

Regina scanned the room before continuing. "They moved up from traveling in trailers, to investing in them. They've purchased dozens of mobile home parks in recent years. Big ones that yield huge rental profits. And with land prices going through the roof, a park an hour west of here sells for over ten mill."

"Ten million? For a trailer park?"

Regina cleared her throat. "A *mobile home park*. Don't call them trailers. They hate that."

"But I still don't see what this has to do with Grant."

"The Travellers want to move up the social scale and become more legit. Or at least appear to be. Word is they're looking for high-end commercial properties to invest in. Like Grant's. And his reputation as a builder of environmentally sensitive dwellings would move them even farther up the ladder."

"But a bodyguard—why?"

"Why do you think? The Travellers want to kill me."

And in that instant, a foreign accent bellowed halfway across the room, "Regina Evans, I'm going to kill you!"

My head snapped so fast I felt tendons pop. Jax sprang in front of Regina, 9mm Beretta in hand. Regina tucked behind him.

Then sneaking a furtive peek from behind her body blockade, Regina gave a teasing smile. "Tinley, you bastard. How dare you startle us."

A model-faced man in a linen jacket and navy slacks strode to our table. He hugged Regina and then extended his hand to Jax. Ignoring the gesture, the bodyguard pushed his gun into his holster.

I weakly held out mine. The man pumped my hand. "Tinley Marks."

Regina folded her arms. "Yes, Tinley, the Tin Man. The man with no heart."

He turned to Regina. "Until you forced me to find mine."

I looked at my friend with raised eyebrows.

"Tinley's a former adversary."

"—of the cunning and calculating Ms. Evans. If you ever go into battle, make certain this beautiful woman is *not* on the opposing side."

Turning to me, he asked, "And you, my lovely, are?"

"Maggie Leman." Glancing between the supposed "adversaries," I said, "Sounds like you two have an interesting history."

Regina gave a suggestive smirk and gestured for us to sit down. "Tinley's referring to his recent divorce. His ex-wife hired me as her attorney. Tinley made the mistake of trying to usurp his spousal support duties by hiding assets offshore. And trying to lowball the winnings of his thoroughbred racehorses." Regina coyly patted his hand. "Poor Tin Man learned I love to play hard ball. He came clean when I threatened him with an IRS investigation. His ex is now living quite comfortably. But you forgive me, Tinley, don't you?"

With a sheepish grin, he said, "How could I not? You showed me the errors of my ways. And how I'd be tied up in court for years if I held out."

"That's right. *Nobody* holds out on me." Regina glanced about our group. "Champagne anybody? My treat. Well, actually Tinley's. But that's the way of the business jungle," Regina said with a pouty smile to Mr. Marks.

Our glasses brimmed with bubbly. Tinley remarked, "Speaking of jungle, an investor in one of my thoroughbreds got himself killed out in Santo Reno." He shook his head. "That town is a nasty place. Doesn't bode well for poor Andrew's legacy."

I almost choked on my drink. "Andrew. Andrew Richmond?"

Tinley nodded. "Did you know him? Seemed like a straight-up guy. I can't believe he was cavorting about in such seedy parts."

"He was a member of my country club."

"Andrew Richmond?" Regina gasped. "His wife called my office. Last week."

I mumbled, "Must have known about his cheating."

"He was philandering?" Regina quizzed. "How would you know that, Maggie?"

Even though I didn't particularly care for Diana, I didn't want to implicate her as the source of the leak. Especially if I needed to use her for future information. I checked my manicured nails. "Let's just say gossip runs through an idle country club crowd faster than Tinley's horses."

Tinley chuckled. "Maggie, you are a card." Then clearing his throat, he said, "But it is a horrible bit of news. Andrew brought his family to the track one day. Nice wife, although a bit on the plain side, two beautiful daughters. Andrew did extremely well with his dental practice—wanted to diversify his income. Hence, his stake in my horses. He also invested in real estate."

"Ramshackle motels?" I interjected.

The group shot me an odd glance.

"Um, I hear they're profitable."

Regina stared me down. "Maggie, what else do you know about Mr. Richmond's murder?"

I didn't want to reveal any more information. But I couldn't hold out on Regina. We'd spilled too many tales to each other over the years. Spewing my guts to her was a conditioned response. "Andrew Richmond was killed by a bullet to the back of his head."

Regina lowered her eyes. "And?"

"And what?"

"What leads you to believe the victim was cheating on his wife?"

"Oh, you know…"

"Know what? If Mrs. Richmond decides she needs counsel

post mortem, I want to be prepared. Particularly since her husband had diversified affairs." Regina's mouth curled into a sly smile. "Excuse me, investments."

I let out a sigh. "Okay. I'm sure it's all going to come out anyway. A frightened maid found Andrew Richmond in a run-down motel. Two glasses of wine sat on the nightstand. Andrew's shirt was off, lying in a heap next to him. His pants were down around his knees. And the dump of a building went into escrow later that day."

"Do tell," Tinley exclaimed. "That nasty boy." He rubbed his chin. "Odd the property was sold that very same day. I wonder if it was Andrew's property."

"Interesting angle," I murmured.

Tinley added, "That dunce. I knew he'd invested in several projects here in Newport Beach. Could have had the good taste to get himself offed in one of those. Better for his family."

"Who cares what kind of building," Regina drawled. "I can't believe the jackass got himself shot with his pants down. Talk about humiliating."

I took another sip of champagne. "Question is, why kill him during the romantic liaison? Either you want it, or you don't."

"Perhaps she took a peek at the goods, or lack thereof, and didn't like what she saw," Regina teased.

"Or, maybe someone else was in the room and didn't like what *they* saw." I shuddered in spite of the warm breeze wafting off the ocean.

CHAPTER NINE

My happy hour group pondered the murder of Andrew Richmond while we sipped our Cristal. Though it appeared my fellow country club member, Andrew Richmond, had achieved both professional and personal success during his lifetime, he'd chosen to throw it all away for a clandestine tryst in Santo Reno. A deadly fusion of lust and bad geography.

Regina chatted with Tinley and me while Jax's eyes furtively scanned the room. The cut of his jaw twitched whenever a bar patron happened by—his right hand never strayed from his gun. Then suddenly, a crack of laughter as two middle-aged men sloshing martinis stumbled to our table. Jax rose like a monolithic tower, barrel chest blocking their path.

"What the hell?" one of the martini men uttered.

Regina sized them up then tapped Jax's elbow signaling the O.K. Glowering, her guard settled back into his seat. The men chattered, or should I say slurred, with Regina for a couple of minutes before heading back to the bar.

Through clenched teeth I mouthed, "Regina, what's going on? Jax is wound so tight I'm afraid he'll shoot any man who asks for your astrological sign. You said the Scottish Travellers wanted to kill you. Why?"

Regina took a deep breath, and then let it out. "Maggie, you're my best friend. I don't want to involve you in this. It's for your safety—and your family's."

"Right. That's why I need to know what's going on."

Again Regina inhaled, exhaled, the neckline of her emerald gown inching lower with each breath. Tinley stared at her perfect cleavage, eyes ready to pop.

"Regina, tell me."

She caught sight of the soaring windows, which gave a view of an outdoor patio. It stood empty. "With all this intrigue I'm feeling a bit claustrophobic. Tinley, would it be terribly rude if Maggie and I stepped outside for a breath of ocean air?"

"Of course not." Eying Jax who was already halfway out of his seat, he added, "I'll hold the table."

Regina and I stepped outside while Jax stood sentry at the door. "Alright, Maggie. I can give you an overview, but I can't reveal too many of the particulars. And certainly not names."

"No big surprise, Regina. I know the drill."

"A young woman hired me. She was born into the Travellers' clan, married one, and desperately wanted out. "

"Why would that make you a target for murder? People get divorced every day."

"Not if you're a Traveller. Once one enters into matrimony, you're bound for life."

"That's ridiculous. If you're unhappy, why stay tied?" I gave Regina a wink. "Otherwise, you'd be out of a lucrative career."

Regina polished off her drink. "I know. But it's not that easy. Travellers grow up isolated from society. Constantly on the move, often one step ahead of the law. And with their tradition practically forcing the young members to marry during their teens, often to a first cousin, it's difficult for a Traveller to cut the marriage tie."

I couldn't believe this. I never imagined the Travellers lived in a secret society with strict social rules that governed their lives. And I could never, ever, fathom my best friend would be marked for murder.

"Regina, I hear what you're telling me. But why would divorce put you on the Travellers' hit list? It's not like you're asking the woman to turn her relatives into the police."

"No. I couldn't attach any fees to that. But my client revealed more to me than she should about the clan. To them, secrecy is sacred. We had one last meeting. She told me she couldn't go through with the divorce. Poor girl was visibly shaking as she relayed me this news. She then went back to her husband—*and* the family. "

Regina paused, staring into empty her glass. "Shortly after, an elder of the clan burst into my office with an ominous warning."

"What did he say?"

"He said," Regina's lip quivered, "I hear you been talking to one of my family members. You best *stay wide*, bitch, or you'll find your body lying on that beach outside your fancy office."

"*Stay wide?* What does that mean?"

"It's a Travellers' term for keep your mouth shut—or else."

"Oh, God."

"Oh, Jax. I hope he's as good as they say."

Still shaken by the story Regina had shared with me, we returned to our table.

Tinley looked from Regina to me. "Well, this is a cheery group. It appears you lovelies could use a diversion from all this nastiness." He raised his hand in a stop motion. "No, I'm not talking about sex, Regina. I know I'm no match for you. After our courtroom battles I can only imagine what you're like in the bedroom."

Jax gave a stealth glance over my friend.

"I have a couple of horses running this weekend at San Marina. I'd like you to be my guests at the Breeders' Club." He nodded toward Jax. "Accessories included."

"That's very sweet, Tinley," I said, "but I have a lot going on—"

"Which is precisely why she'll be attending," Regina countered. "We'd love to join you."

Tinley smiled. "It's the last race of the season. You'll have a fabulous time." Looking to Regina, he muttered, "And who knows, the outing may loosen up the armory a bit."

Regina eyed Jax and then leaned across the table, her bosom nearly busting the damn. "Oh, Tinley, I don't want Jax loose, I want him tight. Like those naughty jodhpurs the jockeys wear."

Tinley looked ready to faint.

I arrived home finding my teens in their bedrooms glued to

their respective electronic devices. Grant had yet to make an appearance. I went to the kitchen, laid down my purse, and checked my text messages. Grant was delayed in a meeting. It wasn't unusual for him to have business gatherings run longer than expected. But I now wondered if it was he rather than a meeting running long.

Ethan sauntered in and began rummaging through the pantry. "Hey Mom, do we have anything to eat?"

"By my calculation, we have close to one thousand dollars of food in storage. You know, that pantry is about the same size as the bedroom I grew up in."

"Yeah, and you had to share it with your sister," he recited. "But as the story goes, you were happy. Because all the electronics in the world can't buy you love. Except for some of the things on the Web—"

"Ethan."

"Just joking. I love to get a rise out of you."

"Very funny."

"But I am starving."

"Didn't you have dinner?"

"Sure, at Brittany's. Their new housekeeper's an awesome cook. But that was two hours ago. By the way, where's Dad?"

In spite of the lingering effect of the champagne, my body tensed. "Working."

"Again?"

"Why do you say, again?"

"It just seems like he's been working a lot lately."

"Well, it, uh, takes a lot of work hours to give you kids the good life. Look at this place. There're enough power cords lying around to run a third world country."

The slam of a door stopped our banter.

Ethan stalked down the hallway leading to the garage, his voice trailing behind. "Dad, I need to talk to you. How 'bout some golf on…"

I took this as my cue to retreat to my bedroom. After our encounter at the club, I didn't want to meet with Grant in front of the kids. I didn't know if he was still steamed about

Todd. And I wasn't particularly thrilled about discussing the Bridget package within their earshot, either.

I changed into a nightgown. Unable to relax, I paced my bedroom floor. A waft of ocean air breezed through the window, ruffling my filmy gown. Grant rushed through the door.

I stopped, stared at him—breath caught in my chest. "Well. It's about time you got home. Ethan was asking where you were."

"Where was I? Where the hell were you? With Todd?"

"How dare you question me when you're sending X-rated cards to Bridget! Who the hell is *she*?"

Grant's face faded to gray.

"Yes. I saw the card—and the bag." I grabbed a pillow off the bed and heaved it at him. "Damn you!"

"Wait, Maggie, I can explain."

"Oh, please. At least you can answer me without resorting to a cheater's cliché." I turned away, too angry to look at him.

Grant moved in behind me and touched my elbow, as if testing the waters. I yanked it hard, stepping away.

Grant continued, "Look, Bridget's a cousin of one of my clients heavily invested in the Optimum Project. You know how much is riding on that."

"Yeah, right. A cousin."

Grant edged behind me, his body encompassing mine. I could feel his body heat through the sheer fabric of my negligee. Nuzzling the nape of my neck, he murmured, "Bridget suspected her boyfriend of cheating. The cousin wanted to help her out. You know, make the guy jealous."

Spinning around I snarled, "You must think I'm stupid."

"I don't. I think you're smart. And sexy," he said, as he pressed against me.

"Stay away."

Grant took a step back. Started unbuttoning his shirt.

My eyes trailed the path of his fingers. His chest muscles still tight, tanned, like when we first married.

He moved closer, our bodies nearly touching. I smelled the

hint of Cognac. His fingertips glazed over my body, fingertips tracing the low V of my neckline. "My investor bought the purse and card. Asked me to leave them with my golf bag in the men's locker room. The boyfriend's a member. He finds it, gets jealous, and comes clean with Bridget."

"I don't believe you." I brushed his hand away. "What about the lipstick stain on the envelope? How'd that get there?"

"Baby, there's nothing sexier than your red lips. I wanted to seal the deal. Really make the boyfriend jealous. I knew your Candy Apple Red would do it. Just like it does it to me." And he cupped my face with his hands, devouring me with a deep kiss. I pressed my hands to his shoulders, trying to push him away. Grant pulled me tight around the waist, thrusting his chest, his entire body against mine.

Passion overtook anger, and I didn't struggle as he lowered me onto the bed. We teased each other's bodies with fingertips and flicks of our tongues, knowing the spots that would exact the most pleasure. As we reached a plateau of passion, we trembled with muted cries.

Grant lay sleeping, but I couldn't seem to drift off. The champagne was wearing thin, and my head began to ache. I wasn't accustomed to imbibing in so many glasses. I padded into the bathroom to retrieve some Advil from Grant's medicine cabinet. He kept them on hand for his golfing aches and pains.

Fumbling between a few bottles, I spotted one in the back I'd never seen before—Oxycodone. Grant didn't use such a strong drug for pain. Never needed it. I'd heard whispers around my club of members using it to enhance their sexual experience. And after our passionate interlude last night, I knew Grant didn't need a drug to enhance his performance, or our sex life. So if Grant didn't need this med for sex or pain, why would he have it? I checked the label. No doctor's name. God dammit, who had given it to him? Oxycodone was dangerous stuff. Worse, if Grant wasn't using Oxy during his lovemaking sessions with me, who was he using it with?

CHAPTER TEN

The morning after our night of lovemaking, I awoke to find Grant gone. I assumed he had an early start to his workday, as that had been his habit for the last sixteen years. I lay in bed, languishing over our lusty session. Somehow, our anger had turned to desire, and I marveled at how we corralled our heightened emotions into sexual pleasure. But visions of the Bridget package kept cropping up, and I couldn't help wondering if Grant's explanation rang true.

The chime of the doorbell tore me from my thoughts. Who would be visiting this hour of the morning? The clock read too early for my teens' school carpool to arrive.

I threw on my robe, scurried down the hall and peaked through the slats of the front blinds. Duncan Reid, my maintenance man, stood outside, shifting his weight from foot to foot.

I swept open the door. "Dun, hi. I forgot you were coming today. I guess it's time for our quarterly check-up."

"You got it. Filters, light bulbs…the usual. Unless there's any repairs you need done."

"Nothing I can think of. Please, come in."

Dun scooped up his toolbox and hobbled into my foyer. A veteran cop, Dun had taken a bullet to the back. Several surgeries later, he still walked with a limp. Given the option of living out his career chained to a desk or retiring, he chose the latter. Dun now ran a successful home repair business. He was a no bullshit guy who worked hard and could be trusted working anywhere within your home. He reminded me of my father.

Dun went about his work as Avery and Ethan bustled in and out of the scene, desperate to get ready for school on time. Because it wasn't my week to carpool, they knew if they missed their ride, they'd be relegated to taking the school bus, a definite no-no in their hypersensitive social world.

After they left, I approached Dun as he changed the air filter in the hallway. "So Dun, how's business these days?"

"Can't complain. Busy every day."

"You know, I went through several maintenance services before I found you. Seems no one wants to do quality work these days. Although I never got ripped off by somebody like those Travellers that used to be around."

Dun picked up his screwdriver and placed it in the toolbox. "Don't kid yourself. They still roam through town. I've been hired several times to clean up after them."

"But there haven't been any recent news reports on them."

"When I was on the force I worked with a couple of the affiliates on those stories. The news coverage dried up because the reporters' investigations kept leading nowhere. Station management told them to shelve the subject."

"Sounds like the Travellers are slick."

"Yep. And now they've moved mainstream. Taking their scamming profits and investing in real estate."

"Can't they be stopped?"

"The cops are under pressure to solve the cases that pose the biggest threat to public safety."

"What's a crummy roofing job compared to murder?"

"Exactly." Dun lumbered down the hall in the direction of a second air filter.

I followed behind. "Speaking of murder, did you hear about the one in Santo Reno? Andrew Richmond, a member of my country club, caught fooling around?" As soon I mentioned Richmond's philandering, I knew I should have kept my mouth shut.

Dun stopped. Stared at me. "How did you know about that? Only the basic facts of the crime were printed in the paper. Who's been talking, Maggie?"

"Oh Dun, you know how idle tongues wag around a club."

"No, I don't. Tell me."

My face suddenly felt hot. I looked down, embarrassed to be caught acting like an idle gossip myself. And I feared legal ramifications if Dun knew I was privy to sensitive investigational material. After all, he was an ex-cop. "Um, I didn't mean Mr. Richmond was caught fooling around. I meant it was common knowledge he was an unfaithful husband. Sad to say his name was brought up more than once during ladies' happy hour."

Dun sighed. "Oh, good. My ex-partner, Nick, now works Homicide, heading up the investigation. I'd hate to think the case was being compromised." Dun splashed a playful smirk. "Any other information you have that I should pass on to Nick?"

"Hmm, tell him to bone up on his knowledge of expensive designer bags."

"What's that's supposed to mean?"

"According to my gossip sources, Mr. Richmond had a fixation on them." With a teasing smile, I said, "But I wouldn't expect a macho cop like your buddy Nick to understand that."

Dun folded his arms. "For the record, Nick's a Nicole, and she comes from money. Ever hear of the Harringtons?"

My jaw went slack. This family ranked the highest of the high on the moneyed scale of Newport Beach. "Nicole Harrington? I remember her debutante ball. Splashed all over the society page. Then nothing. I'd wondered what happened to her."

"She chucked it."

"But why become a cop?" My eyes shot to Dun's back. "It's so dangerous."

Dun widened his stance. "You know why Nick's a cop? Because she likes it. She's good at it. And for your information, she knows all about designer bags. Even ones not made by Baggie."

CHAPTER ELEVEN

That evening I received a call that shook my faith in machismo manhood. It was Todd, whimpering. "Maggie, I can't go through with it. I can't do the CC."

"CC? What are you talking about?"

"Magpie, where have you been since the latest verbiage paradigm shift? CC. Country Club. The mixer you want me to attend."

I sighed. "Todd, the only paradigm shift I've noted in the last decade is my withdrawal from the career world to life in Disneyland. I don't mean to sound like a complainer, but sometimes the place that guarantees the most fun on this planet isn't what it's cracked up to be."

"I know you're dealing with a lot now," Todd breathed, suddenly sounding like his flirtatious self again, "but let me say you've always been my fairytale princess."

I cupped the phone and leaned against the countertop. My muscles felt limp. I could swear I detected a hint of Todd's exotic leather oil seeping through my cell.

Forcing myself back to reality, I asked, "Okay, Todd, what is it that has you shaking like a school girl wearing a miniskirt in January?"

"Like the ones you used to wear to my office?"

"Todd."

"Alright. I'll put that thought on the back burner. The very hot back burner."

"Todd, the CC."

"Oh, well, um, I can't do it."

"Why, are you busy that night?"

"Mags, I'm never too busy to socialize."

"Then what's the problem?"

"I'm scared."

"Of what? This assignment is perfect for you. You've practically made a career out of romancing the opposite sex. All you have to do is flirt with Bridget so I can learn what's going on."

"I know. But this is different."

"How so?"

Todd cleared his throat. "When I'm out looking for sex, flirting comes naturally. I'm free to ask whatever questions needed to get the job done. But this is different." Todd's voice dropped a bare whisper. "If sex isn't the objective, I don't think I can pull it off."

I felt like screaming at Todd, "Does it always have to be about sex?" But I took a breath, which I hoped Todd didn't interpret as heavy breathing. "Todd, you say when you're trolling for a sexual encounter, you gather information on the woman. Right? Well, think of this as a fishing expedition without the end result being two fish wriggling about on your boat deck."

"But I like wriggling."

"God, you are impossible."

"Maggie, I have an idea. How about if you shadow me at the mixer? You can stay in the background so Bridget won't see you, but close enough to coach me if my fishing line hits any snags."

Moving across the room, I mulled this over. Gazing out my expansive living room windows overlooking the waves crashing along the shoreline, I muttered, "That's pretty risky. What if she spots me?"

"You're a member. You have every right to be there. Wouldn't you love to see this Bridget in the flesh?"

At that moment, I pictured my husband and Bridget entangled in the flesh—naked. I felt a surge to tear into their flesh.

"Okay, Todd. Let's do it."

"Maggie. Are you coming on to me?"

"I don't mean do it. Todd, get a grip. This is my life."

"Sorry. Need to focus. With you there, I think our plan will work. If I run into any problems, you can signal me on what one is supposed to say when they're having a sexless conversation. Ooh, I don't even like the sound of those two words coupled together."

"Todd, do you ever think about changing some facets of your life?"

"I have. And besides you, Dear Magpie, I wouldn't change a thing. See you Thursday."

CHAPTER TWELVE

The next morning I strolled onto my back patio with my morning cappuccino and nestled into a cushioned chair. I sipped my aromatic java but felt twitchy. Too much happening. I sank deep within my downy seat. Still couldn't relax.

I grabbed the morning paper and thumbed through The Newport Beach News. No updates on Andrew Richmond's murder. Diana's cousin, Johnnie, must have pulled in multiple favors to keep the story out of the public eye. I scanned for any other newsy tidbits I might find interesting, but my focus wasn't there.

As I made my way out of town up the 55 Freeway, my mind wandered back to my conversation with Regina about the Travellers owning several mobile home parks located inland from Newport Beach. I couldn't squelch my overwhelming need to return to that area to see what had become of them. There was one in particular I needed to see.

Growing up, I played almost every day with my best friend, Leyla, who lived in a mobile home with her grandmother. One day I romped into Leyla's and found her grandmother sitting on her fading floral sofa. My friend held her sobbing grandma in her arms.

The elder woman's voice cracked as she lamented that her mobile home park had been sold. The new owner raised space rents well beyond their family's means. I drew in close and soothed, "Hey, it's going to be all right. That guy can't just come in here and raise your rent. There's got to be something you can do."

She looked up at me with tears tracing the creases of her face. "The neighbors and I already tried talking to the owner. He says it's his right."

"Doesn't sound right to me."

"I know, Maggie. Greedy outsider. Not even from around these parts."

"What can we—?"

A loud thudding on the door had interrupted my question. Leyla's grandmother pushed herself up and hobbled to the door. Her slow speed must have angered the intruder, because the thudding rolled into an incessant banging.

A man who looked early twenties with black sideburns cut to his jaw and a cigarette tucked behind one ear pushed halfway through the doorway. "My dad tol' me to pay you a visit. Seems you didn't pay yur full share of space rent. I'm here collecting."

Leyla's grandmother stammered, "It's more than I can afford."

The man stepped into the cramped room. His dark eyes sliced to Leyla and me. With an accent I couldn't quite place, he growled, "Best tell this old woman she better pay up. My family and me don' take no charity cases. Ya' can't pay yur rent, yur out." And he backed out of the doorway, slamming the door so hard it rattled the mobile home.

Shortly after, Leyla was moved to a great aunt who lived on the east coast. One day an ink-smeared letter arrived from my friend. It read:

Dear Maggie,

I'm so sad. I can't stop crying. My grandma was killed by a fire in her home. The police said she was drinking and fell asleep with a cigarette butt burning. That it set her couch on fire. Burned down her mobile home. I don't believe this. I think the police are stupid or lying. My grandmother would never do that. I loved her so much. I miss her so much. And I miss you. Love, Leyla

Shortly after, her letters stopped coming. I assumed the past, which included me, was too painful for her. Like Leyla, I couldn't block my questions surrounding her grandmother's death. The police story about the fire didn't add up. I'd seen Leyla's grandmother have an occasional holiday toast of sherry, but never drink to excess. And she'd bragged on more than one occasion how she'd quit smoking years ago.

There was something phony about that fire. I couldn't stop wondering who would know a stump of a cigarette could spark a deadly mobile home fire. Someone who lived in one? Or someone who was in the business of owning them?

CHAPTER THIRTEEN

When I finally reached my former homeland of West Bernardo, I drove past my old house. My parents sold it several years ago, and I lamented how the new owners had painted it an ugly shade of gray.

Leyla's mobile home park had been razed and a strip mall built in its place. I was startled at the name printed on a For Sale sign planted out front—Leman Land Development. I didn't realize Grant held parcels in this outlying vicinity. He'd always emphasized his belief to condense his business to the coastal area. What was he doing a good sixty miles from his usual territory? And, if he'd purchased this property from the former mobile home park owner whom I suspected was a murderer, what was he *really* doing?

I spent the rest of the day in a numbed state. I drove aimlessly, past my old schools, stopping to gaze at houses where former classmates lived. I didn't know exactly what I was looking for or why I was wandering the town. I felt questions tugging at me and that the seeds of my answers lay here. But I didn't know how to find them.

When I headed back to Newport Beach, I became ensnarled in the usual southern California rush hour. I thought I'd left myself plenty of time to beat this mess, but the heavy traffic hour now started in the early afternoon.

When I pulled up to my house around six, several Newport Beach police cars were parked out front. As I edged into my driveway, I spied uniformed officers milling about my front door. I stopped, buzzed down my window. I felt their eyes bearing down on me. A rush of nerves kept me from continuing into the garage. I turned off the key, frozen to the seat of my car.

A stunning woman who could double for a fashion model, except for a slightly more athletic build, strode up. Though her moss green pantsuit ranked conservative, the tailored cut exuded quiet elegance. And her Manolo Blahnik heels screamed money.

She leaned through my open window. "Mrs. Leman, I presume."

I nodded.

"Hi. I'm Detective Nicole Harrington. We need to talk. I'm afraid I have some upsetting news. I'm so sorry...can we please go inside?"

My stomach gripped so hard I could barely breathe. "What are you saying? Are my kids okay?"

"Your children are fine."

She gently tugged my arm, coaxing me out of my car.

"Tell me, what's going on? Is it Grant?"

"Mrs. Leman, I feel it best if we step inside. I'd like to give you some privacy," the detective murmured as she guided me toward my front door.

I took a couple of steps. Stopped.

"You didn't answer my question. Does this have something to do with Grant? I want to know."

Detective Harrington looked down at my stone pathway and took in a breath. "Mrs. Leman, we need to discuss this. But not out here. Please..."

"What has happened to my husband?"

Exhaling, the detective met my eyes. "I'm so...so sorry to tell you, but your husband is dead."

My mind clouded black, and I felt myself shifting to autopilot. In a leaden voice I said, "I don't believe you. I just saw Grant this morning. I mean, last night. He was home. Safe." I stood transfixed. Though the detective prodded me forward, my body refused to move.

I don't know how long I stood there. My mind finally started to reconnect with reality. "Grant dead. It can't be." I repeated those words until my nervous system started kicking into gear, and my voice climbed to a piercing cry. "Why are you saying this?"

"Mrs. Leman, if you could just step—"

"I want to see my husband."

"You can't."

"Why?"

"I don't want to discuss it here."

"I said, I want to see my husband. Right now."

"I'm sorry, but that's not possible."

"Why not, dammit?"

"Because…"

"Because why?"

"Because he's lying in the county morgue."

"No! That *cannot* be true."

"I'm so sorry, Mrs. Leman. We checked his wallet. He was carrying I.D."

"What…happened?"

"It appears he met with foul play. The preliminary evidence points to murder."

"Murder? I don't believe you."

"Mrs. Leman, I know this is a terrible shock. But we need to get started with the investigation. You'll need to identify Mr. Leman's…body. But first I need to ask you a few questions."

"I'm not answering any questions until I see my husband."

"Please, this is a very difficult situation. Let's not make it any tougher. I would appreciate your cooperation on this matter."

"Matter? You say my husband is dead, possibly murdered, and you're trivializing it to a *matter*?" My eyes burned so hot, I felt them scorch into the detective's.

She stared back at me with steel blue eyes. My shock at hearing this horrible news, coupled with her increasingly cold demeanor, sent my emotions broiling. I felt an explosive urge to reach out and slap the perfect features of the detective's face. But a spark of clarity suppressed it.

"Yes, Mrs. Leman. It's a police matter. And if you're not

going to come inside and discuss it, then I regret to say we'll have to talk at the precinct."

"We can talk after you've taken me to my husband. I don't have time for chit chat right now."

"I'm sorry for your loss, but you're going to have to make time. It's police protocol." The detective cleared her throat. "Speaking of time, where were you today between the hours of eleven and six? We tried to contact you, but couldn't. We talked to several of your neighbors and friends to in an attempt to locate you. They all said you attended Bikram Yoga every Tuesday at The Wave Studio. Never missed a day. But when we contacted the club, we found you didn't show."

Yoga. My God. I'd completely forgotten about it. The detective was right—I never missed a class. I was so preoccupied with the incongruity in my life I'd neglected to attend the one activity that kept me centered.

Taking a deep breath as if I was in yoga class, I tried to calm my nerves. "Oh, I can explain that. I drove out to my hometown, West Bernardo. Wanted to visit old friends."

The detective pulled out a pad and pencil. "Can you give me their names and phone numbers?"

"I actually didn't see anyone. Nobody was around. Guess they've all moved on. I ended up driving around, checking out my old neighborhood."

Detective Harrington raised a perfectly waxed eyebrow. "For a whole day?"

"Yes. For a whole *day*. It's quite a drive out there. Then of course, I got stuck in traffic. If you were so anxious to talk to me, why didn't you call my cell? Surely someone passed along my number to you."

Detective Harrington folded her long, chiseled arms. "After your husband's body was found, we made numerous attempts to reach you. But your phone went straight to voice mail."

Instinctively I reached into the side pocket of my bag and slipped out my iPhone. The power was off. I always made it a point to be in electronic contact. But not today.

A second detective, male, with peppered hair wearing a

stained sports jacket joined us.

I glanced from him to Detective Harrington. "I must have forgotten to turn it on."

The male officer snickered. I detected a hint of alcohol on his breath. "That sounds like B.S. to me. You must be the only Newport Beach lady I know who tiptoes outside her front door, let alone takes off in her Mercedes without her cell. Don't ya' think so, Nick?"

"I wouldn't necessarily call it BS., but it does seem odd."

"What are you two implying? That I killed my husband?"

The second detective grinned, his voice dripping with sarcasm. "I didn't say nothin' about murder. Did you, Nick? Hell, we haven't even determined one hundred percent he was murdered. Sounds like she knows a little more about this than we figured."

Knows more than they figured. Neurons exploded through my brain. I felt light-headed, detached from my body. My mind whirled back to yesterday morning. "Why would you say that? You sound like Dun. That's what he said when—"

"When what, Mrs. Leman?"

"Oh, nothing, Detective Harrington. We were just talking."

"Then I suppose you wouldn't mind sharing?"

I knew I didn't have to share, but after the cell phone activation lapse, I thought it would be best to appear forthcoming. "Dun and I were chatting yesterday about the murder of Andrew Richmond."

"You just happen to be talkin' murder with a former homicide detective. Doesn't sound like nothin' to me," the older detective said.

Detective Harrington shot him a deadly glance.

"Murdock."

That's all she had to say. He mumbled an apology to me. My guess was that Nicole and Murdock had discussed the proprieties of investigative questioning before.

"But Detective Murdock does have a point. What did you find so fascinating about the murder of Mr. Richmond that you felt the need to discuss it with my former partner?"

I didn't know how much I should divulge. I wished Regina were here to coach me. Even though she specialized in divorce law, at least she was a lawyer. But I'd seen enough detective television shows to know if I asked to speak to a lawyer or refused to answer their questions, I probably would need one.

Clearing my throat, I said, "Dun and I were talking about how Mr. Richmond was a member of my country club. That he was known to cheat on his wife and loved designer shopping bags."

Murdock grunted, "Like the one—"

"Detective!" snapped Nicole. Then she turned to me. "How do you know this information? Dun couldn't be your source. He's retired and isn't part of the investigation." Slicing a sideways glance at Murdock, she breathed, "Although I wish he was."

Then eyeing me, she said, "Strange you would mention a designer bag. Nothing about one has been reported in the news. Even the gossipy country club members we interviewed never broached the subject. And believe me, I know how those people love to talk. So tell me, Mrs. Leman, how do you know so much about this case? And where *were* you today?"

CHAPTER FOURTEEN

After hearing of my husband's death, I called my long-time neighbor, Angie. Managing to keep my demeanor together, I told her I had a personal emergency. Could she take my kids for a while? Without asking any questions, she agreed.

Fighting back tears, I gathered my teens, told them the police needed to speak to me about an issue at the country club, and gave them reassuring hugs. Their faces bore looks of innocent confusion, and they peppered me with questions. But now wasn't the time to tell them their father was dead. I needed to process this horrifying news, if that were at all possible, so I could relay it to them in a way that could somehow lessen their inevitable pain.

After they left, the tears I'd been fighting to contain flowed like waves of the ocean. I sank into my living room couch, clutching one of its plump cushions to my chest. The last time I'd been with Grant we'd made passionate love. Sure, I'd been angry when I'd found the designer Gitan bag. But he had an explanation for it.

Grant was gone. Dead. I'd never hold him in my arms again. My children had no father. I couldn't take it all in. This wasn't my life. This was something you read about in the paper or saw on the nightly news. Not my near perfect life in beautiful Newport Beach.

Detective Harrington cut into my thoughts. "Mrs. Leman. Maggie. I need you to answer my questions."

"Where do you get the nerve to bother me at a time like this? You told me my husband is dead. I can't talk to you right now. Don't you have any sympathy?"

Detective Murdock sneered, "That's right. We bust our asses day in and day out twenty-four seven to solve cases for rich people like you. We got no sympathy."

Nicole Harrington held up her hand to silence her partner. She pushed her thick, blond ponytail back across her shoulder. "This is a possible murder investigation. As homicide detectives, our job is to move as quickly as possible. If your husband met with foul play, and the evidence so far is pointing in that direction, then time is of the essence."

"Evidence? What kind of evidence are you talking about?" I shrilled.

"Take it easy, Mrs. Leman. I need you to stay calm so we can go through today's events, step by step."

"Yes, Detective. Let's go through today's events. First off, how did Grant die?"

"It appears he received a fatal shot—"

My voice rose two octaves. "Appears he was shot. Either he was or he wasn't."

"I can't give conclusive information until the coroner's conducted the autopsy."

"Where was he shot?"

"In the chest cavity."

"No. I mean, where was he shot? Where was he?"

Detective Harrington hesitated.

Murdock didn't hesitate to step in. "Your husband was found at the Chrystal Point Motel by housekeeping. He was nude, with—"

"Murdock."

My body went completely numb. I could hear myself speaking, but I was not in control of the words. "What would Grant be doing at the Chrystal Point Motel? Isn't that in Santa Reno? He only deals with properties in Newport Beach. He wouldn't touch one of those Santa Reno dives."

"Well, he was doing some touching today."

Detective Harrington stood to her full height and bore down on Murdock. "Keep your mouth shut unless you want to be put on administrative leave."

"Just try. You rich bitches are all alike. Quit pussy footin' around and lay the facts on the table."

"Detective, shut the—"

Murdock kept going, his red facial capillaries looked ready to burst. "If her husband wasn't messin' around, then what was he doing in a crapped out motel with an empty Oxycodone bottle under the bed and two glasses of wine on the nightstand?"

"Enough," Detective Harrington seethed, clenching and unclenching her fists. "My bet is you've been drinking again. Hang up the bottle, Murdock, or kiss your career goodbye."

"You know where you can kiss mine." Murdock spat on my angora throw rug as he turned and stormed out of the room.

Nicole sat back down beside me. "I'm sorry you had to witness that. Brass has given him more chances than he deserves, and he keeps screwing up. Can I get you something, coffee, water?"

"No. Yes. Maybe some filtered water. Grant just had the Ecor Environmental filter installed." Saying Grant's name made the reality of the situation dig deeper into my heart, and my eyes filled with tears again.

Nicole placed a calm hand upon mine. "I know it's tough. I'm sorry, I wish there was something I could say. I'll get you that water."

The detective strode back into the living room a few minutes later, carrying a turquoise Grand Cru glass that matched my home décor. Placing it between my shaking hands, she glanced around the room, making small talk as if to calm me down. "You have a lovely home, Maggie. I like the way your color scheme blends with the environment of Newport Beach."

"Thank you. I worked with Akemi Hayashi. Perhaps you've heard of her?"

"Oh yes. Akemi and I attended the same prep school. I always admired—" The detective's eyes shot to the left of my couch. "What's this?" She whipped out a pen, crouched down. Turning to me, she held a clear plastic bag with her pen hooked through the handle. The bag bearing my angry message, I am not a plastic bag. The Gitan that Avery had kidnapped and then most likely tossed aside.

With a nervous chuckle, I said, "It's a Gitan. One of those environmental shopping bags everyone's so crazy about these days. "

"I know what a Gitan is. Why is it desecrated with this scrawl?" Her eyes bore down on me. "Whose bag is it, and what's it doing here, in your home?"

My head pounded, and I could feel myself falling back into the altered state of not being in control of my words. "It's Grant's. Was Grant's. Actually, I stole it from him and gave it to my daughter, Avery. She thought it was so cool the way I scribbled on it. My childish way of getting back at Grant."

"What were you getting back at your husband for?"

"I, um, I was angry he'd spent so much money on such an ugly gift. Can you believe these silly bags retail for $899 at Saks?"

"I'm aware of that. I own one."

"Oh."

"If you were so upset about the price, why would you deface it?"

"Because—"

"Mrs. Leman, it's your husband's pricey expenditure. Why would you ruin it? Why not simply return it? I'm sure you're aware of Saks' generous refund policy. Why, Mrs. Leman, would you do such a thing?"

CHAPTER FIFTEEN

Detective Harrington glared at me, still holding the defaced satchel by her pen. A bead of sweat rolled down my left temple. "Because it came with a card marked, My Bridget. I thought he was having an affair. And now, after what Murdock told me, it appears he was. Just like Andrew Richmond. What is it with these cheating golfer husbands and Gitan's?"

Nicole's face froze. She stood in silence for what seemed an eternity. Then she spoke with low, clipped words, "How did you know about Andrew Richmond and the Gitan bag? Murdock never stated the specific brand. And the paper didn't report it. How is you're so certain it was a Gitan found at the scene of Mr. Richmond's murder? It's not a mainstream label that would roll off one's tongue."

I felt I was sinking into quicksand. I decided to come clean and let her know I'd heard about the bag from Diana Hutchinson's cousin, Johnnie.

The detective shook her head as I told her my source. She mumbled under her breath, "Johnnie. Such a scumbag. He'd sell his mother."

"So you know him? Is his info reliable?"

"I'm not divulging anything. Except we've suspected him of playing loose with the truth on previous cases he's managed to ingratiate himself into. The guy likes to play both sides of the law—just like other members of his family."

"So his family's dirty."

"We've never proven anything on Johnnie's family. They're a slippery bunch. He's the only one who's stupid enough to get caught. But the rest of them...let's just say we have our suspicions but have yet to prove them."

My front door burst open and a blaze of red hair swept into the living room. Regina. She flew into my arms and held me tight. "Oh Maggie, I'm so sorry."

Detective Harrington glowered at Murdock who trailed behind Regina, obviously ineffective in blocking her entrance to the scene of Detective Harrington's interview.

"What the hell is she doing here? Of all people. I want her out of here—now."

Regina's eyes pierced to Detective Harrington. "Are you taking Maggie into custody?"

Nicole opened her mouth, seemingly ready to give Regina a retort, but stopped.

"That's what I thought," said Regina. "I have every right to be here to console my friend over her husband's demise."

Detective Harrington took a step toward Regina. "How did you know about Mr. Leman's death? The body was only discovered earlier today."

I cringed as the term body spilled from of the detective's mouth.

"Police scanner. I keep it on at all times."

"What for? You're a divorce lawyer. Not criminal. Although it was criminal the way you held my feet to the fire during my divorce. God, the money I had to pay out to that dumb ass of a so-called husband."

The thought blazed across my brain that he must not have been too much of a dumb ass to hire Regina. She rarely represented a man. Specialized in helping scorned wives. And judging by the conversation, it appeared Detective Harrington had to part with a hefty chunk of her family money. I was happy to have my friend here to comfort me in my time of crisis but not thrilled to hear Nicole Harrington had been one of Regina's casualties. I hoped the officer wouldn't hold my association with Regina against me.

Nicole glared at Regina. "You didn't answer me. What do you need a police scanner for?"

"Not that it's any of your business, but I like to be

informed about my clients' activities, or their soon-to-be exes' escapades. I need to know anything that could hurt or help during court proceedings."

Nicole blasted Regina with a look that could have come straight from her police-issued Smith and Wesson.

"You really are a piece of work."

"Yes, I am, as I have to work for a living. Unlike some people who were born sucking an engraved platinum pacifier."

Detective Murdock stirred, looking like his old cop's instincts were alerting him the air reeked with the beginnings of a catfight. He stepped up to Nicole and tapped her elbow. "Hey, Nick. Brass says we gotta' get a positive I.D. on the vic. Now. Let's get Mrs. Leman down to the morgue."

I shuffled along the gray hallway toward the glare of stainless steel doors. Regina flanked my right side, giving my hand a comforting squeeze every few steps. Detective Harrington edged my left elbow, prompting me toward the doors. Murdock led our party. He stopped. "Okay, Ms. Divorce Lawyer. End of the line. Next of kin only."

Grant lay on a slab of gray steel, his body shielded by a white cloth. Detective Harrington slipped the cloth downward so I could see my husband's face. I don't know what I'd expected or hoped for—perhaps a mistake. With Grant's average build and common brown hair, I had clung to the possibility that another man lay victim here. That wish proved to be futile. It was Grant. The man I'd been married to for the past sixteen years. The man I thought I'd live forever after with.

"Maggie," Detective Harrington almost whispered. "I need to know. Is this your husband?"

Through numbed lips I murmured, "Yes, that's Grant. But he doesn't seem real. None of this does." Glancing to Nicole I said, "I want to see his wound."

"There's no need for that, Maggie. We have a positive I.D."

"I need to see it. I need for this to be real."

"I really don't think you should."

"I do."

Nicole sighed. "I have to warn you. Death is never pretty. And a fatal gunshot wound can be particularly shocking."

"Please. Let's do this."

Detective Harrington slid the sheet past Grant's midsection. I didn't move—my feet cemented to the concrete floor. I thought, she's right. Death isn't pretty. Grant had looked so sexy that last night we'd made love. But seeing him lying here under the glare of the morgue spotlight—his golfer's tan now ashen, graying chest hairs poking through dried blood…death is never pretty. Particularly with a bloody hole blasted through one's torso.

CHAPTER SIXTEEN

After I identified Grant's body, the coroner confirmed the obvious—my husband was murdered. Unfathomable for me to comprehend, but I felt it was a step on my way to closure. But how to find the words to tell my children this horrifying news? I couldn't imagine how I could find the strength to do this.

Fortunately, with so many arrangements to make, the next few days whirred faster than a Santa Ana wind. I would have preferred a simple burial, but with Grant's leadership in Green Building, a small affair wouldn't pay him justice. Somehow, it all came together, and my husband was laid to rest. I only wished my questions about the Gitan bag and My Bridget were buried along with him.

After saying my last goodbyes to those who attended the gathering after Grant's service, I kissed my teens good night and crawled into bed. Exhausted, I fell asleep as soon as I cozied beneath my down comforter. But the incessant ringing of my cell soon interrupted my sleep. After the third round of rings, I gave in and picked up.

"Maggie, I just flew in from Cabo and heard word of Grant's death. I am so, so sorry. How are you doing?"

I felt like saying, "As well as can be expected until you woke me up." But Todd was trying to be a good friend, and I didn't want to sound rude. Plus, I think it was the longest string of words I'd ever heard him say that didn't include a come-on line, and I didn't want to discourage a perhaps new and improved Todd.

"I'm fine. Relatively speaking. It's been beyond hectic handling all the funeral arrangements. I think that's been a blessing."

"You've already had the funeral? I missed it?"

"Yes, Todd."

"I am sorry. I should have been by your side to comfort you."

Picturing Todd's idea of comforting, I silently thanked God he'd missed the service. I could almost hear the cackle of local gossip if Todd had been here to comfort me.

"That's okay, Todd. Regina was a big help. And thank heavens for my kids. Somehow, we managed to get through it."

"How are they handling Grant's death?"

At the mention of the word death, tears sprang to my eyes. I plucked a tissue from my nightstand. "It's hard. But teens are resilient. While I was making the arrangements, I made sure they were kept busy, surrounded by their friends. I just want them to return to their normal, teen-crazed schedules. Less time to dwell on their father's mur...murder."

"And it goes without saying that course of therapy applies to you as well."

"What do you mean?"

"You need to keep moving. There's nothing to be gained by dwelling on the past. Unless it's our past relationship—"

"Todd. For God's sake. My husband was just murdered. Can't you put down the pick-ups for one conversation?"

"Maggie, you're right. I've been doing this leather-coating Playboy gig for so many years I don't even know how to carry on a normal conversation."

"Don't beat yourself up. It's hard not to become a product of the Newport Beach scene."

"Speaking of the NB scene, we have a bit of scouting to do."

"What are you talking about?"

"Bridget."

"Bridget! How dare you bring that name up now."

"Maggie, don't you remember? You wanted the two of us to check her out at the club's mixer?"

"Oh, right. But I can't do that now."

"I know this is incredibly hard for you. But if this woman was having an affair with Grant, doesn't it sound plausible she could have something to do with his death? Maggie, you've always been a woman of action. And I'm not only talking about in the physical sense."

"Todd. I can't go cavorting around my country club now. I just lost my husband to a brutal murder. I saw the gaping hole in his chest."

"Which is all the more reason to find out what went down."

Thinking back to Detective Harrington's accusatory attitude, and Murdock's slimy one, I said, "You're right. I need to take action. What's the plan?"

"Okay, Mags, this is how it goes…" and Todd filled me in on more information about how men manipulate women in social settings than I cared to know.

CHAPTER SEVENTEEN

As the time of the social mixer rolled around, I met Todd in a dim corner of the Newport Hill's parking lot to discuss last-minute strategy. Normally I use valet parking, but I wanted to remain incognito.

Once again, Todd's nervousness broiled over. I wished I had a handful of Valium to calm his nerves. But my Kors held only non-animal tested cosmetics and a packet of chai tea. What was up with him? He was not acting like the unflinching hunk in his infomercials who could ad lib to millions on the fly. Was he starting to shed some vanity and become more humanlike? Or perhaps he was going through a forties midlife crisis whispered about as male menopause?

Whatever, I was losing patience faster than a receding tide. I grabbed his muscled bicep. "Todd, cut the whimpering. You've always been able to pull it together for an audience. Pretend you're filming an infomercial. It's show time. You're on!"

Todd mumbled an apology and then asked me if I remembered how I'd calm him down before he hit the air.

I scowled at him. "You're not talking about the time we had sex on the desk in your back office?"

"No, I meant how you'd give me a hug and a peck on the cheek right before the cameras rolled."

Blushing at my racy thoughts, I mumbled, "Oh, right. Good luck," and brushed my lips across his cheek. My lipstick left a red smudge, so I grabbed a tissue out of my bag and tried to rub it off. But my Candy Apple Red proved stubborn, leaving a trace of my lucky charm.

Todd strode across the dining area of the club heading to their expansive bar. I held back a safe distance, hoping no one would spot me. But I didn't need to worry about being discovered. Almost every head in the place turned to follow Todd. Even at mid-forties, he still lit up a room with his sizzling male mystique. And his fitted Rufskin jeans framing his taut derriere added to the mystery.

Todd ordered a drink and then subtly surveyed the room in search of single females. Though his body and eye movement were so slight as to be almost nonexistent, I'd seen Todd in enough social situations to know when he was trolling.

Todd slid down the bar to the only female who appeared to be solo. He signaled the bartender with a "we'll have some drinks" gesture. This woman wore a professional workday pantsuit and short scissor-cut hair. I didn't take her for the Bridget type. But knowing Todd, who was smarter than his gorgeous looks betrayed, I assumed he was sidling up to her to appear democratic in bestowing his charms. And who knew? Perhaps this woman was the sexalicious Bridget socializing in a benign disguise.

While Todd was chatting it up with this gal, a leggy blonde with big hair sashayed in from seemingly nowhere and slunk next to him. She immediately drew his attention, and the two quickly clicked into conversation. So much for the Democratic Party.

I strained to study this young woman from my covert position. Her over-blown hair shadowed her face, making it difficult to discern her features. I moved in closer. She appeared pretty even with her minimal makeup. And though she sprouted over-sized hair, she didn't strike me as flashy. Her clothes hung stylishly without being overly revealing.

But upon examining her further, I detected something strange about this woman. Her hair sat too perfect. It never swayed or bounced as she moved. And when she tossed back her head in a jovial response to Todd, her waves never varied an inch. That hair could not be real. It had to be a wig. Unless someone was gravely ill and needed to wear one, artificial hair made me feel the person donning one, especially such a big one, was hiding something.

After much passing of heat between these two strangers, Todd finally asked this woman her name. I thought I heard the name Beatrice muttered from the confines of her umbrella wig. Damn. I was certain this woman was Bridget.

As the flirting between the two continued, it appeared Todd was losing the battle to dominate the conversation. I moaned as I viewed puppy dog wagging of his head and a nearly constant blubbering movement of his lips. Beatrice occasionally spoke, but she remained cool, like a sexy spy extracting vital information from her prisoner. I could barely hold my nerves under reign. Todd was here to sift information, not play pansy to an attractive female. I needed to know if this woman had an affair with my husband, and if she was somehow connected to his death. So frustrated, I could barely contain my impulse to scream at Todd, "You've spent the past twenty years manipulating women. Can't you put this woman under your spell and make her spill her inner secrets?"

As the evening dragged on, Todd downed cocktails while Beatrice drank what looked to be soda water. To his credit, it sounded like every now and again Todd had the clarity to pump her for information, but she would steer the conversation back to him.

And then Diana Hutchinson burst into the picture. She zeroed in on Todd and his newfound friend. Stepped right up to them. Diana attempted to interject herself into their conversation, but they ignored her. She responded by throwing disapproving glances at them, unable or not caring to hide her sour disposition.

Did Diana have no pride? I almost felt sorry for her. Until she said, "Well, Todd, what do we have here on your cheek? A lipstick smudge. And the bright scarlet doesn't look like it came from your new friend. Looks suspiciously like the red Maggie Lehman wears. Looks like you're having fun here, but maybe some fun with Snow White?"

Todd brushed her off with a drunken wave. "Diana, don't

know what you're talking about."

She glared at Todd with flaming eyes. Thankfully, before she combusted Diana was called away by a staff associate to pacify a member who was painfully singed by an out of control Banana Flambé.

As the evening ended, Beatrice muttered a quick good night, then made a hasty withdrawal. I tracked her clipped footsteps from a distance. But like a ghost, she slipped through a backdoor of the club I didn't know existed. She was gone.

I scooted back to the bar and nodded to Todd to meet me out front.

I quizzed him about what he'd found out. "Who's Beatrice? Could she be Bridget? Was she having an affair with Grant?"

He stumbled over his words as he reported that he couldn't remember much, except she had a sexy lilt to her voice and a fixer-up property she wanted to sell.

CHAPTER EIGHTEEN

I wandered to my Benz and slipped into the driver's seat. My car's normal smell of new leather was overpowered by a sour stench. A man sprang from the back seat, grabbed my chin, and twisted my head so I was staring into his face. His mouth pulled into a sickening sneer. A golden glint from his front tooth told me this was the same man who had nearly accosted me in the club—Grant's client. I tried to jerk my head, but his grasp locked tight. "It's not safe to keep your doors unlocked. Never know who might get in."

I choked out the words, "This is a private club. No outsiders allowed. No reason to lock them."

"Well, Missy, there's a funny thing about outsiders. If they want to get in bad enough, they'll always find a way."

"Let go, you asshole."

Releasing his grip, he mocked, "Hmm, don't we have some spunk? Guess that's why you're out clubbing just days after your poor soul of a husband was buried. But I seen you mostly tucked in the corner. Maybe you're the one who doesn't belong."

"I've been a member of Newport Hills for years. I have every right to be here. But you don't seem to. What the hell were you doing here, spying on me?"

"Nah, not spying. Although you acted awful suspicious. Just trying to warn you about the danger a single woman who doesn't have the smarts to lock her car door could run into. Especially one who looks to be snooping around. I hope you don't have a big mouth. Wouldn't make for a good combination."

He opened the door to exit. Turning back to me he said, "You best be safe. Keep your doors locked. And as the Scottish saying goes, a closed mouth catches no flies. A shut mouth keeps me out of strife." He smiled back at me as he climbed out of my car, gold tooth glimmering in the moonlight.

I peeled out of there fast, checking my rear view mirror every few seconds to make sure the scumbag wasn't following me. I didn't want him knowing where my children and I lived. I hoped Grant had kept their business relationship professional and hadn't divulged any personal information. But my burning gut screamed this man knew more about my family than I ever wanted him to know.

The more I replayed this event in my mind, the tighter my hands gripped the steering wheel. This man had to be a member of the Travellers. His talk about "outsiders." The Scottish warning to keep my mouth shut. That sounded like Regina's description of these modern day gypsies. The clan had threatened her life. Had the Travellers taken Grant's life?

If this guy thought he could threaten me, thinking I'd act like a weak, bereaved widow, he was wrong. He didn't know anything about me. He couldn't know I'd take whatever action necessary to protect myself and loved ones. And growing up with a cop for a father, I knew just how to do it.

My first step—get my teens to a safe place. I made a mental note to call my friends Jay and Sondra Peterson the next morning to see if they'd house my kids until this situation blew over. The Petersons' son, who played on Ethan's golf team, was kidnapped. The Petersons were hit up for a five million-dollar ransom. Thanks to the FBI, the kidnappers were captured, and their son came home safe. After that, the Petersons hired the best security firm in the world. They now had round-the-clock bodyguards and a compound outfitted with the most advanced hi-tech security system five million dollars could buy. Their home was more secure than a California super prison.

Shortly after dawn, I called the Petersons. I didn't worry

about waking this power couple. Sondra meditated every morning before the sun rose, while Jay connected with the foreign markets.

"Hi, Sondra. I hope I didn't interrupt your meditation session."

"Oh no, Maggie, I finished an hour ago. I was about to head off to my Tai Chi session at Corona Cove. The transcendental moves along the shore do wonders for my spirit. You should try it sometime. After things settle down, of course. Darling, I can't describe to you how sad Jay and I are for your loss."

"Thanks, Sondra. I appreciate your family showing up for the service. Your support means a lot."

"If there's anything I can do."

"Actually, there is. Can my teens stay at your place for a while?"

"I understand. You need some time to yourself."

"No, it's not that. I think my family may be in danger."

"Oh God. What—?"

"I don't know all the details yet. But I think Grant may have become involved with a group of less than ethical businessmen. I feel they may have hurt him and could decide to target… I need to know my kids are safe. And your home is the most secure place I can think of."

"Of course. Don't give it a second thought. I'll have Jay pull in an extra bodyguard."

"Sondra, you don't have to do that."

"I insist. They only charge $900 per day."

"Nine hundred dollars per day for your security force? That's so much money. Adding two more teens…I wouldn't dream of imposing."

"Maggie, I'm talking $900 per guard. But you're not imposing. They're the best of the best and worth every payroll. I wouldn't trade a fashion week in Milan for my kids' safety— or your family's. You'll be staying with us, right?"

"No, Sondra. I'm staying put. I have too many things to take care of."

"Maggie, you can't stay in your house by yourself. If you feel your children aren't safe, then you certainly can't be. I can bring in my personal assistant to take care of your affairs. You won't have to worry about a thing."

"I appreciate the offer. But I need to handle this situation myself."

"Maggie, there's no reason. I have the resources. How will I know you'll be okay?"

"Remember when I told you my dad was a cop?"

"Yes..."

"Well, he taught me more than not to talk to strangers."

"What do you mean?"

"I mean I have the training to handle myself."

"You have a gun?"

"I do. And I know how to use it. My dad trained me since I was sixteen and drilled into me to always keep my skills sharp."

"And you're your father's daughter, right?"

"You better believe it."

CHAPTER NINETEEN

My kids packed off to the Petersons' fortress, I was ready to put my protection plan into action. I strode into my bedroom closet and made my way to the recess of the corner. The five-hundred-square-foot alcove was outfitted with customized storage units designed to make the most scattered person more organized than a consummate Virgo. Our safe was hidden behind an ornate wooden cabinet. It held not only my most expensive jewelry but also a weapon whose caliber is derived from the Latin phrase, *Si vis pacem, para bellum*. Meaning, "If you seek peace, prepare for war."

My fingers swiftly twirled the dial to the correct combination of numbers. Having been a marketing exec, numbers stuck in my mind. But there was another reason I knew the combination so well—every month I opened this safe, not to collect my jewels, but to retrieve my Ruger.

I drove to the upscale gun club where Grant and I held a membership. Its entry adorned with downy sofas and plush chairs, this indoor facility looked more like a social club than shooting range. But with its steep monthly dues it should look inviting.

I signed in, gathering the required earmuffs. I also picked up a set of rubber earplugs that sat in a bowl deemed optional. The earmuffs made the blasts of the range weapons tolerable. But I wanted total silence. I needed to focus on my target like I was shooting for my life.

I strode along the Plexiglas-lined stalls until I reached the end of the row. I inserted the magazine into my pistol and pressed the electronic button, which signaled my paper target to zoom into range. Eyeing the center of the bull's-eye, I raised my pistol and fired. Close, but not good enough. I needed to pop off some more shots to get warmed up. This didn't make me happy. If danger came my way, I wouldn't have the luxury of a practice session. Real life wasn't a round of golf where you got a Mulligan. The first shot had to be one hundred percent accurate.

I blasted through several more rounds, now hitting dead-on. Though my focus was zoned on the target, my mind kept retreating to thoughts of the hideous man with the gold tooth. I now pictured him as my target, and my shots pierced through where I imagined his dental enamel to be.

My morbid fantasy abruptly halted at the touch of a hand on my shoulder. My thoughts racing back to the Traveller in my car, I nearly turned my weapon on the intruder. Luckily I didn't, because the one interrupting my target practice was Detective Harrington.

"What the—" I stopped myself before I hurled a profanity at her. I found it bold, no stupid, to startle a person holding a gun. My nerves were frayed so edgy, Detective Harrington was lucky I hadn't blown her head off.

I whipped off my headphones and tore the earplugs from my ears. "Detective, you startled the bejeezus out of me. What are you doing?"

The beautiful cop pulled her mouth into an unattractive smirk. "Question is, what are you doing? Your husband's been in the grave less than a week. Instead of acting like a bereaved widow, here you are, blasting away. With an amazing amount of accuracy, I'd have to say."

I didn't like the biting tone to her voice. "What the hell does my choice of activity have to do with anything? My husband was shot. I don't want to sit at home, worrying I could be the next victim. So I'm doing some target practice. What does it matter to you?"

Nicole pulled herself to her full height, glaring down at me. "I'm just wondering if you're a sad widow or a black widow. I hear you and Todd Williams have been cozy lately. Practicing for another marital round?"

"Todd's my former boss. I have every right to communicate with him."

"From what I hear through the society scoop you were very good at playing office politics. Taking up where you left off? Or should I say on?"

I seethed venom through every pore of my body. But I kept my voice steady as I countered, "I won't even dignify that remark with a response. But I will add that your lack of professionalism is shocking. Keep it up, and I'll bring you up on harassment charges."

"What do you know about harassment? Except hanky-panky with the boss kind."

At that moment, I wished the detective had startled me into shooting her. "I'll tell you what I know. I may look like a pampered Newport Beach housewife, but I grew up with a cop for a father. And he shared his war stories around the dinner table. So I know a lot more about police politics than you'll ever know. What did your family talk about? Menu items for your next dinner party?"

"That's of no consequence. So tell me, what else did your dad teach you? How to take someone out?"

"My father taught me how to handle a gun—with safety."

"I can see. By the way, nice Ruger. Did your daddy give it to you?"

"No. I bought it myself."

"Interesting…"

I ignored her snippy remark and pulled my head phones over my ears, zeroed my weapon on my target, and shot five straight rounds—right into an imaginary forehead. Only this time I wasn't thinking about the creepy Traveller. I was picturing Nicole's beautiful face spattered throughout the range.

CHAPTER TWENTY

Sunday morning I picked up my buzzing cell and heard Regina's sexy drawl. "Morning, dear."

"Same to you."

"Maggie, you sound sleepy. Dare I ask what you were you doing last night?"

"Sleeping."

"You're kidding."

"Yes, Regina. That's how I generally spend my midnight hours. What were you up to on your Saturday night? The Samba at the latest hotspot?"

"I was up most of the night. But not dancing. Glued to a brief. But it was worth the lack of winks. This soon-to-be divorced asshole's really going to get the smack down. Just picturing our day in court gives me the same adrenaline rush as boogying the night away. Who needs to hit the bars when one can hit a cheating louse in the pocketbook?"

Regina cleared her throat, raspy from most likely too many hours of work and salivating over her victim's diminishing assets." Mags, you do remember what day it is, don't you?"

"Sunday?"

"True. But more importantly, it's the day Tinley's horses are running at San Marina. We promised the Tin Man we'd be there. You know, as a lawyer I'm legally bound by my promises."

I wasn't sure if that was true. Most lawyers I knew spent their careers trying to skirt the truth. But Regina had always been a loyal friend, and to me her word was gold. I hated to flake out on her. But my God, with Grant's recent death, the idea of attending the races rated a negative ten on my social calendar. I needed time. To myself, to decipher my emotions, to heal…

Regina jolted me from my thoughts. "Maggie, I sense your hesitation. But moping at home will do you no good. You've got to move on. That's always been my modus operandi."

"Regina, you always had the power to call off your affairs. It's not like your loved one died from a shot to the chest."

Regina gave a languorous sigh. "But Maggie…"

"Regina, I love you, but please save your courtroom theatrics for your clients. I just buried my husband, and he's not coming back. This is not divorce court."

I heard a sniffle from the other end of the phone and the plucking of a tissue. "I'm sorry. How could I be so insensitive? I've been playing the venomous snake for so long it's hard for me to separate my cases from my life. Please forgive me."

"I will—on one condition. After this mess is over, we take a much-needed girls' trip to Belize. I think we both could use some stress reduction."

"You've got it. Now the plan for today is…"

Around noon, Tinley's stretched limo pulled into my front driveway. The chauffer opened the back door, and I found Regina nestled into a cavern of leathered seats, clasping a flute of champagne. Jax nudged close to her side. She passed me a glass of bubbly, and we were off to the races.

We sipped our way along the lengthy trip to San Marino Park, which sat at the base of El Sabrino Mountain. This sport of kings complex had been a fixture in southern California since 1934 and had played host to movie stars and multi-millionaires throughout its history. The structure exuded the finest large-scale art deco architecture found anywhere in the Golden State, and time had only enhanced its graceful beauty.

The limo driver assisted Regina and me out of the vehicle. He then passed us off to a man who introduced himself as Aster. With a shallow bow, Aster announced he would be Tinley's co-host for the day. Between his crisp uniform and perfect British accent, I felt royals had adopted me.

Aster led us through a side entrance where an elevator, which carried us up several stories, feeding into the Chandelier Room. We stepped into the private lounge, aptly named for its massive crystal lighting fixtures. Regina whispered, "Looks like the Tin Man has gone all out for this event."

The gentlemen in the room dressed in starched blazers replete with bow ties. The women donned hats that rivaled the best at the Kentucky Derby. Thank goodness, I had worn one of the few I owned, a tiny cap accented with a single red rose.

My observation of the racing crowd was interrupted by the lilting welcome of Tinley as he swept into the room, besmirching us with European kisses. "Regina, Maggie...um, Jax, you're looking chipper today. Maggie, I hate to spoil the day's festivities, but I wouldn't be a proper gentleman if I didn't extend my condolences to you for the loss of your beloved husband. I do hope today's recreation will lift your spirits."

"Thank you, Tinley. And thank you for inviting us. Perhaps this is what I needed."

"And what you need is a bit of bubbly."

I tried to signal to Tinley that I wasn't ready for more champagne, but he waved me off. "No idle hands here. Time for a pre-race toast. Then we'll proceed to the Turf Club to view the races."

Regina cooed, "Oh, Tinley, you do know how to entertain a girl. This setting is lovely."

We enjoyed our drinks and then moved on to our next party destination. Although the Turf Club was not as old-world elegant as the Chandelier Room, it too rang first class. The restaurant displayed floor to ceiling windows, providing a splendid view of the track. And its larger than life bar at the back of the spacious room would certainly keep the party rolling.

After settling into prime seats by the window, I again scanned the crowd. This group also dressed in fine racing attire, except for the group of boisterous men entering the room dressed in tacky-edged clothing that barely met the Turf

Club's strict fashion standard. Squeezed into low-end synthetic garments a size too small, they reminded me of the suspect business associates I'd seen Grant lunching with at Newport Hills a day before his death. They settled into a large table to the right of Regina and Jax. A minute later three women joined them. They dressed in bland skirts with buttoned-up blouses, and did not wear fancy racetrack hats. Would a group that suspiciously looked to be Travellers spoil my day at the races?

Thankfully, Tinley tore me from my dreary thoughts. "Maggie, allow me to tell you what I've ordered for today's meal. I hope it will bring you a pleasurable culinary diversion." He then began describing the delectable delights we'd be savoring throughout the day. But as his voice trailed on, he was drowned out from the rising cacophony from the table of shoddy dressers.

Tinley shot them a disapproving glance. The men were too busy laughing and clinking chilled mugs of dark brew to notice our host's proper British attempt to tone down their social rudeness.

I took a long sip of champagne and studied this clan. I noted the women sat quietly, barely engaging in conversation, avoiding consumption of beer. A stark contrast to the behavior of the "gentlemen" seated among them. Either these women didn't like to party or, I suspected, weren't allowed to. I couldn't attest to it, but I perceived an air of unhealthy male dominance permeating this group.

Then to my surprise, Beatrice entered, and I almost spewed champagne bubbles across my table. What was she doing here? Sliding into a chair at the far side of the table, she took a seat amongst the troupe. Two women nodded a silent greeting to her, but the men kept blathering away, giving no recognition of her entrance. With Beatrice's long legs and lush hair, you'd think one male in the group would acknowledge her. But her presence seemed to go unnoticed.

A cocktail waitress ambled up to her, but Beatrice brushed her off. She sat as demurely as the other women at the table.

One of the male constituents of the group leaned behind

Beatrice and gave the waitress a predatory yank of the wrist. He bellowed, "Hey, woman, us gentlemen be needing another round of brew. And add a line of shots. Scotch. And don't give us none of the cheap stuff. Only the best for my cousins."

The group's voices rose with each tip of their shots. "Ay, Johnston, how's your horse be running today?"

"Keith, going to be making up for last week's losses?"

"McDonald, next round's on you. Let's keep those shots coming."

As their bantering continued, Regina grasped my arm. "Maggie, do you hear those names? Those are common Travellers names."

Regina then flicked her hair, and Jax moved in even tighter. My guess, her hair fling was a silent signal for her bodyguard to move in close. In a muted voice she said, "Maggie, I believe those are the men who want to kill me."

"I thought you said it was one man that threatened you at your office."

"Yes, it was one man who visited my office. But he said his boys could care of me. Said they were keeping an eye out for me. Look at that crew. Tell me, which one would it be?"

CHAPTER TWENTY-ONE

Though the Scottish clan had planted themselves at the table to my right, I was still separated from them by Jax and Regina. I needed to move in closer to get a better take on this crowd. "Psst, Regina. Let me switch seats with Jax. I can't hear everything they're saying."

"Are you crazy? Those men are dangerous. Why do you think I'm paying top dollar for Jax?"

I wanted to say, "Because he's incredible in the sack," but tucked my tongue.

I glanced at the Travellers. These men could have played a part in Grant's death. And if they did, I would stop at nothing to get even. Grant might have been cheating, but I still loved him, and no one was going to leave my kids without a father. Nothing could spark a mother's revenge hotter than that. I shot Regina a glance that let her know if she didn't give me Jax's seat, I would appropriate it from him. Jax and I slipped into each other's chairs.

Most of the men's chatter focused on the races and how well they'd done or not done with their betting.

Like, "Hey, McDonald, too bad your luck sucks, seeing's how you're paying for these shots."

That drew an uproarious laugh from the guys, along with slaps on the back, saying, "You bein' a peevy today."

Peevy, what kind of term was that? Every time the men cracked a joke, I'd hear that word. And then one of them said, "You peevy. Aye, you're a drunk."

Oh, that's what peevy meant. A drunk. I had to agree, with their loud behavior, they did seem like a bunch of peevies.

But I also heard bits of conversation that sounded suspect. "Stewart, you're a smilin.' What ya' do, pay a special visit to the paddocks? "

Two of the men seated a bit farther down the table leaned close to each other, muttering words hard to make out. Sounded like they were talking about something like bronco. I couldn't make out the end of the word. But they tagged it with the phrase, "Having wind." Then I heard them mumbling about cobra venom.

Cobra venom. Did I hear them right? I understood why these men might be talking about "having wind." Sounded vital to an elite athlete, like a thoroughbred, winning a competition. But what was up with the mention of snake toxin? Sounded like a poisonous way of getting rid of one's competition, or someone. We were seated at one of the most esteemed racing establishments in the world. What was going down?

During a lull between two races, Beatrice slipped from the table and headed out the door. I wanted to tail her but didn't want the travelling men to see me. I bided my time. At the end of a particularly exciting race followed by cheers and more peevy slaps about the Scottish group, I made my exit.

I spotted Beatrice in the lobby. "Hi there. So good to see you again."

Beatrice stared at me with vacant eyes.

I extended my hand, babbling, "You're a member of Newport Hills Country Club, right? I saw you at the Social Mixer with Todd Williams. Todd and I have been friends forever."

With the mention of our esteemed club and, I suspect more importantly, my connection to Todd, Beatrice seemed to let down a bit of her perfectly styled hair.

"You're close with Todd?"

"Oh, yes, Todd and I are very tight. I used to work for him. When he was just starting out. Amazing how well he's done. Who would have thought miracle car leather cream would rake in millions. Actually, tens of millions."

"Todd's done that well? He said he worked in the

automotive accessory business but I didn't realize that could add up to such big money."

"Speaking of money," I said, pulling out a wad of greenbacks, "I need to place some bets." I ruffled the money across the palm of my left hand. Beatrice's eyes gaped at the fluttering of hundreds.

She stammered, "You sure came prepared."

"I'm always ready. That's one thing Todd taught me when I worked for him." I thought about the other things Todd coached me on but didn't think I should flaunt them to this particular young lady. Especially since I wanted to pump her for information.

"You're probably too young to remember them, but Todd's sexy T.V. infomercials skyrocketed his success."

"No, I don't. I've never watched much television."

"What I'm saying is, when the cameras rolled, it was my job to make sure everything was ready to go—the set, the slathering oil, Todd's tighter than tight tennis wardrobe."

"Oh, my."

"That was the public's reaction. Those television spots made Todd."

"Todd mentioned he wanted to venture into real estate. Sounds like he has the money to back up his plan."

"He has the money alright. And he's eager to venture out. Not only into real estate but in his personal life. I happen to know he's on the lookout for a beautiful woman to help him enjoy the fruits of his labor. Or should I say, the guacamole of his career? Todd's always been an avocado man." Sighing, I added, "Poor Todd. All that money and no place to spend it, except for his collection of exotic cars."

With each mention of Todd's money and sensuality, if you can call avocados sexy, Beatrice's eyes grew a centimeter in size.

"How do you know Todd's on the lookout for a woman?"

"Even though we haven't worked together for years, we've remained friends. Actually, more like confidants. Todd's discussed his desire to marry many times. But now with his recent breakup with his girlfriend...so sad. And of course, all that's money's he's dying to invest. Oh my. He mentioned you had a listing on some prime property. What a perfect fit."

At that moment, a cocktail waitress sidled by, and I touched her elbow. "Excuse me, I'm absolutely parched. Could you bring me a...what are you drinking, Beatrice?"

The young women's eyes scanned the lobby as if she was trying to spot a Traveller who might catch her consuming alcohol. She cleared her throat. "Greyhound. Can you make it a double?"

"Sure thing, hon," the waitress said, "A double on the way."

I chimed, "I'll have the same. It's on me. A drink for my new friend, or perhaps, business partner?"

Casting an odd glance, Beatrice asked, "What do you mean 'business partner?' I thought you said Todd wanted to invest."

"I did. But the idea of jockeying with high stake real estate sounds like fun. Tally ho!"

"You have money to invest?"

"I will. My recently departed husband left behind a hefty trust." Leaning closer to Beatrice, I added, "And unbeknownst to the IRS, he kept a shitload of cash in safety deposit boxes. Yes, I have the money to buy. Only the best. I'm looking for beachfront property. I'm willing to pay top dollar. After all, there's only so much coastline available in California. Or any other oceanfront state."

The drinks arrived. Beatrice and I clinked glasses to our newfound partnership. To my surprise, Beatrice downed hers in one gulp. I'm not normally a guzzly drinker, but I followed suit. My throat burned raw. Ouch. It always looked so easy in the movies when one slugged a drink. I guess they used either colored water or alcoholic actors. Definitely not acidic grapefruit juice coupled with a double shot.

The drink maven made another pass. Though my throat was scorching, I hailed another round. Once again, the two of us downed our drinks. With the champagne I'd consumed leading up to this, I couldn't believe I was still coherent, let alone chatting it up with Beatrice. But the notion she or her relatives played a part in Grant's death kept my heart racing and me sober. I maneuvered the conversation with the expertise I had when I was a marketing exec on the prowl for information that would snag a new client.

On the other hand, Beatrice didn't fare so well. Her lanky body swayed, and her speech slurred with a bit of a Scottish accent. I guess her gulping the alcohol wasn't from experience but her haste to get in a bit of fun before one of her clan spotted her. I knew this was my moment to pounce. I signaled the waitress for another round.

CHAPTER TWENTY-TWO

I nudged Beatrice toward a table at the back of the lobby. "Let's get comfortable and confidential so we can talk some serious business. If I'm going to be entrusting you with a fiduciary responsibility, I'd like to know a bit about your background."

"Like what?"

"I don't need to know all the details of your life. Just an overview of your real estate experience, what kinds of deals you've closed. Particularly ones in recent months...your love life."

With a slightly sloppy tongue, Beatrice began a rambling of her professional background. "Let's see. I've been in real estate since I got out of school. Never went to college. Actually, I didn't finish high school. Dropped out after my second year. I figured, why sit in a classroom when I can jump into the game and make some fast money?"

"I hear you. I wasted six years of my life doing the higher education thing. And for what? Thankfully, I married well. My husband knew how to take care of me."

"That's what men are for, right? Providing for us women." And with a devious grin she added, "And of course, for sex."

With her comment, an alluring image of Todd flashed before my eyes. And then blazed through my body. I practically moaned, "Of course, of course."

Bringing myself back to reality, I quizzed, "So why didn't you snag a rich guy and forget the whole career thing? A pretty gal like you? I bet you could have had your pick of the herd."

"I had my chances. Been dating someone recently. But I

don't think it's going to pan out."

"Oh, too bad. So what's kept you from connecting with a moneyed mate?"

"It's complicated. We moved around a lot, making it hard to get involved with someone outside the fam…"

"The what?"

Beatrice fumbled with her emptied glass, as if taking the time to choose her words. "The military family. My dad was in the army so we were constantly on the move. Soldiers are a tight group. It's hard to meet anyone outside your circle. And then there was the financial thing. You know what military men make? Next to nothing. How was I going to find a rich guy in that crowd? I decided I needed to branch out and find a way to make decent bucks. After all, I do like the good things in life.

"But I don't regret being shoved from one end of the country to the other. Gave me a good eye for real estate. I can spot a deal like that." And she tried to snap her sluggish fingers.

I tried to keep quizzing Beatrice about her real estate background and her love life, but her answers grew more vague with each sip of her drink. I wasn't used to this type of reaction to alcohol. Whenever I wanted to extract juicy gossip from one of my gal pal golfing partners, cocktails got them yapping faster than a Yorkie begging for a new diamond collar. But Beatrice had a lower tolerance for petro than I anticipated, and I knew we'd hit the end of Inquiry Lane.

I suggested we move back to the Turf Club. But the sudden pop of her eyes told me told me Beatrice did not want to join "the boys" in her current state.

"No need to worry, Beatrice. You're not that buzzed. Besides, the guys are too wrapped up in the races and too drunk themselves to detect you've had a bit of alcohol."

"You don't understand. My family forbids the womenfolk to drink. It's inexcusable. Ya git ma meaning?"

I didn't, but her slurred statement, coupled with her panicked expression, made me feel a tad guilty for getting her drunk to extract information. I snagged the cocktail waitress and ordered a round of coffee.

While we sipped our java, I tried to soothe Beatrice's nerves so she could make a seamless reentry into her family. I reassured her that the men at her table were slugging down the booze so fast, when she returned they wouldn't even notice she'd been gone.

As we made our way back to the Turf Club, she seemed to regain her coordination and self-confidence. She wouldn't have passed a Breathalyzer test, but she looked okay to me. "Why don't you go ahead? You'll do fine."

I held back for a couple of minutes and then strolled back to my group. Taking my seat, I glanced at Beatrice. One of the men placed a determined arm over her shoulder. With a low voice I could barely make out, I heard, "So Beatrice, you've been gone a long bit. What were you two womenfolk talkin' about?"

CHAPTER TWENTY-THREE

Regina also had her attention locked on the Travellers. Observing the overbearing nature of the man with Beatrice, she clutched my wrist with the power of a vice. Her strong hold told me she wouldn't let go until I told everything that had transpired during my meeting with this woman.

"Maggie, what were you thinking? That man did not look happy when he realized you and Beatrice were missing. The women of the clan are not allowed to socialize with outsiders. Do you want to get yourself killed? Thank God we have Jax." Regina let out a heavy sigh. "But he can't protect you if you choose to exceed the boundaries of his protective jurisdiction. And believe me, he has a loose definition of boundaries."

I thought about how only Regina could be obsessing about sex while living within the shadow of a death threat. But I couldn't fault her. If you're going to be taken out, perhaps by the Travellers, why not enjoy it in a blaze of sexual glory?

The wait staff swarmed our table hoisting silver platters displaying gourmet delights. The delicacies comprised every variety of oyster recipes one could imagine. My guess, Regina had ample input into this aphrodisiac menu. I love those devilish shellfish, but my stomach was grumbling for something more substantial. I needed some carbs to calm my digestive track and soak up some of the alcohol I'd consumed. Luckily, one waiter added baguettes of French bread to the mix. I tore into the basket, eating more bread than I would ever admit to my rail-thin, gluten-free, yoga instructor.

Regina and Jax busied themselves devouring the delights. At the rate they were going, I wondered if they would make it to Tinley's first post time before the oysters' magic kicked in.

I was right. Regina whispered to me that she needed to use the ladies room. Moments later, Jax heard the call of nature. I didn't time it, but it seemed quite a while before they returned to our table, their clothing and hair a bit skewed. At least Regina was being well protected by staying close to her bodyguard.

Tinley leaped to his feet, nearly upsetting our decadent feast. Clasping his hands to his chest, he burst, "This is it. My lovely's race. Montelucia is running. Oh, baby, this one is yours."

Regina snatched miniscule binoculars from her clutch bag. Not that she needed them. We had prime seats. But with Regina's legal background, she always came prepared.

The young thoroughbreds pranced into the starting gate. The bell rang, and the announcer bellowed, "And way they go!"

Montelucia exploded out of the gate. Her jockey, clothed in a mixture of green and black checks, hunkered low, giving the filly her lead. He let her set her pace, striding abreast of the others. As they rounded the first turn, Montelucia made her way to the rail and gained two more lengths in front of her competitors. She held the lead as she careened into the final stretch.

As she neared the finish line, two horses that trailed her burst forth with an energy that seemed to belie the ability of the strongest of race horses. They streaked past Montelucia just under the wire. Tinley's filly finished third.

Tinley slammed his fist on the table, nearly tumbling his flute of champagne. The vein in his left temple pulsated faster than his horse's hooves. I rose from my seat, reached over to clutch his trembling hand. "Tinley, Montelucia placed third. It was a tough race. Isn't that something to be proud of?"

"No, it's not. Montelucia was slated to win. All her practice times paced well ahead of the family's horses. She should have taken this race. Believe me, this isn't the first time this has occurred. I've heard rumors about them doping their horses, but I'm now starting to think they're true."

I relayed to Tinley the conspiratorial bits of conversation I'd overheard from the clan's table. How their mutterings about bronco something and cobra venom seemed odd.

Shaking his head, Tinley muttered, "No, not odd. But illegal."

"What do you mean?"

"Bronchodilators and snake venom are used to increase a horse's performance. Kind of like Olympic athletes using steroids."

"That sounds serious. Especially with so much money riding on these races. I'd think the race authorities would keep a close eye out for this sort of thing. If the Travellers are doping their horses, aren't they afraid of getting caught?"

"It's difficult to detect all of the substances being used. And with the stranglehold these gentlemen have on the racing scene, I suspect there's money passing hands."

"But Tinley, it seems like such a risk. Don't they fear being sanctioned or banned from races? Even prosecuted?"

"Maggie, if the Travellers have threatened Regina's life over a divorce of all things, do you think they're afraid of a little race tinkering?"

CHAPTER TWENTY-FOUR

I took a long sip of champagne. Tinley was right. If the Travellers threatened to kill one of Newport Beach's highest profile attorneys over a minor legal action, what would stop them from cheating on the horses? And what would prevent them from getting whatever they wanted, and by whatever means?

I'd come here today to fend off my sorrow over Grant's murder. But the Travellers had overshadowed my VIP getaway and robbed me of a day without worry.

They say life can turn on a dime. With the big money floating around Newport Beach, I'd say luck flipped like a hundred dollar bill. Mine certainly had. Grant's possible cheating—his sudden death—my best friend's life hanging in the balance. Before these horrible events, I felt my life had been a Snow White fairy tale. But now it was as if I'd bitten into the poison apple, and the evil witch who proffered the fruit was poised to finish me off.

I surveyed the gallery. At the back of the room, halfway hidden by its expansive bar, stood Dun Reid. Seemingly so conservative, I didn't take my handyman as the high-flying horse racing type.

He held racing forums in his hand and gave cursory glances toward the track, but didn't seem focused on the race action. His eyes scanned the Travellers' table.

Spotting me seated in close proximity to their group, Dun's eyes locked with mine. Brow furrowed, his expression looked none too happy. With a jerk of his head, he motioned me to join him. Easing out of my seat, I hoped no one, meaning the

Travellers, noticed my second sudden departure.

"What the hell are you doing here sitting next to the Travellers? They are not a friendly group."

"What am I doing here? I'm watching Tinley's thoroughbreds run. What are you doing here?"

"I'm here to enjoy the races. Why else would I be here?"

"I don't know, but the way you were lurking behind the bar, it looks to me like spying. What's your agenda, Dun?"

"I don't have an agenda. Like I said, I'm here to watch the horses."

Eyeing my friend, I said, "And why don't I believe you?"

Dun shifted his weight from foot to foot. This signaled to me his back was hurting, an ailment he lived with on a daily basis. But to me, it was also an indicator he was feeling uncomfortable. What was up with Dun?

"Okay, Maggie. I'll let you in. But this is speculation and purely confidential. I don't want it being passed around your country club."

"Dun, you know I would never do such a thing. Unless it's juicy. But for you, I'll make an exception."

"How mature of you." His eyes darted about the room. "You're right. I'm not here to watch the races. Except for Nick's."

"The detective has horses racing today?"

Glancing at his watch, he said, "Yes. Two. The first race is coming up, so I'll make this quick. I do have more than a passing interest in the Travellers. When I was shot, Nick and I were working the Fraud Unit. I, um, we were convinced the Scottish clan was into more than just shoddy roofing jobs. We trailed them for months. But with their constant name changes, forged IDs, and ghostlike ability to flee before we could question them, we found little. But I knew we were on the right track.

"Nick started receiving threatening messages. Calls to her house late at night. Disturbing messages about her family. That really shook her up. You know how public her family is."

I voiced my thoughts. "The Harringtons are in the society

section all the time. Their social outings would be so easy to track. Certainly an easy target if someone were intent on harming them."

"Exactly."

"Were you able to trace these cryptic calls?"

"No. All calls were made from disposable cell phones or ones that were stolen. Conversations stayed brief. I do remember the time I picked up a call and detected a Scottish accent."

"So you're sure it was the Travellers making the threats."

"Not one hundred percent. At that time, we had a shitload of fraud cases. Newport Beach may not have much violent crime, but with its big bucks crowd and high stakes corporate dealings, there's more than enough greed and fraud to go around. Needless to say, Nick and I worked one of the most overloaded units."

"So you never found out who was threatening Nick and her family."

"No. But I have my suspicions. And a short list of suspects."

"Okay, Dun. You're off the force, and Nick's now working Homicide. Life moves on. Nick was threatened, but she and her family are healthy and well. So why the fixation on the Travellers?"

"Because I believe they shot me."

My breath catapulted from my chest. "How can you be so sure? You said you had little evidence on them."

Dun closed his eyes, seemingly going back in time. "The night I was shot I was on my way to Nick's house."

I raised my eyebrows. Was their relationship more than police partners? Dun was a married man at the time.

Dun continued his story, not seeming to noticing my look of surprise. "Nick called me begging for me to help her. She'd just received a particularly disturbing call. She's tough. But this one made graphic threats to her family. They described how they could take them out in a slow, gruesome manner. During that call Nick believed she detected a Scottish burr."

Again, Dun shifted his weight. He stared across the room like he was conjuring up the painful memory. "I cruised a half block past her house, parked, turned off my lights. I crept up to the iron gate which marked the entry to her house. Eased it open as slowly as I could. I knew it had a piercing creak I'd been meaning to fix for Nick.

"But she'd passed it off, telling me my time was too valuable to bother with a squeaky gate. I cringed as it signaled my approach. I pulled my weapon, suspecting I'd compromised my position. As I crossed the limestone pathway leading to her front door, a blast exploded from behind. Next thing I remember was waking up after surgery, being told I'd be lucky to ever walk again. I vowed I'd catch the son of a bitch that ripped my life apart."

CHAPTER TWENTY-FIVE

After Dun's story of his shooting, a pall of sadness passed between us. I hoped that when we stepped back into the Turf Club, the posh surroundings would raise our spirits.

But Dun hardly needed a mood booster when he eyed a striking blond with cascading tresses striding up to us. She was sheathed in an orange Vera Wang with a cinched waist and puckered V-neck that revealed just enough—topped off by a demure C. K. Nobles hat that accentuated her designer dress without overpowering it.

I did a double take before I realized it was Detective Harrington. What a switch from the button-down pantsuit she'd worn during our first encounter. Talk about a transformation.

Her demeanor threw me off as well. Greeting me with a friendly nod, she gave Dun an even friendlier hug. She didn't appear to be the same woman I encountered the day she informed me of Grant's death—when she portrayed herself as a law enforcement officer encased in armor. The horrible day she'd switched from asking benign questions about my day's activities to grilling me about my exact whereabouts.

I stammered, "Hello, Detective. Nice to see you again."

"Relax, Maggie, I'm off the clock. I'm not here to question you. Why don't you call me Nicole?"

"Oh…sure, *Nicole*. What brings you here today?"

"The horses, of course."

"Right, silly question."

Dun interceded our awkward conversation. "When Nicole says the horses, she means *her* horses." Turning to his ex-partner, he beamed a wide smile. "You have two running today, don't you?"

What was up with Dun? He was not behaving like his usual self. I wanted to scream, "Dun, we just discussed Nicole and her horses. What's up with the gushing over your ex-partner?" But I zenned my mind to stay silent.

Nicole said, "Yes, I do have two of my babies on the track today." Checking her Cartier Pasha, she added, "Their post time's coming up. Dun, Tinley's asked us to join his table."

I cleared my throat. "Well, good luck, Nicole. So, you know Tinley?"

"Of course. Even though we're competitors, the racing crowd is a tight group. There may be a lot of money and ego at stake, but we have each other's best interests at heart."

"Oh. I didn't realize. I thought it would be a cutthroat business, um, sport. Are the Travellers part of this altruistic group?"

Nicole's smile faded. "No, they're not. In fact, their presence on the circuit is beginning to tarnish horseracing's long-standing ceremonial traditions. My father was appalled at the Travellers raucous behavior the last time he attended."

"So the Travellers like to party..."

"San Marino Racetrack has always upheld the highest standard of service—and expected the same from their guests. That's one reason my father's not here with me today."

I cleared my throat. "Seems your father has more to worry about than sloppy drunken behavior."

"What do you mean?"

"Well, from my discussion with Tinley, it appears there may have been some major cheating going on."

Nicole lowered her head, pressed her index fingers to her eyes.

Was she trying to expel unpleasant tears from her mind? Or press out fake ones?

She held up her head, gazing at me with dewdropped eyes. "I will confide to you there was more to my appearance today than watching my horses race. The Travellers try to legitimatize themselves by running blue ribbon money. But it still doesn't mean they can separate themselves from their ingrained family values—or lack of. Meaning, their con games. From what I've seen, they will cheat and steal from any vulnerable soul. And take from them whatever they can."

Her eyes cut to Dun. She sniffled. "Not only stealing one's life, but possibly committing murder."

I quizzed, "What are you talking about?"

Nicole exhaled like she'd been withholding a secret for a long time. "I think this clan is connected to several cold cases in our area. I'm sure you're aware Newport Beach has an extremely low murder rate, but you may not know there're unsolved deaths out there I'd bet my trust fund are tied to the Travellers. And when you take into account the less desirable surrounding cities—"

"Like Santo Reno?"

"Santo Reno?" Nicole hissed.

My mention of the decaying town seemed to reignite a burning spark in her brain. Straightening her spine, the detective stared me down. "Speaking of Santo Reno. Like I said, I'm not here to question you. But my professional training can't help me from wondering what you're doing here so soon after your husband's death."

So taken off guard by Nicole's casual manner, or faked theatrics—I wasn't sure which persona to believe—I hadn't stopped to think how my presence here today might seem inappropriate to a police officer. "I, um, I'm a guest of Tinley's. I didn't want to attend, but he insisted."

"So soon after viewing Grant laid out on a morgue slab?"

The heartless phrasing of Nicole's question almost caused my champagne to lurch from my throat.

Dun must have sensed my distress. He clutched Nicole's arm, nudging her away from me. "Hey, Nick, you don't want to miss your horses' races."

"We have time. I'd like Maggie to answer my question."

I squelched the emotional bile I wanted to spill on her designer silk dress. "Okay, Nick. I'll come clean. I *am* a party guest of Tinley's. But I'm not here for fun. My true motive for being here is also the Travellers. I heard they'd have horses running today."

"And that brought you out of mourning?"

"Look. I know the stories about the Travellers. Today I learned it looks they're infiltrating the race world. It appears they ingratiated their way into Grant's business, which I believe played a part in his murder. There's no way I could resist the urge to investigate on my own."

"Pardon me, Maggie. You're a Newport Beach housewife. What would you know about inspecting a group like the Travellers?"

"What would I \know? Let me tell you, Nicole. Following my internship with Todd, I was a top-rated marketing exec at Bratham and Brothers. You must know of them. The firm that made almost every successful company in Newport Beach— including your father's. When I was employed there, I did research. And when I say research, I mean I'd take a client and their adversaries and pick them apart bit by bit. I'd learn their strengths *and* their weaknesses—and every little secret in between."

Nicole waved me off. "Research. Doesn't sound like police investigating to me."

I was tempted to wag my finger in front of Nicole's nose, but good sense told me to hold off. "Detective, most of my investigations would make your police work look like a cartoon version of *CSI*."

Nicole took a step toward me. Dun grasped her arm tighter.

Tinley swept through the Turf Club's exit and joined our trio. He brushed Nicole's cheeks with kisses. "My dear, Nicole. I was wondering when you would arrive. I was fretting you'd miss the running of Daddy's Princess. Let's hope she has better luck than Montelucia did earlier."

"Tinley, wonderful to see you again. But what is it you're saying about Montelucia? You don't mean..."

"It's a sordid story. I'll fill you in later. Let's get back to the club. I'm sure you don't want to miss your Princess's race. We best take our seats."

"You're right. I'd die if I let my darling down."

We shuttled through the elegant lounge toward our party's window-front table. About halfway to our seats, Nicole skidded to a halt. "And what the hell is *she* doing here?"

I followed the trajectory of her stare, which led to Regina and Jax, cozied in their chairs.

Regina looked back at the detective, returning her daggered stare. "What am I doing here? Why aren't you out flatfooting it on your beat?"

Oh God, how could I have forgotten the bad blood between Regina and Nicole? They both looked ready to pounce. I looked to the men of our group, who seemed frozen in shock.

I stepped between the two women. "Whoa, slow down, ladies. Nicole is here because she has horses running today. Regina is here because...after Grant's murder, I felt I needed protection. And who better to fit the bill than a macho-type like her legal assistant, Jax? I glanced in the direction of the Travellers, and lowered my voice." Since I'm here to check out the Travellers, I felt it prudent to bring along some body armor."

"Assistant. I bet. Assisting in a clandestine affair is more like it." Nicole shook her finger in Regina's face. "I've heard the stories."

Now *I* was ready to pounce. Nobody badmouths my best friend. And Jax looked ready to pull his weapon.

Tinley finally snapped to attention and intervened. "Now, now, my dears. Looks like the perfect time for a soothing flute of champagne. And there're oodles of oysters to enhance your moods. Chop, chop. Let's get back to my party." Peering between the members of our group, he added, "Besides, we don't want to miss the next race. Hopefully this one will be a fair one."

CHAPTER TWENTY-SIX

We took our seats, putting aside our differences as we delved into Tinley's delectable delights. Just as I slurped a shellfish into my mouth, Nicole called out, "Look, it's Daddy's Princess." Her sudden burst caused my mussels to slip into my lap. I wrapped the slimy being into my napkin and eased it onto the floor.

A parade of thoroughbreds pranced onto the track, calming escort horses flanking their sides. The workhorses guided the sleek racing machines to the starting gate. A couple of horses fought the bit as the track handlers led each horse into their slot.

The announcer boomed, "And away they go!" The gates sprang open, and the horses shot out faster than bullets from an AK-47. They sped down the first furlong, Daddy's Princess two lengths behind the lead.

I glanced at the racing monitor perched upon our table. The filly's odds advertised her as a strong shot as the winner. She ran steady, holding her pace in the pack. As they rounded the final turn, she held the rail, making her move, taking the lead.

Nicole cheered, "Come on, Princess! You're almost there."

My friends and I, caught up in the moment, rose to our feet.

Nicole cheered, "Run, Princess, run! That's it, baby. You've got it!" But at the closing furlong Johnnie's Girl emerged out of nowhere, edging out Daddy's Princess by a nose

Nicole threw down her racing forum as a tiny glisten peeked from her eye. She leaned into Dun. He hugged her shoulder. Silence overtook our spontaneous eruption. Even Regina, and more notably, Jax, looked deflated.

A roar from the Travellers' table burst throughout the room. "Hey, Johnnie, your filly beat out that prissy Princess. Way to go!" Clinks of beer mugs rang.

Tinley leaned into Nicole. "That's what I wanted to tell you. About Montelucia's race. Same thing happened. She was favored five to two. The Travellers horse shouldn't have even been in the money. Then out of nowhere, their horse burst forth with an ungodly speed. During training runs, that filly didn't even come close to her winning time. Seems a bit sinister to me."

Nicole nodded. "I agree. I suspected something like this would happen today. I spoke to my father about this, and he, too, is suspicious of the Travellers' winnings. Father's been pressing the racing board to tighten the drug testing. But even with his influence, he felt they weren't taking the issue seriously. I'm sure there's not only doping but money changing the outcome of these races."

Tinley's head bobbed up and down. "That's what Maggie overheard. Well, maybe not the money angle but definitely the possible use of enhancement drugs. Maggie, what was that you overheard from the Travellers?"

Nicole added, "Let's hear it. Please."

Shocked the Homicide Detective would be asking for results from my snooping, I stammered, "I heard them saying one of their horses was a sure thing. They muttered about bronco-something—and cobra venom. I didn't know what that meant, but it sounded strange, and suspicious."

Nicole clinched her fists, breath coming fast. "God dammit! Those sons of bitches."

Dun touched Nicole's arm. "Hey, calm down. I can't imagine how frustrating this may be. But it's just one day of the season. Surely the Travellers can't be in every race you're in."

"Dun, it's not just one race. And it's not the money— although as you know, my family invests millions in our horses. It's to carry on the sport—the tradition." She spread her arms.

"Look at our surroundings. This racetrack has been a southern California landmark for over a century. I remember my father's stories of mingling here with the likes of Jimmy Stewart and Natalie Wood. I'm afraid this shady news will just about kill him."

The announcer sounded the beginning of the next race. Nicole gripped her hands, almost in prayer. She whispered, "Please, Phoenix Rising, do it. Do what you were born to do."

Sadly, the race turned out much like the last one. Only worse. Phoenix came in third, outrun by what I guessed were two of the Travellers horses. And my suspicions were confirmed when their cheers once again erupted, and the acrid smell of sloshed beer permeated the room.

Nicole looked physically defeated. Though I didn't care for the detective, I could feel her pain. Her horses, cheated from winning. Like one's child robbed from his birthright. Robbed by the Travellers.

My eyes targeted on the group. They stood as if on cue, abandoning their drinks, brushing through the Turf Club's exit. I assumed these enthusiastic drunks would stumble their way to the Winner's Circle for more revelry. But when jockey and horse strode into the ring of honor, greeted with a gleaming trophy and wreath of red roses, no owners were there to greet them.

Tinley's eyes followed mine to the winner's arena.

I mumbled to him, "Owners nowhere to be seen. Isn't celebrating in the limelight part of horseracing tradition?"

"Yes, it is. But my guess is the Travellers want to vanish before the spotlight points to them. I view their hasty retreat as the ultimate snub to this esteemed establishment." His voice cracked as he added, "We used to call thoroughbred racing the sport of kings. Now, kings of the gypsies is more like it."

CHAPTER TWENTY-SEVEN

I awoke Monday morning with remnants of champagne hammering my temples. The food—or to be more accurate, oysters—tasted delicious. However, their lack of carb-infused substance did little to stave off a hangover. I should have downed more bread.

But there was no time to lament about my partying woes. Motherly instinct told me to make sure my teens had set their cell phone alarms and were now getting ready for school. I scuttled down the hallway in my Crocs slippers, only to screech to a stop. In my hangover haze, I'd momentarily forgotten my kids were in protective custody at the Peterson's. Thank God for this dear family, keeping my teens safe.

I quick-brewed a cup of Keurig mocha-flavored coffee and wandered onto my patio. I needed to relax, absorb all that had happened. And, I needed time to grieve.

Though nobody has the perfect marriage, I'd always believed Grant and I would have a forever life. Like in the fairy tales...where love and passion trails on and on, happily ever after.

How had our marriage gone astray? Had it? Even though my head screamed Grant had cheated on me, my emotions kept telling me he hadn't. I pondered his story about trying to make the cousin at our club jealous. Was it true? Perhaps. Maybe he had planted evidence in his golf bag and left it to be found. And thinking back to the envelope sporting the sexalicious card that Grant ridiculously sealed with my Candy Apple lipstick smooch, I wondered, why would he add such an amateurish come-on to the card? Did he think that was sexy?

Or was he leaving behind a clue that the message in the card wasn't for real?

And then I received a text message from Carmen I did not want to read.

I dressed in a Tahari pantsuit with accentuating sleek pumps and climbed into my car. It was time to visit Grant's office and find out what was really going on.

I entered the lobby in which Leman Land Development leased a floor of office space. Signaling a perfunctory wave to the security guard, I strode past the elevator and into the stairwell. I mounted the one hundred eighty steps leading to the sixth floor, which Grant's company occupied. Between my sweaty Bikram sessions, tennis and golfing outings, I didn't need the exercise. It was company policy. Grant's green business model prohibited the building's elevator from stopping at the sixth floor—my destination.

So I was relegated to climbing and climbing. This No-Elevator policy meant less wattage waste, trimmer employees. Dual win-wins in the emerging emerald world.

If I'd been lazy, or smart, I could have taken the elevator to the seventh floor and walked down one flight. But out of respect for my deceased husband and his firm belief in his company, I made the trek.

Huffing through the double teakwood doors of Leman Land Development, I greeted the receptionist, Tina, and asked to see Carmen. "Certainly Mrs. Leman. I'll buzz her now. And I am so sorry for your loss."

"Thank you, Tina."

Carmen marched into the lobby, greeted me with a curt condolence, and then nodded toward the conference room. I never cared for Carmen. She always seemed so abrupt. But then I realized that perhaps her silent head signal, coupled with pursed lips, was her attempt to let me know something was up. And judging by the lines crossing Carmen's face, it didn't appear to be something pleasant. I breathed a thankful sigh of relief I'd dressed as a businesswoman from my professional past and not in my usual yoga garb.

I peered inside the spacious meeting room with floor to ceiling glass wall and MOSO bamboo flooring. The vibes Carmen radiated to me were confirmed. Seated around the expansive yet minimalist conference table were three men and a woman wearing serious suits and grim expressions. Their staid attire and stern demeanor signaled they weren't Travellers. No popping shirt buttons or raucous back slaps here. I'd expected at worst to find the clan sitting here. This group certainly wasn't. A good sign or bad?

My hand trembled as I pressed my palm upon the glass door. I held my pose for a moment, taking a deep cleansing breath, determined to settle my nerves.

The woman rose, her well-built frame towering what seemed six inches above mine. With a firm grasp of my hand, she said, "I'm Inspector Wolperg from the California Building Standards Commission. We have some questions to ask you about your deceased husband's recent business activity. These are my associates…"

The names and faces of the group blurred my mind. I struggled to focus. Then without a chance to absorb what was happening, the group barraged me with questions and accusations about Grant's business not complying with green building codes.

I shook my head. "Wait, stop. I can't even hear what you're saying. Please, I just lost my husband. At least have the courtesy to question me in a civil manner."

The four sat somber-faced, looking stiff in the sleek, ergonomic conference chairs. "I'm sorry, Mrs. Leman," said Inspector Wolperg. "But we're under a great deal of stress to flush out who's responsible for the degradation of the environmental building in Newport Beach."

A man in the group with a face drearier than his gray tie spoke. "Since the enactment of the environmental standards of LEED, your husband has been a leader in the eco-building movement in this community, and he helped champion the CALGreen initiative. Your husband was very public in promoting construction utilizing low-pollutant materials and energy-saving devices. I know this is a difficult time for you. But to be blunt, Mr. Leman's business is grossly out of compliance. Not only with CALGreen, but with LEED."

"Grant would never fall out of compliance."

Dreary Tie seemed not to hear me and continued, "I'm certain you're aware of the environmental rating system of LEED."

"Yes, it's been in effect almost as long as Grant's been in business. So?"

"For years, Leman Land Development held the esteemed Platinum rating. Two years ago, they slipped to Gold, then Silver. During inspection of recent projects, I'd have to say they're in jeopardy of landing on Certified, meaning the company is way out of code."

"I hear what you're saying, but I don't believe you. I would know if this was happening. I may not be involved in the day-to-day business operations, but I'm listed in the corporate documents as successor to the company. Grant put that in place in case...anything should happen to him...so I would have the authority to run the company. With this being in place, I'm certain Grant would have confided to me any major problems within the company."

He continued as if he hadn't heard me—or didn't care. "With the company's noncompliance with the newer, more stringent CALGreen criteria, it appears Mr. Leman has compromised not only his business standards but his long-held personal ones as well."

"Like I said, I'm not privy to every detail of Grant's business. But I know what kind of businessman he was. How passionately he believed in environmental building. He would never jeopardize what took years to establish."

Inspector Wolperg chimed in. "That's what's so puzzling. During our recent visits to his projects, we found his company wasn't installing low-pollutant flooring such as the bamboo in this office. Nor the required energy-saving air-conditioning systems. They were installing cheaper versions. Not ones consistent with Leman's Platinum standards. And it appeared their seasoned workforce had changed." She sighed. "I guess they do business differently in Scotland."

"What does Scotland have to do with my husband's business?"

A beep erupted from the hip pocket of the woman's pantsuit. Checking her cell, she said, "Looks like another green building being compromised."

She glanced about her group, then at me. "Mrs. Leman, we'll have to continue this discussion at a later date. I advise you to take a hard look at your deceased husband's business and find out what caused him to jeopardize everything."

Springing from my chair, I shouted, "Everything! What on earth are you talking about?"

The man with the gray tie rose to his feet. "Let's keep it under control. We're just here to let you know that unless Mr. Leman's business successor, you can get these projects up to CALGreen standards, we're going to have to shut down operations."

Inspector Wolperg stood, and stepped between gray tie and me. She managed a cracked smile. "I know this isn't pleasant for you. But it's our job—and obligation. Being the beneficiary to Mr. Leman's business, like my colleague said, it's in your best interest to find out what was going on and get the projects up to code. Before our next meeting."

CHAPTER TWENTY-EIGHT

With that cryptic remark, the group whisked from the room. I slumped into a conference chair. As much as one can slump in a sleek, ergonomic piece of furniture.

I didn't know how long I sat there when I heard a faint tap on the glass door. I looked across the room. Carmen held a coffee mug in one hand, a thick file in her other.

I gestured for her to enter. She approached me, offering me an aromatic cup of java. "I thought you could use this."

"You don't know how much—especially after the news I just heard."

I relayed to her how the commission had reported to me that Grant's business practices had been compromised. "Carmen, do you have any idea what's been going on? As Grant's administrative assistant, you were stationed just outside his door. You screened his calls."

She glanced away, as if she were afraid to answer my question.

"Please, Carmen, if you know anything, you need to tell me."

Carmen stared at me with somber gray eyes. She fingered the file she'd brought with her. "Mrs. Leman…"

"Please, call me Maggie."

"Okay, Maggie. There were some odd things going on. I don't mean to disrespect your husband, but for several months, God, even longer, the company hasn't been operating in its normal, professional manner. At first I thought this was due to the fact he was such a busy man and was pulled in so many directions—overseeing new projects, working with investors, all the while inundated with public appearance requests and interviews about the future of eco-building."

"Yes, Grant was busy. But I always felt he was good at multitasking and could handle it."

"He was. But it came to the point where he became too over-burdened to thoroughly research the backgrounds of the new investors."

"What are you talking about? Once Grant established himself, he never needed to seek out investors. He worked with an outstanding group of people. We socialized with them many times over the years. Why would Grant be taking on people whose backgrounds needed to be checked?"

Carmen dropped her voice. "With Mr. Leman's success, more and more outsiders wanted in. And they were willing to invest. Big time. Mr. Leman saw this as an opportunity to take the company to a whole new level."

"Grant provided our family with a comfortable lifestyle. We didn't need the money."

"It wasn't about money. Mr. Leman relayed on several occasions how this influx of funds could spread his vision of sustainable building beyond southern California. Perhaps even globally."

I thought about this. Grant had confided to me his desire to expand. I'd taken it as a normal step in his career path. I didn't realize his fervor to change the face of world construction. How could I have missed this? Was I too caught up in my Newport lifestyle to listen? Or had Grant shut me out of his dreams?

Carmen's voice rattled me from my turmoil. "I didn't like what I was seeing. These new investors seemed too anxious to get in on projects. When I'd give them the required Leman due diligence documents, they practically waved them off. Didn't want to be burdened with paperwork. I brought this up to Mr. Leman, but he assured me these people had come highly recommended and not to worry."

Carmen continued, "I felt something was amiss in the company, so I started compiling this file. I'm sorry, Mrs.

Leman, I mean Maggie. I probably over-stepped my grounds."

"No, Carmen. I'm glad you were concerned. Please, go on."

She cleared her throat. "I copied documents that looked suspicious. And being in and out of private meetings, sometimes I heard things that seemed amiss. I'd commit them to memory and then write them down as soon as I could get back to my desk."

"What types of things are you talking about?"

"As first-time investors, the amount of money these people brought to the table was staggering. One proposed an initial investment of half a million dollars—in addition to taking an unheard of low percentage on his capital return."

"Did Grant push him into this deal?"

"No. The man offered it. Promised to bring in additional investors."

"Sounds like a profitable situation to Leman."

"At first, that's what I thought. But then I noted odd entries on docs. Not the normal partnerships or trusts I was used to reviewing. These investor lists contained surname redundancies. Like Johnston, or Stewart multiple times."

Johnston, Stewart—those were Travellers' names! What the hell was going on?

"Carmen, this sounds like some shady things were going on."

"I agree. And there were other factors that raised red flags."

"Let me guess. Unusual accent, tacky attire—not to mention vulgar manners."

"Yes."

"The investigators from the Building Standards Commission mentioned something about how 'they build things differently in Scotland.' Did any of these suspicious investors appear to be of Scottish descent?"

Dropping her voice, Carmen said, "Not the ones who initiated the deals. Except for their exceptionally high initial investments, these new clients seemed to be aboveboard businessmen. Or women. They often used a female real estate agent to handle their preliminary meetings. She was young, but conducted herself professionally. Until the day she announced to Mr. Leman that the primary investors were too busy to handle the mundane tasks and introduced him to their subordinates. These new contacts spoke with Scottish inflection—and appeared shady from the get-go."

"If you had such a suspicious vibe from these people, how could Grant have let them into his inner business circle? I know you said he was busy, but…"

"Your husband was busy. But he was a smart man. Too busy to check out these people himself, he had his lawyers conduct financial and criminal background checks on these people."

"And let me guess—they came up clean."

"Exactly."

"So tell me, Carmen, what could have gone so terribly wrong?"

"Diana Hutchinson, for one."

I sprang from my seat. "What? How could she be hooked into this? She sells memberships at my country club!"

Carmen grasped my hand, coaxing me back into my seat. "I know. She's such a tacky bitch. After the original investors handed over the reins, she tagged along with the real estate agent who'd been the go-between. Then she started popping in on her own. Nudged her way into business negotiations, gushing how she'd known these investors for years. Bragged they'd been premier members at the country club she'd worked at—and had a penchant for not only hitting the greens, but investing in Green."

"So, by promoting the country club connection she made them appear to be more respectable."

Carmen chimed in, "Appear is the operative word. Grant didn't like Diana. Confided to me he felt there was something off about her. But she was so pushy."

"I know. I can't believe she works at Newport Hills. Let alone has access to enter the door. Question is how'd she get through to Grant?"

CHAPTER TWENTY-NINE

Carmen slipped me the file and returned to her sentry post. I wandered back into Grant's personal office. I knew I had to take control of this situation, but my mind and body were knotted in paralysis. As Diana Hutchinson had recently and so rudely pointed out, I'd been out of the workforce *so long.*

But then the thought of Diana playing a role in the compromised state of Grant's business sent shocks piercing through my nervous system, blasting away my feeling of helplessness.

I slapped Carmen's file onto Grant's desk and rifled through its contents. Scanning the pages Carmen had Xeroxed and the notes she'd taken, I searched for a clear picture of what had transpired in the months leading to the degradation of Grant's company. An ominous pattern began to emerge.

My concentration shattered when Carmen shouted down the hall, "Stop right there! Just where do you think you're going?"

I couldn't hear the intruder's answer—just a clacking of heels along the bamboo floor, the echoes heading my way.

Carmen barked louder, "I said, where the hell do you think you're going?"

And then Diana Hutchinson barreled through Grant's door. Her heels screeched to a stop when she spotted me seated behind the desk. I cringed at the damage her stilettos had done to the expensive eco-flooring.

"Maggie. What you doing here?"

Springing from my chair, I glared into her squinting eyes. "Me? What are you doing?"

Diana backed up a couple of steps, stumbling on wobbly heels. Grabbing a chair, she clumsily regained her balance. "I, uh, I came to pick up a list of potential country club members. Grant told me, before his passing…that he had some new investors interested in joining."

"And you came for them now?"

"Hey, Maggie, you understand how the system operates. Either you produce, or you're out. I need that list."

At that moment, I wanted to catapult the desk and throttle her skinny, pathetic throat. But I glued my feet to the floor, knowing assaulting Diana would only add to my troubles. Besides, Diana had always chosen to take the low road, and I steeled myself to stick to the high one.

"My husband's just been murdered, and you're so classless you break into his office for a list of wannabe country club members? Not only is that incredibly disrespectful, it's beyond suspicious. Diana, why don't I believe your excuse? Why are you really here?"

As Diana started to mumble some sort of answer, I spied her clutching a Gitan.

I strutted around the expanse of Grant's desk, pushing in close to Diana. "The country club victims have all been found with Gitan bags next to their bodies. And now you're carrying one. Ever since I've known you, you've always carted a cheap purse. Now you're holding a nine-hundred-dollar bag. Kind of makes me think you're closer to the country club murders than you're letting on. Tell me, Diana, what's your role in all of this?"

CHAPTER THIRTY

"You're implying I can't afford a Gitan? I've been working my ass off for the last umpteen years while you played Miss Disney. Wow, talk about a tough life. You, not having to work. Me, always worrying about bringing in new club members. Often one step ahead of the commission checks that would keep me above water. But look now. Prince Charming's been knocked off, and the fairy tale princess has to climb down from her hoity-toity tower and work. How sad…guess with Grant's murder, life may have a way of evening the reality scales."

"Say what you will, but I still sniff a phony, polymer scent on you even with your change from tacky to designer. When we worked together, you didn't know a Gucci from a got-it-off-the-rack."

Diana placed her hands firmly on her skinny hips. "Why shouldn't I treat myself to a nice bag? I'm now making good money. Say hello to the new President of Newport Hills Marketing Department."

"Whoopee. Who'd you have to sleep with?"

Diana flinched like she wanted to attack.

I smirked, "Don't even try. I'll have security here faster than you can run down the hallway on your cheesy heels. But let's get back to the bag. Even with your promotion, I can guess what you make for a living. And I bet a Gitan would still put a hefty tug on your paycheck."

"What are you talking about? You've been out of the game so long I'd say your payroll knowledge of Corporate America is skewed. Or maybe your ergonomic position with Todd

Williams is screwed, oops, I mean skewed. But then, Todd would make the perfect rescue prince. Especially since your marriage with Grant may not have led to the happy land you hoped for."

"How dare you. Grant and I had a wonderful marriage. Todd and I are just friends. I never would have cheated."

"Apparently your buried-six-feet under husband did."

With that remark, I lunged at Diana, desperate to rip her birdlike eyes from her face.

Carman burst through the door, grasping my hands with an amazing show of strength. "Maggie, let it go. Diana's not worth it." Turning to Diana, "It's time for you to leave."

"Wait, Carmen, I need Diana to answer one question."

Diana attempted to smooth her straggled locks. "Well, if you promise to back off, go at it. After that, I'm out of here."

Taking a minute to think how I would confront this woman, I stammered, "Why were you always in and out of town when we were colleagues? Your abrupt departures meant having to continually restart your career, sticking you at the bottom of the pay scale. That's what made me doubt your ability to purchase a Gitan. Tell me, Diana, why were you always traveling about?"

"I wasn't traveling about. I needed to visit my relatives. Help them when they were in a pinch. In my family, we take care of each other."

With that remark, long-forgotten rumors of Diana's family swirled through my brain. Cousins under suspicion for a variety of crimes. A close-knit family allegedly involved in all sorts of con games. But nothing concrete was ever proven.

"That's right, Diana, your family. If I recall correctly, years ago there were several newscasts about their shady business practices. Hmm, let me think. Like the one about their phony roofing scam and the one about leaving a widow's driveway halfway paved before taking off with her money. And, the one—"

"How dare you talk about my family like that? Those S.O.B reporters were just out to make a name for themselves. Caught wind of one rumor then they all piled on. My family has always worked their asses off. Not like some people who spend their days flirting around."

"What are you implying?"

"I saw your red lipstick stain on Todd's cheek at the club mixer. Looked suspicious to me. What are the most common motives for murder? Money? Sex? Looks to me like you're hitting both bullets. Word around town is Grant's business isn't the shining example of green it used to be. Made it difficult for him to bring in the green you were so used to? And around the time your husband shows up dead, looks like you and Todd have rekindled your old romance. Who's the one looking fishy now, Maggie?"

CHAPTER THIRTY-ONE

After Diana's insulting remark, I ordered her out of Grant's office. Pushed my mind back into attack mode. Carmen's hand-written files shared a great deal of information, but I needed more. I tried to log onto Grant's computer but was stumped when asked to input his password. I'd made hundreds of visits to his office. How could I not know such basic information?

I looked to Carmen still standing by the door. "I need to logon onto Grant's computer. Do you know his password?"

She cleared her throat. "Thankfully, yes. Mr. Leman gave me access, in case...as he said, in case anything should happen."

The grip of my throat almost choked me. "You're saying he felt threatened?"

"I can't say that with certainty. But in recent weeks, Mr. Leman began asking me to serve refreshments during private meetings. Before, I'd always been instructed to set up before such a conference began and stayed at my desk during their discussions. It was almost as if Mr. Leman wanted me to have greater access to what was transpiring.

"It gave me a strange feeling. I became even more vigilant about noting my observations. I'm sorry, Mrs. Leman. I know I was overstepping my bounds, but I wanted to protect Mr. Leman."

I grasped Carmen's hand. "Please don't think that. With Grant's murder, not to mention the Building Standards Commission breathing down our backs, I'm grateful beyond words. Now let's get into the brains of this computer and find out what's really going on."

I searched through file after file on Grant's building projects, scrutinizing the capital outlay versus cash flow. My cursory scrutiny told me Grant's recent project expenditures soared way beyond his previous ones. And I was taking into account the stricter CALGreen construction costs. But what screamed from the computer were the names of recent major investors—Stewart, Johnson, MacDonald. Travellers. Just like Carmen had said. Seeing this directory with my own eyes made me feel Grant was sending a message from the grave. And the shudder down my spine told me that message was nothing short of cryptic.

I noted there was a pricey project with Stewart and Associates going up down the road from Grant's office. This venture looked to be soaring way above budget. Worse, a change of title burst from the screen. Stewart and Associates had jumped from role of investor, to being sole owners. I wanted to scream into the computer, "Grant, how did you allow this to happen?" But hysterics were futile.

I ripped up Coastal Road, weaving in and out of tourist traffic like I was Danica Patrick. So hyped over my findings, I almost passed Grant's building site. I stomped on the brake and cranked the wheel into the parking lot. My Benz bounded into it in rhythm to the honking of the angry couple that nearly rear-ended me when surprised by my crazed driving.

Bouncing through the rutted parking lot, torn up during the construction process, I surveyed the structure. The building site was in the stage where it was just beginning to take form. Although the exterior walls were still bare-boned, I noted how the stone indigenous to our coastal cliffs provided the structure of the supporting pillars. This lot had been previously tagged with a bland cement slab medical building that had been an eyesore. I was happy to see it being replaced with a work of local pride.

Walking around the property, I found only two workers at the site. They huddled at the back of the project, sorting through mounds of stone. Where was the rest of the crew?

Looking at my watch, I noted the time stood just past noon. The rest of the guys must have shuttled off to grab some lunch. Better for me. Safety in smaller numbers.

The two men appeared to be in their late teens—twenty at the oldest. Although they toiled at heavy construction, their clothes looked pristine, like they washed and pressed them twice a day.

Waving my hand, I tried signaling them. They continued working. Perhaps not understanding my gesture, or choosing not to, I bellowed to them, my voice rising above the grating noise of their stone sifting. "Excuse me, I'd like a bit of your time." The two kept working. I raised my voice an octave higher. "I said I want to speak to you."

One of the young men, slouched over the pile of stones, slid a sideways glance to his coworker. The two stopped, stood tall to their full height. My eyes met with two muscled chests. Their machismo so strong, I thought, how stupid to be hidden behind a nearly deserted building site. How I could put myself in such a vulnerable situation?

I managed to thrust back my shoulders and keep myself from quaking. Through my years of marketing, I knew if I appeared vulnerable, I would never obtain the information needed to close the deal.

"Looks like you two are busting your butts to get this job done. I have to say, nice work. But where's the rest of your crew? Deserted you two to do the grind work?"

I knew they hadn't been permanently deserted. But I wanted to inject a slice of jealously as to why they were stuck working while the rest of the boys were off. Nothing like driving a poisonous wedge between cohorts to get one talking.

The slightly taller one, who possessed a super-sized physique built by hours in the gym or hard labor, stepped forward. "Lady, either you don't know nothin' about putting up a building, or you're full of shit. My guess, both."

He exchanged a knowing smirk with his buddy with the Crisco' d hair and unshaved stubble.

"Okay, smart guys, then where did the rest of the crew go?

My guess is they're slopping down a few brews over a cozy lunch of prime rib sandwiches while you're stuck here. But I'm sure they didn't tell you that. I bet they said they were going to Santo Reno to grab a quick bite off the lunch truck and promised to bring you back some. Am I right?"

The smirks slid from their faces.

"So you newbies are left here sucking wind while the old boys are yucking it up about how gullible you are. Get over it. That's nothing on the ladder of life. Think about your cousins who haven't been slick enough to evade the law and are now warming their butts in a sterile jail cell."

The second guy bulging less muscles, but who still looked like he could easily take me down, chimed in. "Now you really don't know shit about nothin'. We got no cousins in jail."

"Yeah, yeah, I know the story. Your family's business dealings are pristine as fresh snow. Have you ever seen the snow in the mountains outside L.A.? It's dirty, polluted. Like your family. Sure, for every one that gets stuck for a while in the pokey, a dozen or two get away. I know your family's history."

The young men started to give me a retort. I shut it by whipping out a quick question. "What I want to know is how Stewart and Associates plays into this project? I have insider info this started out as a Lehman Land Development deal. Now Stewart's sole proprietor. What's up with the switch, boys?"

At the mention of Stewart, the second worker's eye twitched. Though he tried to emulate masculine security, I detected bravado-veiled fear. I took a step forward. "Like I said, why the change of players?"

The man started to speak. Stopped.

Damn. I felt so close to getting information from the Travellers who probably weren't the most schooled at keeping family secrets. I had to find a way to make these young men talk. My knowledge of the Travellers told me crispy cash would be the best way to get them yapping.

Dipping my hands into my slacks, I fingered a wad of bills.

Thank God, I'd reused the pants I'd worn at the track. That was the one day I carried real money instead of my credit cards.

I snagged a bill, leafing it in front of the young men. Following its path, their eyes bulged at the sight of a Ben Franklin.

"I see you like money. Very good. Tell me, who are Stewart and Associates? And how have they taken over this project?"

I stopped fluttering the hundred and held it within sniffing distance. The muscled one cleared his throat. "The Stewarts, they're our uncles."

"You want this money, be more specific."

"It's true. Stewart and Associates are three of our uncles. But the top one is Charles Stewart."

"So Charles is the man in charge."

The young man's Adam's apple pulsed. "Yeah. Charles—"

The roar of testosterone-motored engines brought a halt to his confession. He backed away from me so fast, he stumbled over a chunk of discarded cement and went down hard.

Whipping my sites between the half-finished walls of the structure, I spied three trucks careening into the building project. Confronting the torn-up parking lot, they laid off their neck-break pace, crawling toward the back of the building. I hoped their slow speed would give me time I needed.

I stuck the hundred an inch from the still standing man's nose. "I don't have time to mess around. My last question, who's Beatrice, and how does she play into this?

The guy snatched at the bill, but my reflexes proved quicker. I held the bill tight.

He stammered, "Beatrice is a part of the family. But she's a good girl. Does our real estate deals. Lives legit so we can do business with the Country Men."

I heard the increasing drone of approaching trucks. I started to give the guy the bill when a spark shot through my brain. "You have a cousin, Diana Hutchinson, right?"

The guy scratched his chin. "Our family's so big, I can't say. But I think I remember a Diana Higgins. If she's the same one, she left the family a long time ago."

"So what happened to her?"

"Not sure, but once you leave the family, you always come back."

I clutched the hundred so hard before his face, I felt the paper would crumble. I'm sure he feared the same, because he blurted, "Okay. I've heard word. There's a Diana in the family who works at some fancy club."

I shoved the hundred into his hand, just as the trucks rounded the curve to the back of the building. It was unnerving dealing with these two Travellers. I did not want to face three truckloads of them. I tore out of there, using the route that provided my only hope of cover—through the middle of the unfinished structure. Climbing over a partially finished wall, I glanced behind me. The men lumbered out of their trucks, swaggering to the work site.

I started to exhale a sigh of victory, when my breath caught. I spied a glint in the California sun. The man with the gold tooth was climbing out of the driver's seat of the lead truck. I didn't think he spotted me, but my instincts told me not to be too cocky. Running the last few yards to my car, I fingered the right pocket of my blazer and grabbed my keys. I also made a silent vow—never again venture into a dangerous situation unarmed.

CHAPTER THIRTY-TWO

I rolled out of the parking lot and hooked my Bluetooth into my ear. So shaken, I wanted to call my teens, have a family gathering. Pull them into my arms. But they were sheltered away with tighter security than the Secret Service. Breaking that shield could not only jeopardize them, but the lives of anyone living within the compound.

I probably should have dialed Detective Harrington to report my suspicions about Stewart, but after her nasty attitude during our previous meetings, she lagged toward the bottom of my list.

My next instinct was to call Dun to get his take on what had transpired.

"Dun, there's some things going down. I need to speak to you. Like now."

"Maggie…what have you been up to?"

"Doesn't matter. It's done. Want to talk?"

"Of course, Maggie. Meet me at Chow Down Chili's."

"The indigestion capitol of Newport Beach."

"As I recall, you used to work there."

"Yes, but I never ate the food."

For the second time in days, my shoes hit the beer-sloshed floor at Chow Down's. I scanned the room and spotted Dun. I flashed him a smile, giving a quick wave of my hand. But my hearty salute faded when I spied the beautiful, yet menacing face of Detective Harrington seated at his side. What was she doing here? Didn't she have some unsuspecting housewives to drill? And why was she here with Dun? For friends, they seemed to spend an awful lot of time together.

Just looking at her pursed, silver-spooned smile made me feel guilty. And I had nothing to feel bad about. Except the thought that if she even breathed a whisper of suspicion about me being involved with Grant's murder, I would rip her thick as rope ponytail from her head. As this vision flashed through my brain, I thought maybe it was a good thing I'd left the house unarmed. I'd hate to take her out in a fit of female rage. But that was a silly thought. I was too well trained to make such an amateurish mistake. If I wanted to do away with somebody, it would be because I needed to—one life sacrificed for another's.

I slipped into their u-shaped, corner booth. I'd expected to have an open-heart talk with Dun. But I found myself seated amongst a surprisingly cozy-looking twosome of nice ex-cop and surly now-cop. My usual chatty nature was missing in action. I fingered the salt and pepper shakers and ever-present bottle of ketchup on the table.

The detective broke the ice, or froze it by stating, "So Maggie, looks like you've been a busy lady lately."

"With my husband's murder I had a lot of arrangements to make."

Nick's glistening smile tarnished a faint tinge. "I'm talking about your uncharacteristic, extended visit to your husband's office. According to my sources, you've been so busy sweating away at your yoga classes you haven't stepped a barefoot toe within Leman Land Development in months. Now you've practically taken over the place."

"And what are you implying?"

"That with your cushy life style, you've been so consumed with his business. Looking for something? Or trying to cover up another something?"

"I have every right to be in Grant's office. For God's sake, we were married for sixteen years. Now that I'm widowed, I have two teens to support. Of course I'm interested in his affairs."

"I bet."

Dun raised his hands. "Hey. Let's all calm down. This

bickering is accomplishing nothing. Look, Nicole, I've known Maggie for years. I say let's listen to what she has to say."

"Dun, I know you do work for Maggie. But—"

"Nick, let's take off the gloves and hear what Maggie has to say. Off the record."

Nicole folded her arms and leaned back in her seat. "Okay. I'm game."

Dun asked, "And the 'off the record' part?"

"Agreed. I just hope this information is worth it." Staring at me, she quizzed, "So what have you found, Maggie?"

So much had transpired this day I almost didn't know where to start suspicions of shady goings on, how I'd surveyed Grant's files and found suspicious transfers of titles.

Then I added, "There was also an odd timing for a real estate transaction associated with the death of Andrew Richardson, killed in a compromising situation in Santa Reno. I believe that Grant may not be the first...murder victim, to have fallen prey to suspicious business dealings. Dealt by the Travellers."

Nicole drummed her fingernails upon the greasy table. "Well, you have been a busy lady. I would have thought you'd be huddled with friends and family grieving. Not traipsing around playing cops and murderers. My mind still can't fathom why a social person like you would have no personal contact, no alibi, on the day of your husband's death. That's what sounds suspicious to me."

Slamming my fist on the table, I sprang from my seat. "You've got to be kidding! Do I look like a murderer to you? Do I look like someone who would shoot my husband?"

Nicole twisted her ponytail. "Murderers rarely do. Judging by the way you handled your Ruger at the gun range, I'd say you have the skill."

"My father taught me how to handle a gun before I could drive. He was a cop. Wanted me to know how to take care of myself. In case..."

"You found your husband cheating?"

I lunged toward Nicole when Dun shot out of his seat and

pushed me down by my shoulders. "Maggie, you don't want to get brought up on an assault charge. And Nick, don't you think you're pressing a bit hard?"

I snickered, "Yes, Nick."

Dun gave me a "cool it" look. "Maggie, as the daughter of a policeman, you know how hard cops have to push to get to the bottom of a homicide. Nick's only doing her job."

"Her job is to solve the crime. Nick should be looking at the Travellers and their suspect transactions. Small crimes often lead to big ones."

The detective stared at me for what seemed forever "Oh, we're looking at the Travellers. But, we're also looking at everybody else. And I mean everybody."

CHAPTER THIRTY-THREE

With that swipe I scooted out of Chow Down's so fast, I knocked a ketchup bottle to the floor. An ooze of red bloodied the dingy floor. How dare Detective Harrington treat me that way? How could Dun let her?

I grabbed my cell and dialed the one person I knew who understood the feline cattiness of women better than anyone. And one who knew how to take advantage of that knowledge. Regina.

I couldn't believe Regina picked up on her personal office number. Often her lunch hour was occupied by crucial business lunches that included extra-curricular activities. Regina swore this modus operandi helped her rise to the top in a male-dominated field. She'd quip, "To run a successful law firm, one has to keep in practice, and learn how to stay on top."

"Maggie, I'm so glad you caught me before I headed out the door." She sighed. "Another working lunch."

Starting to hyperventilate, I struggled to find the words to describe my anger to my friend.

"God, Maggie, it sounds like some perv has stolen your phone."

Regina's weird sense of humor brought me back down. "No, it's me. I'm just so…"

"Pissed."

"Exactly. Please, Regina, I need to see you."

"You've got it. I'm canceling my afternoon and meeting you at Swag."

"Isn't that exclusively a night hotspot?"

"It is. But I know the owner. I'll text and explain how I need them to open the doors early for us. It will make for a totally private meet-up. Nobody will see or hear us."

I smiled for the first time in days. "Perfect. Meet you there in—ten."

For the third time in days, I met Regina at a happening place. I hadn't had this much social action since I dated Todd Williams. Todd? What was I thinking? How could I let a glimpse of his oil-slathered body into my head now? If Nicole Harrington could channel this thought, she'd probably have me cuffed and sprawled on the cement slab of a jail cell in ten seconds flat.

Pulling into Swag, I was greeted by a valet in a white dress shirt opened to his navel. He bent down to open my door, ropes of gold chains laced around his neck swinging like pendulums. I cringed, envisioning his bullion collection scraping my Benz, resulting in a fifteen hundred dollar bill of Bavarian touch up paint.

The interior was dim, and I was briefly blinded. I whipped my Versace sunglasses from my face. How do movie stars maneuver their way in such places wearing designer shades? Faithful handlers guiding them. That's why the ones who choose to go it alone end up toppled before popping paparazzi lights.

A middle-aged woman with dark as night hair dressed in black leather appeared from a side entrance. She clutched my arm. Survival currents jolted me from her grasp. I started to bolt when the woman blocked my path.

"You must be Maggie. I'm sorry if I startled you. Let's start over." She extended her hand. "I'm Zera, owner of Swag. Regina asked me to greet you. Please, allow me to lead you to your friend."

"Um, thank you. I didn't mean to be rude."

"I'm used to it. Most people take me for a barmaid or worse, dominatrix. Obviously, I'm neither. But this," Zera ran her fingertips down the length of her leather, "is my work attire. It's what people expect. After all, this is Swag."

She escorted me through a narrow hallway of curtains that led to a booth so deep, I could barely see Regina. I joined my friend and sank into cushions more comfortable than a down bed at the Ritz.

"Regina, thank God you had time to meet. You wouldn't believe the treatment I've been getting from Nicole Harrington."

"Let me guess—Nicole Harrington's trying to make you out to be the monster."

"Not just a monster—a monstrous killer."

CHAPTER THIRTY-FOUR

The detective's putting the screws to you. I'm not surprised."

"Why?"

"As a lawyer who's been around Newport Beach longer than my driver's license reveals, I know Nicole dons a beautiful facade and comes from money. But underneath, she sports claws sharper than a female tiger protecting her cubs. She can be ruthless. It's in her twenty-four karat genes."

"I get the fact she likes to zero in on a target, namely me. But I don't see anything ruthlessly genetic in her. All I see from her genetic pool is exceptional beauty."

"In that gene pool swims a force of family fortitude no one would ever want to challenge."

"But their press. The Harrington's are such philanthropists. I've never read or heard anything bad about them. How would you know?"

Regina clasped her hands together, causing her breasts to swell above the golden sequined camisole beneath her professional blazer. "How do I know anything?"

I smiled. "From your liaisons in the sack?"

"Not this time, darling. You know I'm much deeper than that."

Regina's statement flashed me an image of Regina's bodyguard, Jax, and I could well imagine things being deeper.

I stammered, "This may be off topic, but where's your new bodyguard?"

"Oh, he's around. Jax has the uncanny ability to make himself visible, or not, depending upon the situation. But getting back to Nicole and her family…"

A swoosh of our booth curtain almost sent me through the ceiling. I looked up to see Vera toting an ice bucket filled with a bottle of vino. "I thought you ladies could use something to imbibe upon while you talk. Am I right?"

Regina cooed, "Vera, you always know what your clientele, or should I say, friends, want—or need."

As Vera uncorked our Chardonnay, she murmured, "That's how I outsmart the cocky male club owners." After pouring our wine, she backed away from our booth and disappeared into darkness.

Regina swirled the stem of her wine glass between her fingers. "Vera. What an astute businesswoman. Another one of my divorce success stories. But getting back to the Harrington's...when I faced down the detective and her family during Nicole's divorce, I saw venom like I'd never seen before."

"Nicole, divorce? I didn't realize."

"It was years ago. Nicole's husband wanted out of the marriage. The Harrington family closed ranks trying to ensure the young man walked away with nothing. Normally, seeing how women get screwed in divorce, I side with the female. But not in this case."

"Why?"

"For one, Nicole's husband had given up his medical internship to play the role of doting husband."

"So what happened? The guy got greedy? Wanted a super-sized slice of the Harrington pie for giving up his career?"

"No, it wasn't money. Down and gritty sex."

"He was cheating?"

Regina shook her head. "The opposite. Nicole was the one carrying on."

"You're kidding. She's a cop. She's sworn to uphold the law."

Regina chuckled. "Maggie, adultery's not a crime in California. This transpired long before Nicole's transformation into law enforcement agent. When she was deeply enmeshed in the money web."

"He was smart to go to you. But if he gave up everything for Nicole, how could he afford you?"

"Maggie, I make a lot of money. But that's not the sole reason I do what I do."

"Right. How'd you meet him?"

"At the dog park."

I nodded. "Ah, Pouchy."

"Yes. Pouchy's personal trainer felt that due to my career, my baby wasn't having enough social time. When I took her to the dog park, I spotted an innocent-looking young man sitting alone, head hunched over his knees."

"So you two hooked up."

"Maggie, I told you. I was there to support Pouchy. My life is not all about sex."

"Sorry. So what happened?"

"We started talking. At first, he was hesitant. Said he was dealing with a high-profile family. But I know how to get people to talk. Once he started, he couldn't stop. He'd had a promising career as a doctor. Gave it up for the love of his life. And what did he get? Chiding by the Harrington's because he wasn't blue blood. His main married obligation was to escort Nicole's Bichons to the dog park while she lounged at the spa—or wherever she chose to go."

"How did he get wind of an affair?"

Regina took a long sip from her wine. "Turns out the Harrington's shouldn't have looked down on his simple upbringing but feared it. The man had the street smarts to contact his high school buddy who worked as a P.I. The friend took a ton of pictures. Nicole made Playboy Bunnies look like virgins. The noble Harrington daughter was cheating in a big way. And in the sleaziest of places."

"You don't mean Santo Reno?"

Regina nodded.

I shuddered. "Why would a society girl like her romp in that seedy town?"

"Anonymity. Nicole's numerous pictures splashed across the society pages made her a familiar face. But Santo Reno—

who'd think she'd be there? If someone saw her, they wouldn't believe it was she."

Regina exhaled, as if the story were too much for even her. "When I handled his divorce, it was not a pretty courtroom picture. I was still green. The Harrington's sat next to their pony-tailed, scrubbed-face daughter, staring me down. Cold as ice. I had to pull together all my mental resources to concentrate on this hearing. And then there were the verbal threats

"Against you?"

"No. Would have been too obvious. Against the P.I. And veiled allegations against the son-in-law."

"The Harrington's stooped that low? Couldn't you bring them up on some sort of charge?"

"I was too busy advocating for my client to pursue it, so nothing was ever proven. But I *knew*. This case made me toughen up quick. I had to ignore the evil force of wealth while fighting for every dime this man deserved. I swear to this day that legal battle made me who I am today. People think I'm heartless and tough. Try going into battle against the Harrington's. That will do it. But I had the ultimate victory."

"Regina, why didn't you ever tell me this before?"

"Maggie. You know about attorney-client privilege."

"Yes, but being dearest of friends, you've crossed that line with me before. Why hold out on this?"

"Maggie, I saw what the Harrington's were capable of during the divorce. Do you think I'd compound their wrath by shooting off a big mouth? Perhaps a wrath that could lead to being shot *in* the mouth?"

CHAPTER THIRTY-FIVE

I left Swag and headed home. My chat with Regina about Detective Harrington and her nasty family left me with a lead-filled brain. What was happening? Everywhere I turned it seemed someone was either involved in crime or falling prey to one.

My daze almost caused me to speed through a red light. At the last second, my eyes flashed to the stoplight. I stomped on the break. A black Humvee whizzed before my eyes. If my luxury vehicle didn't have the ability to stop on a tire tread, I would have been Desert Storm T-bone. I sat before the intersection, fingers gripping the steering wheel like they were permanently glued.

Then the rev of a motor really sent my nerves flying. My head snapped to the left, where a vintage Porsche sat gunning. A second that seemed like an hour went by before I realized this wasn't an aggressor, but Todd. He flashed me a bright smile and a cardboard sign attached to a popsicle-like stick that read, UR Hot.

To any other female with half an ounce of independence, this sign would have screamed, "Annoying!" But I remembered Todd had bought a slew of these message boards years ago. He was so handsome and drove such flashy cars, women were always trying to signal him along the roadway. Told me their gestures proved so distracting he'd narrowly avoided several collisions. He'd bought a collection that relayed messages like, Hey Babe or Red Lt-Green? Todd boasted these not only saved his life, but also snared several dates. I couldn't believe he still kept them after all these years.

Todd laid down his placard and gestured for me to pull over. With my world spinning so fast, I relished seeing a friend with signs from my past. Signs of a happier, less complicated time.

I turned into the first parking lot I saw—my favorite organic food market, Simple Means. Normally I would have whipped out my canvas environmental bags and snagged some fruits and vegan meals. But I assumed Todd's pulling me over didn't include boosting his Vitamin C or antioxidants. I resisted my urge to shop. As Todd strode to my car, I buzzed down my window.

"Maggie, I hope you didn't mind my stupid sign. I was taking my 1955 baby out for a spin. Have to keep these touchy ladies in shape."

My eyes must have rolled at Todd's macho comparison of females to cars. He cleared his throat and said, "Sorry, Maggie. I don't mean to sound so, like me. By the look on your face I'm either a jerk or totally out of date. What is it?"

I held out my hand and squeezed his. "No Todd, you're just you. Trust me. That's not a bad thing. You may come off as a brazen male, but I know there's a sweetheart inside. Though I do have to ask, what's up with the sign? If I recall correctly, you purchased those ditties about twenty years ago. You've held onto them? Or have they brought you such female luck you couldn't let go of them—or the women?"

"You always loved to call me on my bad boy behavior. You're right. The signs are juvenile. I just never removed them from my Porsche. Felt they were part of the car's charm. When I spotted you, I remembered how I'd flashed you once or twice."

Leaning into my open window, his fingertip brushed my cheek. "Hmm, do I detect a hint of a blush upon your Snow White skin?"

"No, Todd. But tell me, you're not still using your signs on random women."

"Of course not. Too impersonal. I like to meet women the old-fashioned way. In a bar, or nightclub. So we can talk face to face—if the music's not too loud."

I extended my hand once again, patting Todd's. "You're right. An alcohol establishment is the perfect place to connect with a woman. It's nice to know some things haven't changed. Now my life…"

Flashing back on the recent, horrific events, my hands grew clammy, my head swayed and my world shaded black. My next recollection, Todd snugged beside me in the backseat of my Mercedes, forcing breaths of air into my mouth. As I came to, the added air into my lungs felt too much, and I pushed against his chest.

He halted his rescue breathing and nudged his tight body an inch from mine. "Magpie, you scared the hell out of me. Are you okay?"

"I think so. How did I, we, get into the backseat of my car?"

"You lost consciousness. I couldn't tell if you were breathing. I didn't know what else to do."

I lay there, feeling oddly secure beside Todd. I knew this wasn't proper widow posture, wanted to spring up and shout, "I'm okay." My extremities felt like fifty-pound kettle balls.

"Thank you, Todd. I'm trying to be strong."

"I can't begin to imagine what you're going through. My most serious worry has generally been whether the salty ocean air would rust one of my classic cars."

"Todd, everything is turned inside out. Seems the silver pillars of Newport aren't what I believed them to be."

"Sometimes the silver ones are covering up the most rust."

"Todd, I'm not talking about cars."

"Neither am I, Maggie. Your husband's been killed. You had me spying for you. And you were just one step away from me calling the paramedics. How could this happen? We've always lived a fabulous life in Newport Beach. I feel something's happening. Something sinister. Am I crazy, or do you feel it too?"

"Todd, you've been a presence in Newport Beach longer than anybody I know. And if you feel the apple has been

143

poisoned, I believe you. Maybe we can put our heads together and find out who's injected the venom. Do you have time to talk?"

"I always have time for you, Magpie. Let's take a drive. Nothing like a top-down ocean breeze to clear the mind. I think we have a lot to share."

CHAPTER THIRTY-SIX

Heading south of Newport, traffic snaked along Coastal Road. The motorway hugged the cliffs overlooking the coastline, and Todd shifted the vintage Porsche gears with every rise and twist of the road. Normally, this hyperactive driving would take me beyond nervous. But I knew if Todd hadn't made a fortune in the oil slathering business, he would have triumphed in the Grand Prix.

We rolled into Laguna Del Mar, a picturesque artist colony. Todd slowed and parked on a side street. Sweeping from the Porsche, he offered me his hand. "Come on, Maggie, let's take a stroll."

We sauntered into a white-latticed gazebo. When Todd and I worked together, we'd sometimes escape the crazy business world for a quiet lunch in Laguna. Todd turned to me, his voice a near whisper. "Maggie, do you know how many times I dreamed of proposing to you in this romantic spot?"

Propose? Todd? I always thought he was adverse, even allergic to marriage.

"Todd, we had great times, but you never gave any signs you were thinking along those lines."

"Well, I was. But you were still in college. So young, innocent. Well, maybe not *that* innocent."

"I was innocent. But not with you. How could I be?"

Todd seemed not to hear or chose to ignore my comment. He continued, "And when my business exploded, I worked ungodly hours. And then you met Grant…"

"And sixteen wonderful years. Until I found that damned Gitan bag. Then everything spiraled out of control."

Todd looked at me. "Gitan? That's how this bizarre twist of events started? You never told me that. I'm a primary investor."

"You're kidding? Although I shouldn't be surprised. Everywhere I turn, someone's either displaying them or carrying one. I don't get it. They're such ugly purses and so over-priced.

"Maggie, they're not just purses. They're *environmental tote bags*. They serve a purpose on this planet."

"Handbags, purses, save-the-earth bags. I still don't picture you as a key ingredient with this designer line. How'd you get involved?"

"Charles Harrington."

"Detective Harrington's father? How'd you hook up with him?"

"I knew him during my younger days. But our business association began several years ago by a chance encounter at a charitable event."

I shook my head. "Harrington Associates is primarily a manufacturing empire. You're telling me they've branched out into the green industry? I'd never peg the big man as the environmental type. Although, being sold at Saks, Gitan *has* gone mainstream. But that couldn't have been the case during the brand's inception."

"True. The making of Gitan began years ago. Before living green was considered chic. Charles Harrington had vision."

"So Harrington's into the green movement. Seems like everybody is these days. But you said you knew Mr. Harrington when you were young. How was that? I don't mean to sound condescending, but the Harrington's have always conveyed such a conservative image. Why would Charles bring you into his inner business fold with your legendary sexier than sexy infomercials?"

"It goes way back...to my great-grandparents...Charles's grandparents. Maggie, I've never confided this to anybody outside my family—my last name isn't really Williams."

"What?"

"My name was originally Williamson. After my mother divorced my father, she changed our name."

"Why? What's the difference between Williams and Williamson? It's not like your name was Willamloshkanovia."

"I don't know the whole story. My mother always told me she wanted a clean break from my father and his family. Hinted he'd been a hard-drinking philanderer, and his parents offered her no support. She wanted to sever all ties. And my mother wasn't the only one who changed their name." Todd continued, his words racing. "The Harringtons also altered theirs"

"You're kidding."

"They used to be the Haringtons."

"That's not a change of name."

"Let me backtrack. Same pronunciation, different spelling. They added an R"

"How would you know this? I'm certain a name change, even one so minor, would be handled with utmost secrecy by people like them."

"My mother worked as their housekeeper."

"You're kidding?"

"My mother had little education. After her divorce, her career options were nil. Because my grandparents knew the Harrington's, the family hired her. Being an incredibly hard worker, she remained a member of their staff for years. At the end of her service, they practically considered her a member of their family."

"Wow. Your connection to the Harrington's caught me off guard."

"I know. Weird how lives twine and intertwine..."

I pressed my hands to my face, taking in this information. "Your mother, working within the Harrington confines, I'd imagine they became so used to her presence she became almost ghostlike. Privy to private conversations."

Nodding his head, Todd said, "I'm certain of it. And with her maid's quarters sitting right off the kitchen, she was usually in close proximity to them. On the other hand, my room was in a converted garage at the back of the house."

"Wait. You *lived* with the Harringtons? You never mentioned this. Why?"

"Maggie, I don't mean to sound shallow, but look at my image. I didn't want to destroy it by advertising my mother toiled as a domestic, and I lived in an old garage."

I clasped Todd's hand. "Coming from humble beginnings is nothing to be ashamed of. I'm sure you remember—my dad worked as a cop, and my mom was a housewife. We weren't rolling in the dough."

"But at least your father had a profession of esteem."

"Hey, your mother must have been damn good at her job to be employed by the Harrington's for so long."

"She was."

"I would loved to have met her. But getting back to the Harringtons and their name change. How do you know about it? Was your mother the source of this information?"

"She never spoke about them—except in general terms. It's like a domestic code of silence. But one time she fell ill with a fever. It hung on for days. I wanted the Harrington's to admit her to the hospital, but their personal doctor made daily house calls, assuring me she'd pull through. One night, so feverish, she slipped. Confided to me that once the Harrington's dipped their blue-dyed blood into Newport Beach society, Charles quietly added an 'r' to their name."

"Did she say why?"

"No, she was so sick she sank into a restless sleep after sharing this with me. I kept vigil at her side that night, as she thrust from side to side. Occasionally she mumbled weird things like, 'Baby. I need to take care of the baby.'

"After she recovered, I asked her about it. Said she was just talking old lady gibberish. Told me to forget about it. And now she's gone."

"Adding an 'r' to one's name does seem odd. Why would the Harrington's change theirs? What's the difference between one 'r' and two?"

"I didn't think much of it until I researched the Harrington name."

"And?"

"And one 'r' denotes the difference between blue blood English, and roots to Scottish descent, to a branch that spouts trouble."

CHAPTER THIRTY-SEVEN

After Todd dropped me off at my car, I crept back to the confines of my home. I strolled onto my deck overlooking the Pacific. I needed the wafting ocean breeze to soothe my nerves so I could concentrate on Todd's revelations about the Harrington's and their possible role in my life's mess.

Shocking, the change of the esteemed Harrington name. One that very likely obscured Scottish ancestry. Could this somehow link them to the Scottish Travellers? A rogue clan I'd believed disappeared years ago. Now they seemed to be everywhere. The Harringtons affiliated with the Travellers? That would rock Newport Beach to the bottom of its sandy shore.

Compounding my suspicions—the fact Harrington had been an original investor in Gitan and brought Todd into this enterprise. Todd, raised on the Harrington grounds. Had Mr. Harrington suspected Todd knew things this patriarch wanted hidden? His mother a hard worker. But father, a scoundrel who sounded like he had multigenerational ties to the Travellers.

Strange how this designer product kept popping up in seedy places. Tied to a sexy-tagged golf bag and two gruesome murders. And, in the unsavory and unlovely hands of Diana Hutchinson.

My gut told me Diana belonged to the Travellers. So many signs pointed to it. I also felt with her abrasive mouth, she could be a faulty link in the family chain of secrets.

I would love to question Charles Harrington about his role in this mess. But getting past his estate's iron gates, not to mention his padded inner circle would be next to impossible. But who knew? I was a widow on a mission. I'd be damned if I would let some phony society patriarch get in my way. But I knew I had to be patient—build my case. I filed Interview with Charles Harrington in the back of my brain. Diana Hutchinson would have to do for now.

I called Newport Hills Country Club and asked to speak to Diana. Her assistant informed me she was out of the office. When I pressed for more information, the underling said Diana was gone due to family business.

Family biz. How apropos. Sounded like a Traveller.

Lucky for me. This would give me the chance to scrutinize Diana's office again. Of course, the staff would be around, but I had a plan to lure her busy bees into a hasty exit.

As I gathered my non-environmental Louis Vuitton and started to my car, I pondered Diana's possible Traveller ties. What would happen if Diana returned from her business while I conducted my business in her office? Worse, what if Gold Tooth or one of his cohorts sauntered in? I'd already encountered some chilling situations. Vowed not to venture into another one unarmed. I backtracked to my closet, retrieved my Ruger and tucked it into my Louis.

Strutting down the hallway leading to Diana's office suite, my mind wandered to the last time I'd visited. When the sleazy gold-toothed man had salaciously bumped into me slathering his sweat. I shuddered. Gross, was one thing, but my later encounters with him led me to believe he was outright dangerous. And played a big part in this twisted tale.

Marching into the marketing department, again I found Diana's troops buzzing about. Damn. With them whizzing in and out of her pod, I'd never get a peek into her affairs. Clearing my throat, I announced to the group, "You'll never believe who's in the lounge chatting it up with your members. Saying he's considering joining your club."

Mumbles of, "What?" and "Who?" reverberated throughout the office. I raised my voice an octave higher. "Charles Harrington has entered the building. Word is, he's thinking of adding you to his list of country club affiliations."

With my announcement, Diana's staff rushed from the suite, each scrambling harder than the next to squeeze through the doorway and down the lane that led to the potential Platinum member.

I slithered into Diana's private office. I had time—but not much. Once the workers realized the esteemed Mr. H. was not in the building, they'd be on a tear to quiz me on why I'd made my false statement.

I'd already scanned Diana's members list, so I went in search of something new. But what? How could I prove Diana wasn't the forthright marketing exec she purported to be? Engrossed in thought, I circled her desk, haphazardly gliding my hand across its surface. I stopped. Looked at my fingers. They were enmeshed with a tangle of hair fibers. Ooh! Red twines wrapped throughout my fingertips. How long had it been since this office had been dusted? Wouldn't such a fancy club keep a white gloved cleaning service on staff?

Forcing myself to examine them more closely, my female knowledge of mane couture screamed these weren't the droppings of real hair, but synthetic ones. Pulling at a fiber, its elasticity didn't snap like a fragile human strand. I'd bet my next cut and color appointment these long, strange threads were fake. And my professional guess—they came from a wig. And I'd bet a very big, suspicious wig.

CHAPTER THIRTY-EIGHT

These hairs had to have come from a wig Diana wore. Sure Beatrice wore one, but when was the last time she visited? My guess, Diana put it on in her office and then styled it before heading out to her family.

This wig revelation proved what I'd suspected for some time. There was something off about Diana. And I'd say the phony tresses on her desk weren't the only thing fake about her—and her family. Thinking back to the night of the club's social mixer, when I first spotted Beatrice sporting a super-sized hairpiece. With her beauty, I didn't believe she wore it to enhance her features. My guess was it made it easier to shadow them. Now Diana could certainly use a hair bustier to enhance her mousy looks. But what were the chances of two young women who didn't appear to be outwardly connected sporting vamped-out wigs? Was this a Travellers ploy to disguise themselves and become somebody they weren't?

The Travellers swapped names to avoid the police. Could they also don subtle disguises, namely wigs, to change facades with their cousins? Make it more difficult to tell one woman from the other?

At that moment, a woman with voluminous russet hair sauntered in. Beatrice. Still holding a fake fiber to my face, I almost choked on it. What was she doing here? Now. During my snoop time?

"Beatrice, how nice to see you. I was checking to see if Diana was in."

"Obviously, she's not." Her greeting was about as warm as our chilly ocean water.

"Um, Beatrice, you impressed me the other day with your story about your real estate career. When we talked about Todd and how I told you about my husband's death. That I wanted to invest in real estate."

"Yes, my cousin, Diana, and I talked about it."

Cousin! So they were related. I wanted to quiz her about this, but continued with my ruse. "As I mentioned, my hubby had a shitload of money stashed away. He also ran a thriving business in the environmental construction market. With his departure, coupled with convoluted green building codes, I'm not sure if I'm up to carrying on with it. Not sure if I could wrap my little head around it. I'm thinking about selling Leman Land Development and cashing in."

Beatrice nodded. Her styled hair never bounced a micrometer. "I'm sure it's tough running a business like your husband's. God, the way the government loves to stick their nose in people's businesses. I know. The stories I've heard from the family—"

"The what?"

"Oh, nothing of consequence. Let's get back to talking money."

"My thought exactly. I feel it may be easier to get out of the Oz biz, meaning green building, and invest in something less regulated. Like good old fashioned land." I gave a fake female twitter, hoping to gain her confidence. "California's coastline property values may fluctuate more than a 4.2 earthquake, but they always bounce back."

Beatrice patted her tougher than hair-sprayed coif. "You sound like a smart gal. Want a piece of the coast. But I'm sure you're aware how beachfront properties are sorely overpriced. Now in some neighboring communities, realty investments are cheap. And I mean cheap as the dirt they sit on. There's nowhere for their values to go but up."

"Have any locations in mind?"

"Several. Depends on what you're looking at."

"I'm thinking small commercial, maybe multi residential. I'm sure this type of investment would pocket more money than an expensive, single house. Why buy one property, when you can purchase multiples?"

"I couldn't agree more. I happen to specialize in those. Are you thinking office complexes, apartments, mobile home parks?"

"I hadn't thought that far. Whatever you think will make my money grow, multiply, and hopefully give quintuplet birth."

Scrolling through her iPhone, she mumbled, "I have several listings in towns near Newport Beach but without this town's ungodly price tag. Where would you be interested in looking? San Juan, Costa Verde, Santo Reno?"

At the mention of Santo Reno, I nearly jumped from my skin. And the approaching stomp of footsteps reverberating down the hallway really made me want to leap from my seams.

"Beatrice, we have a lot to talk about. But I hear Diana's troops approaching. Why don't we find a more private place to talk?"

"Sure. But I need to speak to my cousin first."

"Don't worry about Diana. She's not with the gang. Her staff assistant told me she was out on family business."

Beatrice took a step back. She edged out the words, "Oh. She didn't tell me that. I really need to meet with her. Can we schedule for a later date?"

"I don't know. I'm anxious to get moving on this. Who knows what will happen in California's seismic economy?"

"I won't put you off too long. It's something I need to take care of. If you'll just give me your phone number, I'll call you as soon as I can. That will give me time to put together some numbers for you."

Reciting my contact info, which I wasn't thrilled to give to someone with a suspect background, I managed to say, "Don't wait too long. You never know what may happen."

"Yes. You never do."

CHAPTER THIRTY-NINE

I wanted to query Beatrice as to why she needed to meet with Cousin, Diana. And other items of interest. If Diana was the weak link to the clan, I felt Beatrice was the bare thread. I knew I only had only a moment. Make that a non-moment. Beatrice darted out the door.

I only hoped she'd be leaving through the front door. I remembered how she'd departed through a back door at the Mixer. But I couldn't cover all exits. And I couldn't follow on her heels.

Waiting near the edge of my club's palatial entry, I tried to cozy behind a flourishing bougainvillea. A zealous valet, anxious to snag my car and my tip, spotted me. I waved him off before he could blow my cover.

A few minutes later, Beatrice strode along the stone exit way, huddled over her iPhone. She looked none too happy. I was just about to intercept her, when Nicole Harrington came out of nowhere, blocking Beatrice's path. Was the Detective here to arrest Beatrice? It would be nice to see someone I believed to be a Traveller do time for their past crimes. But then again, I hoped not now. I wanted to pump Beatrice for family information and couldn't do it with her sitting in the pokey.

I was shocked to see Nicole give Beatrice a swift hug, then fall into cadence with her. As the two sauntered down the path, I slipped from my hiding spot. Followed behind them at a safe pace. I remembered my dad's stories of shadowing a suspect. Stay close. Walk softly. Keep to the shadows. The two engaged in conversation. But with the buzzing of Jags and Beamers entering and exiting the club, it was hard to hear their words.

I did decipher, "Our dad," and "Profits." But I couldn't tell which woman had spoken. As the two approached a silver BMW, Nicole beeped her key. She'd parked next to a thick grove of eucalyptus trees. I slithered my body within them.

Nicole nudged her face so close to Beatrice's they were almost touching. She muttered something that sounded like, "Done at the wedding, not in the wedding." She then gave Beatrice a swift hug, slipped into her car, and sped off.

What did her strange combination of words mean?

I expected Beatrice to also exit the premises, but she backtracked toward the club entrance. I stepped up my pace and closed the gap between us. I rifled in my purse as if I were searching for my valet stub. "Oh, dear, where did I leave my ticket? This Louis is so big it's like a black hole."

Glancing to Beatrice I chirped, "Oh. Hi. Hey, did you have any luck locating Diana?"

Beatrice kept walking.

I pushed on. "I'm glad we ran into each other. I know you haven't had time to examine your listings, but your coupling of office complexes with mobile home parks fascinated me. With my limited real estate knowledge, I would have thought they'd be two different animals, or at least in different jungles."

With the mention of a possible real estate deal, Beatrice stopped. "In a way they are—and aren't. Both profitable investments. But commercial office space is trickier. You need to buy closer to a metropolitan area, which of course, prices them higher. And that market is more volatile. Now mobile home parks, they're extremely lucrative."

Beatrice's eyes darted toward the upcoming roar of a large, shiny truck.

"Really? What makes trailer parks so valuable?"

"Mobile home parks. Please don't use the T word."

"Oh, sorry. So why are they such a good investment?"

"Stability. Mostly senior citizens live in the parks. Quiet; pay their space rents on time. Once these people are settled in, they're basically stuck for life. Don't have the means or energy to move. Do you know how much it costs to relocate a double or triple wide? So a new owner, like you, can go in, do some minor upgrades, and then raise the space rents. Bingo. Your investment almost doubles overnight."

"Isn't that tough on the residents?"

"They should consider themselves lucky. Let's face it, where else could retirees afford to live in beautiful southern California? On a bluff like you, overlooking the ocean?"

The approaching truck revved louder. I glanced back, expecting to see a valet sitting behind the wheel. Christ, it was Gold Tooth.

My eyes shot to Beatrice. "How do you know where I live?"

Beatrice spun and darted to the menacing truck, either not hearing my question, or choosing not to.

CHAPTER FORTY

How could Beatrice know where I lived? Worse, did she pass along this information to Gold Tooth? Thank God I'd shuttled my teens away. Did I, too, need to abandon my home? And what was up with Beatrice's cozy relationship with Detective Harrington? That seemed odd—and beyond suspicious. Particularly after Todd's revelation of the Harrington's name change from Traveller Scottish to regal English.

Who could I talk to? The sun hadn't even set, and I felt I'd depleted all my sources of information. I still wanted to question Diana, but where was she? Her staff said she was out of the office on family business. Knowing her family, that could mean anywhere from down the street to across the country. I needed to discuss this with someone I knew I could trust—and one who had first-hand knowledge of the Travellers. But who?

I could only think of one person. I'd already bothered him today. But with my depleting resources, I had no other choice. I needed to speak to Dun Reid.

I plucked out my cell. "Dun, I'm sorry to trouble you again, but I need to talk to someone I can trust. You wouldn't believe the information I've uncovered."

Dun stammered, "Maggie, what are you doing? If you're talking about Grant's murder, as a friend I need to warn you, this is an ongoing police investigation. You can't get yourself involved."

"Well, I am. And in a big way."

"Oh, Maggie, you don't know the danger you're setting yourself up for."

"Dun. Somebody killed my husband. The police, or should I specify Detective Harrington, don't seem to be out there looking for the killer. They appear zeroed in on me. You know I could never harm Grant even if he was cheating. And I still doubt that. There're some very strange things going on in Newport Beach. In fact, I just spotted your friend, Nicole, cavorting with someone I suspect to be a member of the Travellers."

I could hear the squeak of Dun's shoes shifting from foot to foot. "Maggie…listen to me. If Nicole was talking to one of the Travellers, and I'm not saying she was, I'm certain she was questioning them pursuant to her investigation."

"Does hushed conversation, mention of 'our dad,' and a cozy hug sound like police grilling to you? Seems the opposite of the treatment that I, the grieving widow, received."

"Maggie—"

Dun didn't get a chance to finish, his voice overcome by the lilt of, "Dun, baby, I'm back. I had such a nice talk with my sister."

The unmistakable sound of Nicole Harrington's voice almost made me drop my phone. It must have had the same effect on Dun, because I heard a series of thumps, then the speakerphone announced a reverberation of scrambled steps. I could almost feel, no hear, his desperation to retrieve it as Nicole rattled on.

"Dun, my sister's in. And Father's coming around. Forget about being at the wedding. I know you're going to be in—"

Click. Dun's phone went silent. Darn, that conversation was so…strange. Yet telling. "In the wedding." Beatrice? Dun? I knew Nicole and Dun looked comfy lately, but wedded?

And this tidbit sounded like Beatrice was Nicole's sister. How could that be? In all the numerous articles published about Nicole and her family, there was never any mention of a sibling. Was Beatrice perhaps a product of Mr. Harrington's long ago indiscretion?

I grasped my iPhone and Googled the Harringtons. A family portrait of Charles, his wife Evelyn, and Nicole popped up. No sister. The article below summarized the business and charitable endeavors of this Newport Beach power family.

Zeroing in on Nicole, I analyzed her features—regal nose, taut jaw line, slim stature.

Beatrice's beauty certainly rivaled Nicole's. But there was something about the eyes, when I could actually see Beatrice's from under her wig. Both she and Nicole shared an intense shade of blue. Beautiful, yet startling. They did share similar physical attributes. But very different upbringings.

CHAPTER FORTY-ONE

Where to go from here? I couldn't meet with Dun. Not with Nicole cooing about. I thought I knew the man. His personal life was certainly his own, but he'd worked within my home for several years and never mentioned any ties to the high profile Harringtons. And by the sound of the scudding speaker call, it seemed he could be tying the knot with their daughter.

Dun had disclosed to me that he felt a member of the Travellers fired the bullet that nearly killed him. When the fateful shot pierced his back, he was approaching Nicole's house. She had been frightened by a cryptic phone call and begged Dun to rush to her side.

Dun said the squeaky gate might have alerted the shooter of his approach to Nicole's house. He'd wanted to fix it, but she kept putting it off.

And then there was the marriage factor. Dun was matrimonially tied during the time of his shooting. His offer to repair the gate could have been an innocent attempt to help a friend and partner. Or was it?

Now thinking about the bits of conversation I'd overheard between Beatrice and Nicole, and more loudly through Dun's speakerphone about how "our dad" didn't want Dun to be "in the wedding"...if Dun and Nicole were having an affair while they were partners, how would Daddy feel about that? Bad enough Nicole cheated on her husband then shed her blue blood obligations to become a cop. But to carry on with one? One that was married and teamed as her professional partner? I'd say her father wouldn't like it very much.

But getting back to the squeaky wheel in these sordid

affairs. If Dun and Nicole were carrying on, perhaps in love, why wouldn't she want him to fix her gate? Wouldn't that gesture of hominess signal to her that he was ready to leave his wife and move on to her? Why wouldn't Nicole want the gate fixed?

At the racetrack, Dun talked about Nicole and him working the Fraud unit, pursuing the Travellers. He said he had suspicions about the clan and wanted to investigate them. Not that they'd wanted to pursue the family. Sounded like Dun was the driving force in tracking the Travellers, and Nicole may have been swept into the investigation by her senior partner.

So much conjecture about Nicole and her family. How could I ever prove any of it? More importantly, how could I tie this to Grant's murder? I wandered through the club parking lot, lost in thought, before realizing I hadn't valeted. I'd lost my car. My life was in shambles. And now felt I was losing my mind.

I wandered about for what seemed forever until I spotted my Mercedes. I snagged my keys from my bag, thumbed the clicker about to hit "unlock," when a hand grabbed my shoulder and twisted me around. "What the hell you think you're doin', messing with the family?"

I faced a slick-haired man with a stubble. The stench of his alcohol breath almost knocked me to the ground. Trapped in a nightmare, I struggled to answer, wanting to speak, but couldn't.

He tightened his grip on my shoulder. "Didn't ya' hear me? I said, what ya' doing pokin' your country club woman nose into our life?"

He probably thought his vice-like grip would scare me, but produced the opposite effect. I glared into his eyes. "What the hell are you talking about?"

"I saw you talkin' with Beatrice. Getting all cozy with her. She's one of us. You best stay away from her, or…"

"Or what?"

"You don't want to know."

I clutched my key tighter, raising the pointed edge upward.

"I do know. All about your family." Then jabbed the sharp metal key into his eye.

Grasping his face, he stumbled backward. "You bitch!"

I punched my freedom button, scrambled into my car, and peeled away. I sped through the club's seemingly endless parking lot, bouncing over speed bump after speed bump, until I hit the open road. Then I punched the accelerator like I'd never done before, racing toward what I hoped would be a safe haven.

I flew over the bridge that led to the Newport Harbor Islands, gunning for the most private of private ones. Reaching my locale, I skidded to a stop, nearly crashing the guard gate. A gate I'd been given access to many times years ago.

The guard station's tinted window buzzed down. An elderly man peered down at me, eyes scrunched.

Crap. I hadn't had a breath of time to call ahead to gain clearance.

The guard slipped on his spectacles. His face cracked a smile. "My, my, is that you, Maggie? Haven't seen you in years. You're still as Snow White beautiful as ever. Are you here to see Todd?"

Shocked this landmarked guard remembered me, I muttered, "Yes, I am. It's so nice to see you again. Mr.?"

"You don't remember my name. No one does. That's okay. I know you. And I know you're Lockett Island quality. I'm granting you access." And with that, the hallowed gate raised.

Happy the guard remembered me but concerned how easily I'd gained entry, I rolled through the gate. With such an easy entree, I hoped this island still provided the privacy and safety it once did. More importantly, I prayed my visit to Lockett Island would unlock some of the secrets plaguing me.

CHAPTER FORTY-TWO

I crept down the central lane of Lockett Island—my speed a far cry from the harrowing pace during my escape from my club. I knew that crazed type of driving would certainly get me offed from this island, probably for life.

Pulling up to a beachfront estate with the initials "T.W." blazed upon its gridiron gate, I stopped at the intercom box. Because my visit was unexpected, it seemed tacky to buzz the annoying box. Announcing my arrival via text, I sat in my car, heart pounding, waiting for his response. I waited and waited. My body urged me to leap from the car and scale the damn gate. But I knew that would earn me a police escort to a place I did not want to visit.

I dialed Todd's cell. It went straight to voice mail. Strange. Todd being such a social person, he never shut down his line of communication. I resorted to buzzing the intercom. Its squealing pitch ramped my nerves ten notches higher. No answer. I punched the device and repeated the process. Still no reply. Drumming my fingers on the steering wheel, I forced myself to be patient.

When Todd had dropped me off after our drive to Laguna, it sounded like he was heading home, calling it a day. But knowing Todd, maybe he'd decided to go out or have a female companion in.

About to set my car in gear, Todd's voice came through the speaker box. "Maggie, what a surprise. L-look to the speaker. C-camera reads face."

"Todd, it's been years since I've been here. That camera would have no record of my face. Unless...you didn't, did you?"

"No, Maggie. Never filmed us. Simple iPhone download. You can…uh…enter."

I rolled through Todd's gate to his sleek home with soaring windows framed by shining chrome. The house design normally projected light. But not tonight. If Todd was home and knew I was visiting, why the blackout mode?

Todd's voice sounded strange, almost incoherent over the speaker. And what was up with the face recognition? Todd's compound always kept him guarded but never paranoid.

I didn't have time to worry about this. I had questions that needed to be answered. I snagged my purse and headed toward the front door. Strutting along the mica-flecked walkway, I cringed at the clacking of my heels upon the stone. I tried to tiptoe, causing my shoes to slip from my feet, my steps reverberating louder. It reminded me of the squeaking gate signaling Dun's arrival at Nicole's house.

I rang the doorbell. The door peeked open. Behind it, Diana glared at me from beneath a broad, red wig. Her staff said she was out on family business. What was she doing here? And what was up with the outrageous headpiece? If her beaked nose wasn't sticking out, I wouldn't have recognized her.

"Maggie, what a surprise. Widowed wife visiting her ex-lover's house. Well, maybe not such a surprise. I know you two had it hot and sexy. But from what I heard about your trip to the chilly morgue, I would have thought your hormones would have cooled."

So angry at her remark, I pushed past her, never slowing to ponder if I was stepping into a trap.

Diana slammed the steel door. I stopped. A prickle of sweat slithered down my spine. I reached into my Louis, checking if my Ruger was in ready position.

"Okay, Diana. I'm here to see Todd. But it's not about what your perverted mind is thinking."

"What I'm thinking is that you're not wanted here. Todd and I are doing business. I'm sure he wouldn't want you and your frivolous whatever's getting in the way of money. Todd may like women, but he loves the dollar."

A shuffle of feet caught my attention. Todd lumbered into the foyer. "Maggie. Hi. Wuz up? Beatrice, Bridget, um whoever, we're talking numbers."

"Shut up, you fool!" Diana shrieked.

Todd slunk his head. "You all seem so much alike. I'm so...confused."

This was not the Todd I knew. In our heyday, we'd done our bit of partying, but I'd never seen him out of it. Usually in. Especially when conducting a money deal. My guess—Diana was at the big-haired root of it. With his millions, and with him in such an incoherent state, it was scary to think what kind of business Diana was planning.

Turning to her, I said, "Todd doesn't seem to be feeling well. Not the time for money pacts. It's time you left."

Diana strutted her bird legs to within inches of me. Tried to puff out her scrawny chest. "Maggie, haven't you noticed? Times have changed. You're no longer a power player in this town. I think it's time you got out and let Todd and me finish our transaction." In a cooing voice she said, "Right, Todd? I'm going to make you millions."

I thought he mumbled something like, "Mark...low...bad ti...ing"

"Diana. Todd's obviously tired. If he wants to do a transaction with you, it can wait until tomorrow. In his office." I fluttered my hands in the air. "Go on. Time for you to fly away like the skinny bird you are."

"I'm not leaving, Magpie." Diana scrunched her eyes. "Now that's a disgusting bird."

Shaking my head I said, "You never got over Todd's attraction to me. How pathetic. I had him as well as a great marriage to Grant. What do you have? A shady family that taught you to deceive innocent people? And by looking at Todd, I'd say drug them."

"Just keep talking. Maybe you'll be the next country club statistic. Like your husband. Talk about a pathetic demise."

At that remark, I wanted to rip my manicured nails into her

throat. I could almost feel my pleasure doing it. But at that moment, the front door snapped open. Diana's family?

I pushed against Diana, lunging her backward. She tumbled onto the floor. I snatched the Ruger from my bag.

Twisting in the direction of the compromised entrance, I leveled my weapon at the figure coming through. My finger gripped the trigger, ready to pull. My eyes almost blinded by fear, all I could make out was another big wig coming through. So surprised at the site of another woman sporting a super-sized hairpiece, I almost fired.

I thought the intruder would be some macho Traveller, ready to take me out. But taking a second glance, I could see it was Beatrice. And she approached not in a threatening manner, but breezed in, as if nothing was wrong.

"Todd, I'm here—"

At the sight of my raised gun, she froze. Not a fake hair on her head quivered.

I almost felt sorry for her. But I needed answers. I fired words, instead of my weapon. "What are you doing here? What are you doing to Todd? Worse, what is Diana doing do to him?"

I heard a moan from behind me. Slid my glance back to see Diana rising from her sprawled position. I turned my gun on her. "You heard my questions to Beatrice. Same goes for you. What the hell is going on here?"

Diana opened her mouth, closed it.

Todd stumbled up to me, resting a heavy hand on my shoulder. "Is okay, Magpie. Bridget's here to make me money. Sell…parks. Worth a fucking fortune."

Todd's eyes rolled, his body swayed into mine, crashing the two of us onto the concrete floor. My hand jolted hard, gun skidding across the room. My head smacked the unforgiving surface. My last thought before I blacked out was I hoped this new wig was a nice wig.

CHAPTER FORTY-THREE

I regained consciousness with a bizarre scene playing before me. Females shrieking, nails lashing, tangled hair flying. I felt I was in the throes of a season finale soap opera catfight. Their piercing screams felt like vocal daggers impaling my skull.

Dazed moments passed before my head cleared. Diana and Beatrice were going at it. They were family. What would cause them to resort to ferocious feline blows?

I reached for my gun. It wasn't in my hand or next to my body. I needed to get to it. But where was it?

I struggled to focus. I scanned my periphery. In the corner of the room, I spotted my weapon, skidded to a halt about three yards from me. Peering at the cat fighters, lashing at each other, they were too preoccupied to notice any movement on my part. If I could just stay low and avoid their range of sight.

Making my move, I found myself stuck. Two hundred pounds of golden hunk lay across my body. Years past, I would have enjoyed this position. Not now. I needed to get to my gun in case these ugly cats reeled their claws at me.

I pushed Todd's shoulder, trying to slide his unconscious body off mine. He didn't budge. I jostled Todd, hoping to bring him around. Again, nothing. Using every inch of my core muscles, I pushed my feet against Todd's body. I edged him a couple inches. Repeating this process, I pressed on and on until I was able to extricate myself.

I slithered along the floor, desperate to retrieve my weapon. As I snagged my gun, an abrupt silence choked the room. I whipped my head in the direction of the women to see what had brought their catfight to a halt.

No! It couldn't be. The slick haired man who'd grabbed me in my club's parking lot had slipped into the scene and wedged himself between Diana and Beatrice, grasping their wrists.

The ladies tried to pull free, but the man clutched with white knuckles. Thank God, I had my gun. Judging by the way this guy manhandled his family, I could only imagine what he'd do to me.

The women's winced faces signaled they were in pain, but they continued their struggle. The man seethed, "Stop you two. This ain't the way we do family business. Stewart heard something was up. Told me to get over here and make sure everything was going to plan."

With the mention of Stewart, the fight in the women evaporated. They retracted their claws.

Beatrice pleaded, "Johnnie, you and Stewart know I'm the tie to the Country Men. They trust me. And I was the one was who was told to…"

"Stop, you twit. I've been working Todd for months at that snot-nosed club. I'm the one who should sell his mobile home parks. He's been sitting on them forever. Prime land worth a fucking fortune. Johnnie, he's prepped, ready to sell. Thanks to me. Cousin, we're talking millions. I earned this deal."

"Okay, Diana. So you got yourself in. But Beatrice is the legit tie. She's clean, and she's blue blood. She's the one brokers for us."

Diana pressed her face into Johnnie's. "Wise up, dumb ass. I've got control here. Look at Williams. Out of it and ready to sign. I had the smarts to stack the deck. Pump him with our Oxy. Give me the family blessing, and I'll have him signing before Beatrice can find a pen. Then…you can do whatever with him."

Johnnie glanced from Diana to Beatrice and back again. For such a tough guy he was either intimidated by his female cousins or ranked low on the IQ scale.

Diana pushed, "What's it going to be, Johnnie? I score big with this, and you get jumbo points with Stewart."

Johnnie looked ready to choose and then hesitated. He

scanned the room like he was buying time. "Hey, what the fuck is she doing here?"

Diana and Beatrice shot glances at me tucked in the corner.

Beatrice stammered, "Johnnie, listen to me. She was knocked out cold. If Diana hadn't lost it, I could have taken care of her."

What did Beatrice mean by that? She always struck me as the most benign member of the family.

Diana chimed in, "Beatrice, you were right in there swinging. Or should I call you Bridget? Isn't that what your daddy calls you?"

With a snap to their wrists, the thug thrust the women to the floor. "Stay wide! We don't want no ref hearing this." He stepped over Diana's body, his menacing steps heading my way. "Especially this nosy bitch."

I didn't see a weapon on him, but he didn't look like he needed one. I raised my gun, sighted on him.

I yelled, "Stop! Now. Not one more step."

Johnnie kept coming. I rose to my knees, tightened my trigger grip. Aligned my sites with the approaching target. I'd honed my sharpshooter skills since I was a teen. My father drilled into me if ever threatened, never hesitate. If you did, you were dead.

Johnnie halted, raised his hands in a protective a gesture. "Whoa, Missy. I wasn't going to hurt you." He cocked his head. "Everything's cool. You can put the gun down."

"Like hell," I spit. "You may be able to strong-arm your cousins, but I'm not some female who was raised to bow down to men. I'm sick of you and your family threatening me. You don't know how much I'd love to pull this trigger." Rising to my feet, taking a wide stance signaling I wasn't bluffing, I added, "But then you'd be no use for me."

Johnnie's jaw twitched. "Hey, I'm just here to protect my family. I don't cause no harm."

"Yeah, right. And I'm Snow White, and you're Prince Charming. You may charm your marks, or should I say victims, but you don't fool me. You and your family are into crime. At first, I thought you were petty gypsies, but the more I study you Travellers, the more I learn. And tonight I've discovered a lot."

A guttural moan from across the room caused my searing gaze at Johnnie to flicker. Todd had come to. Thank God, he was okay.

Johnnie took my second of weakness to lunge at me. I fired my gun, hitting Johnnie dead on. He stumbled backward, collapsing upon the floor. Blood spurt from his gut.

I started toward Johnnie, wanting to check for signs of life, but Diana and Beatrice outpaced me. I held back, gun ready— in case they turned on me. Let them check their cousin's pulse.

The women hovered over his body. Diana leaned into his face, like she was listening for signs of breath. Beatrice quivered beside her.

Diana pleaded, "Johnnie…you asshole. Stay with us."

God, what had I done? I'd been prepped almost my entire my life for such a situation, but I never thought I'd shoot someone. How had I gone from Country Club Mom to trigger shooter?

I didn't know if he was dead or still amongst us, but I knew my obligation. Call 911. But my cell was stashed in my bag on the other side of the room, and I didn't want to risk my life among these crazy people trying to retrieve it. I yelled, "Someone Call 911!"

The two women stared at me like I'd just committed a worse offense than shooting Cousin Johnnie. They didn't move a muscle. I repeated my order. "Get help. Fast."

Diana looked at me. "Not gonna happen. Not until we're gone. Magpie, you're in big trouble."

I sneered at Diana's beak-nosed face. "I may be, but right now I don't give a shit. I'm the one holding the gun, but you're refusing to get medical help. I'd say we're all in a heap of trouble. So while we're waiting for one of you to make that call or for poor Johnnie to bleed out, let's have a girl-to-girl chat. I want answers. Now."

Diana snickered, "Forget it. What are you going to do,

shoot us? Then you'd have three times the blood on your hands. Go ahead. Do it."

My hand trembled, feeling the weight of my weapon and where it had taken me. So angry, I wanted to pull the trigger. But my dad's training screamed, "Let it go."

A deep mumble came from the other side of the foyer. "The po… the cops on the way."

Diana and Beatrice's eyes shot to the sound of Todd's warning.

Beatrice gasped. Holding a shaking hand to her lips, she whispered, "The police. That can't be. Diana, we have to get out of here."

"Can it. He's faking. He's so loaded he can't even talk, let alone dial 911."

I laughed. My sizzled nerves couldn't contain the irony of Todd's emergency signal. "Diana, do you think Todd has to dial for help? He has more electronic gadgets than the CIA, which are more than capable of doing Todd's talking for him."

Diana's eyes popped, probably thinking back to the camera recognition device installed at the entry gate. I knew somehow that Todd had the police dispatched. And with Lockett Island's monetary status, I'd wager it'd take them only a minute to arrive.

I fingered my gun, signaling I had the firepower to enforce my inquisition. "Okay, ladies. It's either the cops or me. Who would you rather talk to?"

CHAPTER FORTY-FOUR

Diana and Beatrice exchanged glances like they were warning each other to remain silent.

"Look, I'm giving you two the chance to get out of here before the posse arrives. You'd better be quick with some info, and you better be truthful, which I know is difficult for con artists. You mentioned family Oxy. I'm assuming you're talking about selling Oxycodone. Your family's into construction cons. What's up with the drugs?"

Diana puffed like she was proud. "Helping people with their pain. We do have a heart."

I smirked. "And a passion for money. This drug's exploded as an overprescribed, abused med. I bet your heart is bursting at pride with the money you're raking in. And judging by Todd's doped condition, I can see how you could use Oxy to manipulate your marks. Like my husband. Or Andrew Richardson. Drug them into a compromising position, then snatch the titles to their properties."

Diana stepped forward. "Hey. If these spoiled CC members were into alleviating their golfing aches and pains, it's not my problem."

"Yeah, right. My husband was into Oxy."

"Well, maybe I gave him a sampling. He was complaining about some back pain. No big deal."

God! That sampling may have cost him his life. Now I really did want to kill Diana. But I forced myself to remain cool. As my father always said, "Keep the focus."

"Diana, Johnnie said Beatrice was legit. That she was blue blood. What did he mean by that? And what about Daddy calling Beatrice, Bridget?"

Todd muttered more coherently now, coming to from his drug-induced stupor. "Maggie, my surveillance app is signaling the police are entering my compound gate. One more to pass through and they're in."

"Todd, those gates are locked. Won't that stop them?"

"No, Magpie. Cops have emergency codes."

Damn, I needed answers—fast. I turned the gun to Beatrice. "You heard me. Who are you?"

She quaked. "I'm part of the Traveller family. But not. It's—"

"Don't say a frickin' word!" Diana screamed. She continued hurling profanities, but they were quickly drowned by the blare of police sirens.

The pitch of the rescue squad momentarily caught me off guard, and I made another rooky mistake. Glanced in the direction of the noise. Out of the corner of my eye, I spied Diana grabbing Beatrice, speeding out of the foyer toward the back of the house. I didn't want to shoot them in the back—I had enough to explain. And with the four thousand square feet Todd's estate encompassed, I knew it would be fruitless to pursue them.

I rushed to Todd's side. "How are you doing?"

"I'm fine. Just help me into this chair. Don't want the police to see me sprawled on the floor."

I hoisted Todd into a low-slung chair, and propped his shoulders into an upright position. I knew he was still buzzing from Diana's poison, but at least his posture looked presentable. With his stature in the community, I could understand him wanting to present a formidable front. I felt confident he could pull it off. Numerous times I'd see him pounding down drinks, then snap to faked sobriety when a sexy woman or business associate sidled by. At least Todd's numerous years of debauchery finally paid some redeeming value.

"Maggie, don't fret about me. I'm worried you could be in serious trouble. You shot a guy."

"It makes me sicker than you'll ever know. But I had to do it. He would have killed us. But no time to get into that. Todd, if I remember, you have a penchant for recording thing. Tonight's events are all on record, right?"

"You know it."

"Then the taped evidence will show I was protecting my life, and yours. One problem—how fast can you delete a smidgen of the recording?"

Todd held out his smart phone, faking a thumbed click. "Like this."

"Good. Then make the last part of the evidence disappear. About Beatrice being blue blood and Daddy calling her Bridget."

"Why? Shouldn't we tell the police about that?"

"In a perfect life, yes. But not now. Our ocean tide holds secrets. Dark ones that I believe are tied to the Santa Reno murders. And with Grant's killing. I feel it's up to me to turn this murderous tide."

Todd tapped his iPhone. "Done. The police will see only what we want them to. Maggie, I want to back you up, but everything's so… hazy."

"Don't worry. Just follow my lead. Quick, scroll through the recording so you know everything that happened before the cops bust in."

Todd followed my orders. "You're right. This proves it was either you—or him. I'll help you handle the police. But, Maggie, there's something I want to share with you that will shine some light on this mess."

Todd didn't get the chance. The police pounded on the door. I heard muffled cries. "Mr. Williams, Newport Beach Police."

Again, Todd tapped his cell. The front door swung open. Police officers crept through, guns hoisted. "Mr. Williams…" The lead cop laid his gaze upon Todd. "We received your emergency call. Are you all right? Is your house secure?" Staring at me he added, "Who's this woman?"

"It's fine. She's a friend."

The police officer repeated his question, "Are you okay?"

Todd shrugged in the direction of Johnnie's bloody body. "That depends on what you mean by okay. Me? Yes. But that guy's not doing so well."

The squad spun around to Johnnie. A path of blood oozed across the floor. They clutched their weapons tight, ready for action. It wasn't necessary. Judging by Johnnie's river of red, I knew he wasn't going anywhere.

Time blurred with a series of calls for medical assistance, backup, forensic experts. Then police questioning, Todd alerting the officers two suspects had fled. And the surrendering of my weapon, followed by more questions. As the evening whirled by, I remember Todd insisting the detectives examine his crime cam. Then more questions, or should I say drilling, directed at both of us.

I prayed that after the police viewed the tape of the shooting, they would see I had no choice. If I hadn't shot Johnnie, he would have overpowered me and I would have been the victim sporting a gaping wound.

After the two officers took a cursory look at the tape, I heard them mumble that it did look like Johnnie had executed life-threatening behavior. I was off the hook for now, but I knew the police would take the recording into evidence, pick it apart. I hoped Todd's obsession with razor-edge technology would obscure the fact the recording had been tampered with.

Then Detective Harrington strutted in. She nodded to the officer who'd been issuing first responder directives. "I'll take it from here, Sergeant." Ignoring Todd, she aimed her sights on me. "So, Maggie. Looks like you have a lot of explaining to do."

CHAPTER FORTY-FIVE

Detective Harrington grilled me like I was a serial murderer on trial for my life. She fired questions with such lightning speed I could barely get my answers out.

This was good, because her rudeness caused Todd to cut in. "Detective, Maggie's already answered your questions. She's fully cooperated. Interview's over. She's not saying another word."

"I'm the Homicide Detective, and I call the shots. If she doesn't give me everything I need, she can accompany me to headquarters. And you won't be invited."

"Maggie's not going anywhere."

"Says who?"

"Me. And Maggie's lawyer, Winston Cunningham."

Nicole shut her mouth. "So you've retained Mr. Cunningham for your ex-girlfriend? When?"

"While you were badgering my friend. Guess you didn't see me hit my legal app. If Maggie needs him, he's on his way."

Nicole stood silent.

I thought, Wow. Winston Cunningham must be some tough lawyer. Nicole didn't throw another query, muttering something about needing to consult with CSI. She turned away and then paused. "Maggie, obviously there's a lot to be processed at this scene. Leather Boy may have bought you some time, but I wouldn't take any more nostalgic trips back to your childhood roots, or any other place out of town. We'll talk soon."

I smiled. "Of course, Nicole. I love gal pal chat."

Judging by Nicole's daggered look, she must not care for

schmoozing with the girls.

I needed to return home. Snuggle into bed and pull my downy duvet over my head. Make this horrible day go away. But I didn't feel I could drive in my nerve-wracked state, picturing myself swerving crazier than a drunk blowing alcohol two times the legal limit.

I thought about calling a taxi when Todd pulled me aside. "Maggie, I can tell you're in no condition to drive. But I don't want you leaving your car here. I'm certain the detective would impound it and process it as part of the crime scene. I have drivers on staff. It will take just a minute, and they can drive you and your car home."

Clasping Todd's hand, I murmured. "Thank you. And thanks for handling Detective Harrington. I don't know what it is, but she seems to have it in for me. I don't even know why."

"I may."

My hand gripped Todd's. "What…are you talking about?"

Todd leaned his cheek against mine. Spoke with hushed voice. "Remember what I told you about wanting to share some information?"

"Yes, but—"

Todd touched his finger to my lips. "Not here. Let's find a safe place to talk. Are you up for it?"

Todd's words squelched my desire to whimper beneath my goose feathers. I nodded. "Let's go."

Exiting Todd's house through his front gate, a Lincoln Town Car rolled up the driveway. A driver in a navy chalk-striped suit donned a fedora shadowing his face and whisked open the passenger door. Todd held my still trembling elbow as we slid in.

Inside the dark confines of the car, its engine droning ever so smoothly, I peered out the back window. "Todd, what about my car? You said Nicole might impound it."

"Not to worry. A second driver is on his way."

"But I didn't give him my key. How's he going to get in, let alone start the engine?"

"He has his ways."

Not wanting to know the ways of Todd's subterranean staff, I moved the conversation in a lighter direction. "Todd, this car's so conservative. Such a departure from your sporting machines. A bit of a surprise."

"You know me, I'm full of surprises. He then touched a button that opened the confines to a mini bar. Todd plucked out a bottle of champagne. "May I pour you a glass?"

Reviewing the unnerving events of the day, I answered, "May you ever." He filled my glass to the brim, the car's smooth ride never causing him to spill a drop. We clinked the crystal, sipped in silence until our bubbly was drained. I made a mental notation to double up on my workouts to expel the toxins the recent madness had poured into my veins.

God, if my life could just go back to normal. But that would never be the case. And with me killing Cousin Johnnie, Detective Harrington would really be sifting through my life. Could chaos be my new normal? These dark thoughts caused my champagne flute to quiver.

Todd laid his over mine. "Maggie, would you like a refill?"

"Yes...please."

We sipped the fine, liquid fruit for a few moments. I cracked the window, feeling the cool ocean breeze flutter over me. I giggled. Tried to stifle it. This wasn't the time to be laughing. But I couldn't help myself.

Todd turned to be. "What's so humorous, Maggie?"

"Nothing. Just nerves. Silly thoughts. With all our cruising Coastal Road, I feel like I'm back in college. I should be home grieving, but I've been up and down this road more times in the past week than in my past twenty years."

"Maggie, we live in southern California. We spend our lives driving. When was the last time you saw somebody walking, besides along the beach?"

"1989?"

"Exactly. And with recent events, you've needed to be on the road. You're not going to solve this puzzle sitting at home."

Todd was right. If I was going to find Grant's murderer, I

had to leave the confines of my house. And in southern California, where a jaywalking ticket was easier to get than one speeding, you drove and drove. I only hoped this ironic gypsy-like movement would help me on my quest.

Todd broke the silence. "Maggie, you said you didn't understand why Detective Harrington seemed so venomous."

"Yes, but..." I nodded in the driver's direction, a silent signal to see if this man could be trusted.

"Former Special Ops. And I mean special." I got it. This man had seen it all and would keep all secrets to his grave.

Todd took a long sip of his bubbly. "Do you remember how I confided my mother served for years as the Harrington's housekeeper?"

"Of course. Your families went back a couple of generations. Mr. Harrington altered his name, possibly to disguise Scottish heritage. What else could there be?"

"Mr. Harrington had a child born out of marriage."

My hand flew to my lips. "Mr. H. had a love child?"

"I believe he did. And from what I could piece together from the sprinklings my mother told me, and from what I saw, this truly was a love child. Mr. Harrington cared for the child's mother very much. And, for his daughter."

"But Nicole's his daughter. You're telling me there's another silver-spooned ancestry out there?"

"Yes, I am. And I'm certain Nicole doesn't want someone with brains looking into their family affairs, finding this child. Someone like you."

CHAPTER FORTY-SIX

"An illegitimate child! How could something so astounding be kept a secret?"

"By loyal staff, such as my mother. And I'm certain the disloyal ones paid off."

"Did your mother confide to you who the child was—or the mother?"

"Not outright. But the time she took ill, I told you she kept mumbling about a baby. A baby named Bridget. I believe this infant was Mr. Harrington's."

"How can you be so certain this Bridget is the Big Man's illegitimate daughter? Did your mother ever outright tell you?"

"No. Nobody did."

"Then how do you know?"

"As I told you, we lived in a converted garage on the outskirts of the Harrington property. I may not have been privy to what was happening within the household, but I detected a number of strange things happening outside my garage."

"Like what?"

"Like Mr. Harrington exiting the property, not from one of the main garages connected to his mansion, but from a single-standing, isolated one just across the way from mine. Late at night I'd hear the creak of manual hinges then the hum of a car engine. Pulling aside my curtains, I'd spy a dark blue Oldsmobile Delta backing out and then heading down the dirt lane to the estate's back gate. I was young, but even then Mr. Harrington's departures struck me as odd. The late hour, slithering out the obscure gate, driving a bland vehicle. He normally travelled in a Benz or Bentley—usually chauffeured ones."

I mulled over Todd's revelation.

"An Oldsmobile sedan would be more obscure than a Rolls or a Bentley. Especially one to blend into the more common areas of town."

"Exactly," Todd said. "Like the neighborhoods where kids with no money hung out with their friends. Kids like me."

"What are you saying? You tracked Mr. Harrington?"

"Maggie, I wasn't old enough to drive at that time. There's no way I could follow him. But I did stumble upon something profound. It happened innocently."

I chuckled. "Todd, there's nothing innocent about you."

"There was at one time." Todd cleared his throat. "When I was around ten, I'd visit my buddies who lived a bit inland. We'd skateboard around, using our change to buy junk food at Ray's Market. One evening while satisfying our sweet tooth, a lady walked in. I happened to be standing next to her at the checkout counter. Her purchases were an odd combination—a box of baby cereal and a large bottle of wine."

"An alcoholic mother with an infant is not a good thing. But what would make you remember this woman after all these years?"

Todd smiled. "Because she was very leggy and had perfect facial features."

I rolled my eyes. "Todd, you said you were only ten."

"What can I say? My way with the ladies started at an early age."

"Oh, God," I groaned. "I guess you were destined to be—Todd."

"Yes, but there's more. She was so beautiful, I stood transfixed as she sashayed out of the store. She stopped at a dark sedan at the edge of the compact parking lot. Tucking her shopping bag into the backseat, she leaned over and kissed a baby, or maybe a toddler. Then the woman slid into the passenger's seat. The male driver pulled the woman into him, languishing her with a long kiss. As the car left the market, it passed under a light. I swear the man driving was Charles Harrington."

"How can you be so certain?"

"When I lived on the Harrington premises. Saw the man countless times walking the grounds. I could always recognize him by his full head of hair, severe jawline, and the regal way he held himself. And I saw him driving that same model car in and out of the back garage more times than I could count.

"But how can you know beyond a doubt it was Mr. H. in that parking lot?"

"When I returned home, I couldn't shake the scene from my head. Late that night, I heard a car, and then the squeal of garage door hinges. I peeked out my window and spotted Charles walking, with a bit of a drunken sway, toward the manor. I tried to sleep, but my racing mind wouldn't let me. Finally, my kid curiosity couldn't stand it any longer."

I whispered, "What did you do?"

"I slipped into Charles's garage, crawled into the car, scoured about. I knew I had to act quickly. I didn't know if a member of the Harrington night-staff was stalking the grounds."

"Did you find anything?"

"Nothing in the front seat."

"And in the back?"

"A receipt from Ray's Market for wine and baby cereal."

CHAPTER FORTY-SEVEN

Mr. Harrington had a mistress and love child. That revelation could lead to social suicide. Was Bridget his daughter? The Bridget who had dubious ties to the Travellers? Todd's mother had feverish mumblings about a baby—her concern for a Bridget. Did his mom fear this out-of-wedlock child would be swept under one of the Harrington's fifty-thousand-dollar Persian rugs?

Cruising along with Todd, I thought back to my horrible encounter at his house, where I'd fired the fatal shot that killed Johnnie. Before his demise, Johnnie insisted Beatrice was the one to do the deal, the legit tie for the Travellers. She was blue blood. Harrington blood?

Going back to Todd's childhood spotting of Charles with his girlfriend, I pondered the facts. Todd said the car was a 1985 Olds Delta. That painted a timeline. Todd also stated the woman bought baby cereal, not jarred baby food. I'd borne two kids and knew this placed the child toward its toddler years—probably about two. And Todd's observation that the child's head peeped just over the bottom of the window, told me this wasn't a baby. Calculating this information, that child would now be around the age of twenty-eight. About the age Beatrice, or Bridget, appeared to be.

Interesting, but I needed more. Thinking about Beatrice's striking appearance—legs that went forever, the sway to her cadence. Her perfect chiseled facial features—when you could see them from under her wig. She sounded like a clone of Mr. Harrington's conspiratorial love. Beatrice's wigs were a subtle red, but what was her true hair color?

Turning to Todd, I asked, "The woman in Ray's market. You remembered a lot about her. Do you recall the color of her hair?"

Todd took a swig of his champagne. "Do I ever. Blonde. Thick golden waves cascading over her shoulders and down her back. And the depth of the color told me it didn't come from a bottle."

Taking another sip from his flute, he added, "Always reminded me of Nicole years ago, romping around her backyard, thick yellow ponytail flailing about. Whenever her mother would come out to call her into the house, I remember thinking, Thank God Nicole doesn't have her mother's hair."

"Why?"

"Because her mother sprouted thin, dullish brown. Nothing like Nicole's thick hair."

"Todd, once you were relegated to living in a garage, were you ever allowed into the main estate?"

"Of course. I lived in my mother's maid quarters until I grew so big our room was too cramped. My mother asked Mr. Harrington if he could provide us move living space. That's when his workers converted the garage for me."

"With all the palatial rooms in his house, Mr. Harrington couldn't give up one for you?"

"He could have. But I think he detected that might mean trouble in the upcoming years with Nicole and me. I was young, but you know who I am. Probably a smart move on Mr. Harrington's part."

"Weren't you miffed when you were downgraded to a garage?"

"At first. But once I grew into my teens, it allowed me certain freedoms. I learned how to sneak my dates through the back gate—like Mr. Harrington. Except mine were coming in, and he was going out."

"Okay, Todd, I get it. You had a love shack on the grounds of one of the wealthiest families in town. Once you moved to the garage did you still have access to the main house?"

"I did. As I said, my mother was one of the most valued

members of their staff."

"So you had free reign."

"Not exactly. But sometimes I did take advantage of my situation."

"Nicole?"

Todd laughed. "Do you think I'm crazy?"

"No. Savvy."

"Exactly. But when Mr. and Mrs. Harrington were away on vacation, I'd take that sliver of time to sneak about the mansion, peeking in places my mother would have slapped my butt if she knew. Of course, she was always too busy mopping floors or scrubbing dishes to keep an eagle eye on me. Fascinating times. Especially when I'd find something I knew I shouldn't have."

"Such as?"

"A faded black and white photograph."

My arms tingled cold. "Can I ask you what was in the photo?"

"A man with thick hair, hugging a woman with luscious blond hair, holding a tow-headed toddler. Standing before a Delta Olds."

"Where did you find this?"

"I can't tell you. I shouldn't have been inside that room, peeking about. I was just so taken by the man's power, his success. I wanted to learn more about him."

"Todd, where did you find that picture?"

"God, it's so embarrassing."

"Tell me!"

"In the bottom of Mr. Harrington's cuff links drawer."

"I thought you were going say underwear. I get that it's rude to rifle through someone's belongings. But what's so embarrassing about a kid peeking about cuff links?"

"Because for the rich, cuff links can provide a link to the past. And sometimes that past is not one they want discovered."

CHAPTER FORTY-EIGHT

"Come on, Todd, how mysterious can cuff links be? They're a one-inch piece of metal that holds shirtsleeves together. Hardly anyone wears them anymore."

Todd glanced at his wrist. "I do—on a special occasion. And Mr. Harrington does. I've noticed them when I've shaken his hand during our professional encounters."

"So Mr. Harrington's a fancy dresser. What secrets could cuff links possibly bear?"

"Family heritage."

"What? Cuff links normally bare nothing more significant than one's initials. Charles Harrington may have added an R to his birth name, but his initials would remain CH."

"No. I'm talking about something much more intriguing than family initials. I'm talking about an engraved family crest."

"Todd. Cuff links. Come on."

"Maggie. I found two pairs of cuff links bearing two different shields. One etched identical to the coat of arms prominently displayed above the Harrington's living room fireplace. I'd heard Mr. Harrington boast many times to visitors about the golden-jeweled helmet displaying the crest. A symbol that represented a tie to British royalty. Another set of links bore a different design. One that looked to be Scottish."

"No offense, but what would you know about ancestry crests?"

Todd heaved his iron-built chest. "Actually, more than you'd think. At the time, my fifth grade class was studying Scottish history. Fascinating stuff."

"I thought the only history you found interesting was your

dating memoirs."

Todd tsked, "Maggie, I keep telling you, there's more to me than you realize."

"I know…now getting back to the cuff links."

"The second pair bore a simple plumed helmet. I etched, so to speak, that design into my mind. Was going to see if it matched one of the Scottish crests, or bore a strong resemblance to the ones in my history book. When…"

"What? Oh my God, did Mr. Harrington walk in on you?"

"No, his lovely daughter, Nicole. And when I say lovely, I'm only referring to her looks. Not her personality."

"Let me guess. Nasty? And not in the sexual sense?"

"You hit it, babe. She stood with hands on hips, as if she wanted to challenge me to a brawl. I was three years older, outweighed her by at least fifty pounds. She charged right up to me, smacked my hand sending the cuff links skidding across the floor.

With a suddenly not so pretty face, she glared at me. "You sneaky thief, what are you doing leafing through my father's drawer?"

"You've got it all wrong, Nicole," I stammered, searching for a plausible reason to be there. "I just wanted to know your father. He's such—"

Glancing to the rifled dresser drawer, she seethed, "What's this?"

"What?" I asked.

"That picture lying there. Where you've been snooping?"

"I, um, I have no idea. It's just a photograph."

"Grabbing the weathered photo, she stared into the smiling faces captured by the camera. Steeling a glance to me she said, "That's my father. But who's this woman? That's not my mother. And that toddler they're holding has blond hair. Like mine. But that's not me. Who are these people?"

"I knew who they were, but I couldn't tell Nicole. I didn't want to stoke her anger by saying Daddy had a secret family. My snooping would certainly get my mother fired. And if I told Nicole what I believed the photo meant, her ensuing anger would most likely cause her to summon her family's security guards. Or, worse, land me in jail on a trumped up charge of stealing."

His story had me spellbound. I prompted him. "What did you do, Todd?"

"The only thing I could. I opened my hands in a surrendering gesture—beamed my brightest smile. "Honestly, Nicole. I don't know who these people are. How could I?"

Flipping her braid, she smirked. "You're right. You're just the maid's son. What could you know?"

I interrupted Todd's recantation, and said, "Apparently a lot more than she thought."

"Exactly, but I knew to keep quiet. I kept my eyes on Nicole, waiting to see if she bought my story. She stared intently at the picture. Her hands trembled. It appeared she was doing her math, putting two and two together to make three. Even at her young age, I'm certain Nicole had already been schooled in her family's place in society and to let telling photos lie buried.

She tucked the picture back into the depths of the drawer. "Tell you what. I won't tell my father you've been poking around in his belongings, if you don't say anything about this photo. And I mean anything. Are we straight?"

"Sure, Nicole. That picture means nothing to me. This all never happened."

"Good. Now pick up those cuff links and straighten the drawer. Exactly as you found it."

"Then she spun around, ponytail flying, and marched out the door. My hands shaking, I could barely reconstruct the perfect order in which I'd found the contents of the drawer. Cuff links in place, I wanted to run from the room, back to my garage, to safety. But I couldn't resist slipping my hand back into the contents of the drawer, careful not to disturb anything, and take one last peek at the engraved pieces I believed were Mr. Harrington's link to a mysterious Scottish crest not boasted above his fireplace."

"Then what did you do?" I asked, surprised at how

breathless I'd become.

"I got the hell out of there."

"What about the cuff link? Did you ever find it had any significance?"

"Yes. Quite interesting. As soon I was back in my garage, I flipped through my world history book, until I came upon the chapter about ancient Scotland and the heritage of the Harrington coat of arms."

"Did you find any pictures identical to the engraving on the suspect cuff link?"

"I wouldn't say identical, but the crest on Charles's link bore several characteristics to the one that was Scottish."

"Intriguing. We already know Mr. H. quietly changed the family name to disguise suspect Scottish heritage and denote regal English. Seems Mr. Harrington isn't who he purports to be. I wonder what other secrets he holds."

"I don't know, Maggie. But the way the Harringtons operate and the power they yield in Newport Beach, I'd say big ones. Charles Harrington doesn't do anything on a small scale."

"There's one thing that nags me. If this man has gone to such great lengths to mask his roots, propelling him into the highest tier of upper-crust society, why would he risk his secrets being uncovered by holding onto those cuff links? And that picture?"

"Why do any of us do foolish things?"

"Sentimental memories?"

Todd smiled. "Possibly. But I'd place my bet on love."

CHAPTER FORTY-NINE

Coinciding with Todd's uncharacteristic sentimental statement, the Town Car pulled to a stop at my driveway. Todd and I sat in silence for a moment. I quivered at the thought of returning to my home. Not only because I knew nasty people most likely had it in for me. But after killing a man, how could I go back to my life as wife and mother?

Todd must have detected my nervousness. He murmured, "Maggie, if you don't feel safe here or don't want to be alone, you can come back to my place."

"Todd, with the heat Detective Harrington's blazing on me, that would raise even more seared flags. I need to present a front of normalcy. My kids are safely tucked away. I'll be fine."

"Magpie. What if another member of the family comes after you?"

"After the female cousins' hasty retreat from Johnnie's murder scene, the heat's not only on me, but them as well. I doubt they'll be bothering me. And if they do…"

"You'll do what?"

"Let's just say I always have a backup plan."

Todd brushed his lips across my cheek. "I bet you do.

Besides learning the horrific news of Grant's death, this day ranked as my second worst ever. But I didn't have time to wallow in my troubles.

The superficial evidence made Grant and Andrew Richardson look like two philandering country club men. Sleazing it out in Santo Reno, downing some wine, doing the nasty deed. Couldn't get their pants down fast enough. This image angered me so much, if I hadn't already killed a man tonight, and if Grant weren't already dead, I'd pull my trigger right now. But the police had confiscated my gun, so that wouldn't happen. Plus, being at home alone, I had no victims to target.

Once my anger somewhat subsided, my thoughts started racing. Diana talked, no, bragged, about the Travellers pushing Oxycodone. A savior for those in true pain, but a dangerous drug for many. I'd witnessed first-hand Todd's lumbering reaction to the drug. For a while, he'd had no control over his movements or clarity of thought. What if Grant and Mr. Richmond had been drugged?

While Todd was stoned, he mumbled about selling, or not wanting, to sell property. Grant had transferred the title of at least one project to Stewart. And the motel in which Andrew Richmond had been killed went into escrow the day he was murdered. Richmond invested in real estate. Was this one of his? Were these men drugged into handing over property?

Strange coincidences? Or staged ones…

I called Carmen. Said it was urgent to see her. Vital to solving Grant's murder.

Carmen responded in a husky voice, like she'd just puffed a cigarette, "Sure, Maggie. I'll meet you at the office. I know there was some hanky-panky going on…uh, unscrupulous people trying to get a piece of Mr. Leman's action. I mean, I believe your husband's success attracted lowlifes to him—those who wanted to worm their way into Leman Land Development. When do you want to meet?"

"Now."

Fifteen minutes later, Carmen strode into Grant's office. She was dressed in casual off-hours attire, but her tight face told me she was ready for business. Once again, we poured through my husband's financials.

"Carmen, this is good information, but it's nothing I haven't already discovered. Do you have anything new?"

Carmen slapped down a new file. "Take a look at this."

"God, Carmen. There're Travellers' names listed as lead vendors for building suppliers and subcontractors. Grant never used these people before. And the prices they were charged for products and services were way beyond what was reported for earlier projects. Worse, Stewart's name is all over these ailing buildings. First as investor, then consultant, project manager…and…"

"Then a quit claim deed making Stewart the sole proprietor."

"Carmen, what else can you tell me?"

"The Scottish men usually met with Mr. Leman after business hours. As my workday was winding down, he'd ask me to order in some hors d'oeuvres and varieties of Scotch."

"Grant didn't drink Scotch."

"It wasn't your husband downing the hard liquor. It was his tacky business associates. Although Mr. Leman would sometimes join them for a glass or two of Cognac."

Cognac. The hint of aromatic breath I'd inhaled before Grant and I made love for the last time. The last time I'd ever catch a wisp of his breath.

Carmen interrupted my thoughts. "These late meetings didn't follow company protocol. Hastily set, not listed on the company's schedule."

"Carmen, that's all very interesting, but what do these happy hour meetings tell us about why Grant would allow himself to be controlled by Stewart? Is there anything else you can tell me?"

Carmen hooded her eyes and spoke in a low, dusky voice. "Stewart plays big into this. I believe he and his family used their money and con skills to derail your husband's business. But…"

"But what? Carmen, what else did you find?"

"Stewart's not the one pulling the strings. There's someone big, very big. One who knows how to play people like puppets. Someone who's been making this town dance like a bunch of marionettes for years."

CHAPTER FIFTY

"What do you mean? All the evidence points to Stewart as the ringleader. His name and slimy imprints are all over the docs. Are you saying there's a Traveller kingpin reigning over him?"

"Someone, but not a Traveller."

"Who? How do you know?"

Carmen twisted her feather-wrinkled lips into an all-knowing look. "It's amazing what people will say before a ghost of an employee who's laying out a platter of food or stocking the office bar."

"As if she were a simple servant, like a housekeeper."

"You got it. These saps were so stupid, they never shut their traps while I was performing my office duties. Treated me like I was low paid temp or minimum wage caterer."

"Carmen. I'm sorry Grant allowed this to happen."

"Mr. Leman always regarded me with respect. It was those low-life Scots men." Carmen let out a guttural laugh, , bosom jiggling. "I'd say I have the last laugh. Those idiots didn't know I could deliver their food and drinks in one sweep. I'd mosey in and out of the boardroom, fumble about with their goodies, taking my own sweet time to listen in."

Carmen smacked her lips as if she were savoring a well-fought victory.

"Carmen, what did you discover? You mentioned a key puppeteer."

"I did. And you won't believe who. Does the name Harrington strike a chord?"

"You mean the Harringtons?"

"The one and only in Newport Beach."

My lips quivered, struggling to get out my words. "My God, could they have played a part in Grant's murder? I'd heard some suspect things about them lately, but nothing pointing to violence."

"Maggie, relax. I need you on this. Take a breath of yoga air, or whatever you're into. I'm not pointing the murder finger at Charles Harrington. I'm just saying he has some dubious connections that indicate he's not the pristine statue of society everyone believes him to be. From what these Traveller guys were chomping about, there's a deep, dark secret in Mr. Harrington's past that connects him to unsavory business associates in the here and now."

Thinking back to Todd, the night he confided Charles Harrington had a mistress who bore him a second daughter, my mind was off to the track and running. If this information became public, it would certainly be a juicy piece for the oceanfront tabloids. Was there more? Could Charles's scandalous past behavior somehow connect him to the Travellers? Or worse, to my husband's murder?

"Carmen, tell me, exactly what did you hear?"

She laid another file on Grant's desk. "This. And these notes are personal family ones. Not financials."

Gazing over Carmen's notes, I struggled to decipher her scrawls.

"Carmen, I don't mean to sound rude, but your handwriting is terrible. It looks like scribble scratch. Couldn't you have rattled it onto a computer to make it more decipherable?"

Carmen pumped her ample chest. "Screw computers. Ever watch those forensic T.V. shows? Everything you type onto a computer is like leaving a fingerprint trail. Worse. A DNA trail. But this," she blurted, waving her hands over her compilation of papers. "This is non-traceable evidence." Carmen cleared her throat. "And the chicken-legged writing? Part of my plan. Maggie, in my day I won the St. Mary's penmanship award three years running. I can write like a nun. But who can decode this?"

I murmured, "Smart move, Carmen. So after deciphering your notes, what would you say is the most telling bit of information you found?"

"That Mr. Harrington had a daughter, who didn't go by the name of Nicole."

"Yes, I know that."

"You do?"

I smiled. "Let's just say you're not the only one who's into intrigue. Please, go on. I'm certain you've uncovered more than I."

Carmen shuffled through her papers, hand resting upon a noticeably crinkled one. "Remember how I said there was a master puppeteer running this town?"

"Yes…"

"Well take a look at this notation here." Carmen thrust her finger at a smeared piece of child scratch. "It states how the Scottish jabber mouths discussed not only edging into your husband's company, but being ordered from somebody very high up, to use Bridget as their front man. Or, woman. These guys didn't seem to have a tiff with Bridget, but the Scots men were none too happy this born-into-money lady would be collecting thousands, no, hundreds of thousands, in realty commissions—when Leman's properties were put on the market."

Bridget. Could this coddled money monger be the Bridget that Grant had sexily written on his love note? The one he'd bestowed an $899 Gitan bag to? Or tried to, before his death? And now she was set to get rich off my husband's hard-earned business? Worse, his death? If she were here, I'd…

"Maggie." Carmen prodded my shoulder. "We need to work together on this."

I struggled to reign in my deviled thoughts. "What else do you have?"

"From what I could gather, Charles Harrington, or someone within his organization, pushed the Travellers to not only muscle in on several of your husband's properties, but take over his entire business."

"Why would Harrington want Grant's company? Mr. H. has been a thriving force in Newport Beach forever. His ventures sift in more money than a full-moon tide. And why would this wealthy patriarch associate with the likes of the Travellers?"

"For love?"

For love. The second time I'd heard that endearment referenced to Mr. Harrington in one day. What was up with this man?

"Carmen, what do you mean by love? What would love have to do with shady business dealings?"

"I'm talking about Charles helping his beloved daughter, Beatrice—I mean, Bridget—put up here. From what I overheard during my times under the radar, it seems Mr. H. preferred the more refined endearment, Bridget. Which, when I Googled it, in English lore, means voyager, Traveller."

A tingle ran through my body.

"So you think Harrington accepted Bridget's ties to the Travellers?"

"Yes. Seems he loved her as much as he did her mother."

I struggled to take in this plethora of information Carmen revealed to me. "Carmen, you said you were in and out of these business meetings. But this story seems to go beyond what someone would say in such a situation. Considering how guarded the Travellers are, and I'm not doubting you, but how could you have uncovered such private matters?"

"Because my spying went beyond the boardroom."

So shocked, my eyebrows shot up like I'd been injected with an overdose of Botox. "What are you telling me?"

Carmen's breasts heaved. She said, "Let's just say my loyalty to your husband's company, and to my financial future, went from boardroom to bedroom."

"You didn't."

"I did. And I'd do it again if it meant getting the goods on these people."

"Can I ask who it was?"

"You don't want to know."

CHAPTER FIFTY-ONE

I was dying to hear the dirty details of Carmen's tryst, when I saw a flash of blond hair whisk through the office door.

"Ms. Carmen Zimmerman, I'd like—" Detective Harrington stopped. Spotted me seated behind Grant's desk. "Mrs. Leman, we seem to be running in the same circles these days. How comfy you look nestled in your husband's chair. Planning on taking over his business...now that he's out of the way?"

Rising from the chair, I said, "I have every right to be here. I backed Grant's business from day one."

Nicole cocked her head. "You did? Not from what I've discovered. Must have been hard work all those years honing your golf game, perfecting yoga poses, dining at your club. Yes, I've talked to your friends. Seems you've led a charmed life."

Struggling to keep my voice calm, I said, "At least I built my life on my own. Put myself through college. Worked my ass off to build my marketing career. I wasn't swaddled in a cashmere blankie like you."

"Yes, my parents have money. But I make my own way in life."

I mumbled, "Probably had to after they discovered your cheating ways."

Nicole slammed her hands on Grant's desk. "What did you say?"

"Oh, nothing. Just chattering away like a ditz-head housewife. May I ask why you dropped by?"

Nicole straightened her tall frame. She took her glaring eyes off me and stared across Carmen's yellow papers strewn about the desk. "I need to ask Ms. Zimmerman some questions about the inner workings of Leman Land Development. Though it's past hours, her neighbor told me I would probably find her here. I need to examine all areas of Mr. Leman's life in order to establish motive. And being that financial gain is one of the major reasons perpetrators commit murder. Along with…"

My disgusted sneer stopped Nicole dead on. I didn't need to hear that sexual exploits were another biggie in the commission of murder. Ever since I plucked that damned Gitan bag from Grant's golf bag I'd tortured over the possibility, or probability, my husband had philandered.

The Detective picked up some of Carmen's note sheets and studied them. Her expertly waxed eyebrows rose. "Oh, looks like we have some very interesting information here. I think you two just made my job easier. Messy writing, but I'm schooled in deciphering sloppy police reports. Ms. Zimmerman, are you sharing proprietary information that could pertain to a current murder investigation?"

Carmen blurted, "It's my duty as Mr. Leman's head administrative assistant to make sure Maggie knows what's going on within the company."

Nicole laid the paper down. "I'm assuming after your little chat session you two were planning on coming forth with this information. I'd hate to think you were conspiring to withhold vital evidence."

I didn't believe Nicole had any teeth in that statement. Carmen and I had done nothing wrong. I knew the detective had it in for me, but now she was taunting Carmen for no apparent reason—other than twisted pleasure.

"Ms. Zimmerman, I'd like to ask you a few questions—alone."

With a flip of her hand she said, "That's all, Mrs. Leman. I don't need any further statements at this time."

I sank back into Grant's chair. "Good, then you two can talk in Carmen's office while I tend to my new business obligations."

Nicole didn't have a comeback for that remark. The two headed through the door and into the hallway when I heard Carmen say, "Oh my, I think I left my business cell in Mr. Leman's office. Detective, I'm sure you'll want to take a look at that."

"Okay, go get it."

Carmen whisked back into the room, swept around the expansive desk, scooping her cell from the table. She leaned down to me and whispered, "I'm afraid she's going to confiscate my notes."

I said, "I don't think she can cherry pick our things without a warrant."

"Well, judging by her rude demeanor, what do you think the odds are she'll get one?" I said, "Pretty certain."

"Exactly. Get rid of these notes."

"What?"

Carmen slipped a key into my hand. She said, "I placed another set at First American Bank. The branch Mr. Leman always used. Safety deposit box number one-twenty-nine."

Carmen started for the door when Detective Harrington strode back in. "Ms. Zimmerman, let's get going, I'm on the clock."

Carmen chirped, "I'm so sorry, Detective. Had a menopausal moment trying to remember where I'd laid my phone."

Nicole rolled her eyes like she had no patience for middle-aged crisis. Probably believed she'd never have to deal with hot flashes. Smiling, I thought, she wouldn't have hot flashes. She'd have broiling ones.

A moment later, I heard Carmen's voice outside my door, "Oh dear, I forgot to remind Maggie about something."

"Ms. Zimmerman, this is a homicide investigation. We don't have time for chit chat."

"I don't think your father would think of this important event as chit chat."

Nicole's voice boomed, "What do you mean about my father?"

"Relax, Detective. I just need to remind Mrs. Leman about your father's charity golf tournament. The Newport Hills Swing Green, Drive Green event. Mr. Leman was supposed to…" Carmen blew her nose, "…was supposed to attend as honoree."

"Yes, I know about the event. I'll be teeing off myself. Go on, tell her about it."

Once again, Carmen popped her head into the doorway. "Maggie, did you hear what I said about the Harrington golfing event? I'm sure you know about it. Mr. Leman was set to deliver an acceptance speech. With him gone, I'm sure you'll want to be the one to speak."

Shaking my head, I stammered, "I don't recall Grant mentioning it."

"That couldn't be. Mr. Leman was to receive the prestigious LEED Award, Building a Greener Future. From Mr. Harrington himself."

Such an honor. How could Grant have neglected to tell me about it? I wanted to ask Carmen more details about this event, but I couldn't resist the urge to find out about her investigative tryst before the detective burst back in. "Quick, Carmen, who was it you slept with to get info?"

She stepped up to me, leaned over, and whispered, "Stewart."

Stewart? Carmen was sleeping with that slime? How could that be? I wanted to hear the juicy details, but Nicole's impatient, "Enough mid-life crisis delays. Let's get on with it, Ms. Zimmerman," told me my questions would have to wait.

I turned my focus to Grant's computer and scanned his schedule. There it was—the Swing Green, Drive Green Golf Tournament, and added to the entry: Award Speech.

I couldn't help feeling angry that Grant hadn't discussed this important milestone with me. And that he'd kept me in the dark about being so passionate about taking his business global, he'd resorted to doing business with suspect investors. But I pushed on. I also couldn't prevent my marketing mind from thinking that if I'd organized this event, I'd have comprised a classier name for a Harrington event. Swing Green, Drive Green sounded to me like a used car dealership promo. Then glancing again at Grant's entry, I noted Diana Hutchinson listed as his contact. Ms. President of Marketing must have come up with it.

This gathering would make for an interesting day. Mr. Harrington and his lovely daughter, Nicole. And if she hadn't skipped town, I presumed Diana would be hovering around. And perhaps some of her cousins. Maybe even Beatrice, or Bridget, depending on the persona she chose to present that day.

Since Grant was gone, I knew I had to take his place on the links and present his acceptance speech. I felt confident about my golf game. My bi-weekly score sheets from my club confirmed this. But it had been years since I'd spoken before a formal group. And the content of this speech was a subject on which I had no true expertise. Why hadn't I paid more attention to Grant's business? Perhaps Detective Harrington was right. Maybe I'd had too much fluff time.

Then thinking back to the mom hours I'd spent with my kids—helping them with homework, driving them to their umpteen activities—golf, dance, you name it. And the amount of time I spent pulling together a nice household. I put in hours, years, as mother and wife. Yes, I'd had the time to work on my mind and body and enjoy my life. But I'd sacrificed a lucrative career and dedicated myself to my family to earn it. And I knew Grant felt the same way. At least until he cheated…?

But I had more pressing things on my mind. Like composing a winning speech. Deciding what designer golf label to wear. More importantly, could any of these Swing Green, Drive Green attendees have played a part in my husband's demise? I felt so sure of it I'd bet my next Mulligan on it.

CHAPTER FIFTY-TWO

About an hour into writing my speech, I heard Carmen's office door open. Detective Harrington's voice echoed down the hall, "I think I have all I need for now, Ms. Zimmerman."

Good. The Detective was leaving for the night. Thank goodness, she hadn't swaggered back into Grant's office, pounding me with more insidious questions. I had a lot to do before the clock struck midnight.

When I felt I'd reached a point at which I'd pulled together a decent rough draft, I logged off his computer. I felt pleased with my work, but my past executive perfectionism told me to seek out expert advice to critique my work. But who?

My mind tangled through the twisted route my life had taken me in the past few days. There had to be somebody I'd encountered who had sufficient insight into the green industry to help me. There was Stewart. He seemed to be implanted as a formidable fixture in Grant's leafy projects. But I doubted Stewart would help me. Hurt me was more likely.

I shivered. How could Carmen have slept with him? She was either desperate for love or on a desperate mission to help my husband. Whatever it was, I silently thanked her for her dedication.

Moving along, I pondered who I knew that had experience in both real estate and the environmental movement. Todd. He held numerous realty investments and was a primary investor in Gitan. Todd was my go-to guy.

I texted him to see how he was feeling after his drugging experience. Would he be able to meet with me?

He answered that he was alert, going full speed ahead, and

up for anything. Todd. Practically killed today by Diana's overdosing, he never let anything slow him down.

I tapped, I'm on my way.

Todd's next text informed me that after Cousin Johnnie's shooting, his house was an official crime scene and the police forced him to leave. His estate was taped off tighter than a home wrapped in Saran Wrap.

Oh my God, Todd was forced out of his home, and it was all my fault. I texted him this sentiment.

He zipped back. Not a problem. He was off-property, checked into his favorite Newport resort, Vista Montagne.

I drove the bougainvillea-lined drive that separated this luxurious property from the hectic pace of Coastal Road. I arrived at the showcase fountains that dominated the entrance. A valet whipped open my door, and I swept through the lobby door.

Assuming I'd have to consult with the front desk to gain access to Todd's room, once again Todd surprised me. Before my second step hit the marbled floor, Todd's former Special Ops guy who'd previously chauffeured me intercepted me. He clasped my elbow, nodded a silent greeting, and then escorted me not to the lobby elevator, but to the back stairs. After my shooting of Johnnie, this action made me assume Todd knew I was in a precarious position and wanted to keep me under wraps.

Thankfully, unlike trekking to Grant's sixteenth floor office, we only had to trudge a three flights Because of strict environmental beach building codes, this resort had to be built to fit in with its natural surroundings, so the upper crust suites didn't require a marathon runner's training to comfortably use the stairs.

Upon entering Todd's room, I should say suites, the palatial surroundings made me I realize why Todd seemed nonplussed about being forced out of his house.

He greeted me with a checked kiss on my cheek and a brim of bubbly. "Nice to see you, Maggie."

"Thank you, Todd. You're always so accommodating. Army escort, champagne dreams, everything a gal fantasizes about when visiting Newport Beach's most eligible bachelor."

Todd sank into one of the white, silk sofas. He sighed. "Maggie, at one point in time, the term 'most eligible bachelor' would have been me. But let's face it. Time is moving on. It's time I grew up and moved on."

I sat down with Todd. "Hey, what's up with you? You'll always be Newport's number one Playboy. You're a legend."

"I don't think I want to be. I'm so tired of straining to uphold my leather boy image. Magpie, I've come to the point in my life where I want to be me. Todd Williamson. Who grew up in a garage—the son of a housekeeper?"

So shocked by Todd's words, I almost couldn't speak. Had his recent life-threatening event caused him to take pause at his frivolous lifestyle?

He continued, "My business success... I was lucky."

"Todd, it was more than luck. You have one of the sharpest marketing minds of anyone I've worked with."

"That's big coming from you. I know you worked with the best. But let's face it—my success is due to the fact I had the balls to put myself, or my tight white shorts, out there on T.V."

"You certainly did. As Newport's female population can attest to. But you knew your stuff. You're one smart guy. But if you're thinking about toning down your lifestyle and letting the real Todd show, I understand."

Sighing, he said, "Yes, I think I'll scale down from socializing seven days a week to five."

"Wow, a big move. Now you can kick back in your jammies two nights a week. If you own a pair."

Smiling, Todd said, "What do you think?"

"I think I don't want to know."

"Plus, this will give me time to get caught up on my Facebook demands. You don't know how many friend requests I have, but no time to respond."

"I can only imagine."

My voice must have resonated a sarcastic tone because

Todd countered, "Maggie, I'll have you know that most of my Facebook contacts are business related."

"I bet they are."

"Yes. You wouldn't believe how many women own cars with cracked leather they're dying to restore."

"Kind of like their SoCal sunbaked skin."

"Maggie. I'm serious."

"I'm sure you are. But I have a more pressing situation than posting on Facebook."

"Maggie, are you having problems condensing to Twitter?"

"Todd, I'm talking about real life. Not phony profiles posted through cyberspace. I need your help."

"Name it. I'm yours."

I'm yours. Suppressing the urge to groan from Todd's response, I took a longer than needed sip of champagne. "It's the Swing Green, Drive Green golfing event. During the awards banquet, Grant's being recognized for his contributions to environmental building. He was slated to give a speech. Which now, I am."

"Maggie, you're a great speaker."

"But it's been so long. The biggest group I've spoken to recently is my yoga class. And I was reprimanded for cavorting during the sacred hour. I'm lucky the owner, Deirdre, let me back in after my motor mouth slip. Do you know how long it takes to tier through her waiting list to get into her class?"

"So what do you need?"

"I was hoping I could run my speech by you."

"Of course. You know I'm always willing to go above and below for you, Magpie."

I ignored Todd's subtle reference to our former love affair. So used to flirting, I'm certain he had no idea he was even doing it.

Todd and I plowed through my presentation until my head was dizzy. I was stressed, exhausted, and had consumed too much champagne. I leaned into Todd's shoulder.

He rubbed my arm. "Maggie, you look wiped. You know I have my drivers. But I can't fathom you returning to your empty house in your wrung out state. Who knows if it's safe? My suite has three bedrooms. Take your pick. I promise not to make any of my legendary moves. Please, spend the night."

Todd didn't need to convince me to stay. My eyes leaden, brain shutting down, I was drifting into dreamland. For the first time in days, I felt secure and at peace...until Todd murmured, "I'm so proud of you, Magpie. Stepping in for this event. And I'm certain Charles Harrington will be happy. You'll be taking Grant's place in the tournament's leadoff foursome. You, Nicole, Harrington, and Stewart. Talk about a powerhouse group. Won't that be fun?"

CHAPTER FIFTY-THREE

Stewart! I sprang from the sofa as if a shark had bitten me. How could Newport Hills allow this con artist to step foot upon their greens? At my club? At the event honoring my late husband. More pointedly, how had Stewart weaseled his way into Charles Harrington's cart?

I must have been barking these questions, because I felt Todd's hand pulling me back down. "Maggie, what's wrong? Stewart's an up-and-coming realty investor in Newport Beach. He also put working capital into Gitan at a time we urgently needed it. Charles Harrington was beyond grateful for that."

I stammered, "With Gitan's steep price, combined with their cheap plastic package, I'd think the company would be rolling in the dough. Why would you need emergency funding?"

"The line started out strong. But our sky rocketing success caused competitors to hop on the Green Express. The company needed to fight back with an aggressive marketing campaign. That costs money."

"But Stewart's a Traveller."

"Maggie, that can't be. Do you think Charles Harrington would associate with someone of dubious means?"

"Who knows? The Travellers are crafty. Maybe Harrington doesn't know Stewart's past. Or present. And if my research, and that of Grant's loyal assistant, Carmen, is correct, Stewart is most likely the local ring leader for the clan's scams."

"Maggie, I'm wondering if the stress of recent events has taken a toll on your imagination. Leading you to see conspiracy connections that don't exist."

"Todd, I tell you, the Travellers are seeping their way into Newport Beach. They started years ago with petty cons, then began buying up mobile home parks. They wormed their way into Grant's business—and it appears, into Gitan. Regina's life has been threatened. Grant and Andrew Richmond were murdered. I tell you, the Travellers are killers! Stewart's fingerprints are all over these disasters. And he's set to tee off with Charles Harrington at a premier Newport event? If this continues, the Travellers will soon be running this town.

"Okay. I get it. There're a lot of crooked dealings you've brilliantly weaved together. But if Stewart's dirty, what's he doing in the same arena as Mr. Harrington? God, this is making my head spin."

"Oh, Todd, what you've been through today. The Oxycodone Diana slipped you must be taking a toll."

"I admit, it is." Todd nestled closer to me. "But before I pass out, let me ask you one more question. You had me shadowing Beatrice, or Bridget, at the country club mixer. So strange how she interchanges her name."

"Todd, that's what the Travellers do. They float their names between relatives, making it difficult for the police to peg their true identity. But Beatrice is even more crafty. One day she's a Traveller. The next, she's Bridget, an upscale real realtor providing a bridge between the Scottish clan and the ref."

"What's a ref?"

"It's what the Travellers call us. People in the mainstream of life. Those of us not enmeshed within the net of modern day gypsies."

Todd sighed. "So strange. One day I'm doing a little flirtatious surveillance. Then I'm police-taped out of my house and relegated to staying in a hotel. After all that's happened, I'm certain you're right. It's all starting to make sense."

I scanned the luxurious living quarters of Todd's Montagne suite. If one was going to have to be holed up for a while, this was certainly the place to do it. I wandered down the hallway of my palatial surroundings, passing two bedrooms before settling into one that looked cozy. I kicked off my shoes and snuggled into a cushy, queen bed. My eyes shut and I felt blessed sleep enveloping me.

The next thing I remember was loud pounding on a door. And pounding in my head from all the champagne I'd consumed the night before. I sprang out of bed, cracked open my door. Barely able to make out the conversation, but too frightened to leave my room, I shivered on the travertine floor, not from the cold tile, but from fear.

Opening my door wider, I detected a woman's voice that sounded suspiciously like Nicole Harrington's. And it did not sound friendly. Then I heard Todd's raised voice followed by a stern closing of the door. I held my spot for a moment, testing to see if all was clear. Silence.

I skirted up the hall to find Todd. He was leaning against the suite's door, shaking his head.

"Todd, what's happening? Was that Detective Harrington? And why was she here at such an early hour?" I glanced at my Marc Jacobs and noted the time was eleven a.m. I guess it wasn't so early. I must have really needed some serious sleep.

"Yes, it was Nicole."

"How did she know you were here?"

"God knows. Worse, she knows you stayed the night."

"Ooh, I bet she thought that looked suspicious."

"She alluded to that. She wanted to question you, but again, I insisted all inquiries were to go through your lawyer, Winston Cunningham."

I patted his shoulder. "Thank you, Todd. I really appreciate your help."

Todd looked straight into my eyes. "You know what really hurts?"

"What?"

"When we were kids, Nicole and I played together. Almost like brother and sister. After she discovered me looking through her father's drawer and found the picture of the mystery girl and woman, she treated me like trash. But nothing like she's been displaying lately. Not only to me, but to you as well. And to think we have to cavort with her at the Swing

Green event."

"I know. I thought she'd opted out of the silver-spoon crowd years ago. Wish she'd stayed out."

"Yes, Nicole's kept a low profile in recent years. My guess, she's making a social comeback. At least for her father's golf tourney. But enough of Nicole."

Todd gestured toward the balcony patio. "I took the liberty of ordering Montagne's signature Eggs Benedict and Brioche French Toast. And of course, double lattes."

With Todd's depiction of our morning meal, my stomach grumbled. When was the last time I'd eaten? I nestled into a cushioned patio chair, and marveled at the delectable delights laid before me. So starved, I wanted to plunge into the meal. But good manners, plus knowing this breakfast was meant to be savored, made me hold my fork. After Todd so gentlemanly served, I enjoyed this meal like it was my last. With all that was happening, perhaps it would be. I pushed that thought from my head, not wanting to spoil this tasty feast.

Upon finishing, I laid down my silver, scanned the resort's scenic beauty. Expansive lawns, as manicured as feathered carpeting spread beneath our balcony. A palette of flowers hemmed the greens, lush as a Monet painting. Hedged shrubs hugged the pathway leading down to the beach. Ocean waves splashed over mounds of rocks dotting the shore, spraying those who ventured upon them.

The buzz of Todd's iPhone interrupted my reverie. He picked up. "Mr. Harrington. How wonderful to hear from you." Todd signaled me he would take the call inside. As he was walking through the patio door, I heard the trail of his voice. "Great news. Looks like Stewart's infusion of capital has really…"

Stewart. At the mention of his name, my stomach lurched. How dare he spoil my exquisite meal? Todd mentioned Stewart had helped Gitan through a tough time, but I assumed that partnership was over. Hearing Todd gush about Stewart in the here-and-now made my stomach do a second flop. If Stewart could embed himself with savvy businessmen like Todd and

Charles Harrington, what hope did I hold for ejecting him and his clan from Leman Land Development?

CHAPTER FIFTY-FOUR

After breakfast, I made my way back home. Todd offered me the chance to luxuriate in the master bathroom's jet tub, but I declined. I didn't need to run the risk of hot-tubbing it with Todd like in our former days. With my luck, Detective Harrington would decide to make a second visit. Plus, I didn't have a clean set of clothes.

While indulging in the shower, warm water streaming over my face and down my body, my mind began to wander. Earlier, Todd received a call from Charles Harrington. Judging from what I'd overhead, I'd bet my next seaweed spa wrap that Stewart was sitting now in the big guy's office, schmoozing with Charles? If so, I needed to get there fast. I had questions that needed to be answered.

I speed-dressed, then headed out to Harrington headquarters, which consumed a premier piece of real estate on the corner of Coastal Road and McKinley Avenue. Less than a five-minute drive from my house. If I hurried, maybe I could still catch the two of them cavorting. I wasn't sure how much information I could garner by busting into their meeting. But I had to try.

I reached the multi-story, glass-shielded building that towered over Newport Beach in record time. Certain the Harrington building was outfitted with as many security cameras as the White House, I pulled into the parking lot of the office next door. I didn't want my car's license number to pop up on Harrington's radar screen.

Head low, I traipsed into Harrington territory. I pushed through the quadruple-paned entry door. Stealing a glance to my left, I noted three security receptionists built like pro wrestlers manning a heavy metal desk. I also detected what I had suspected—every corner of the place outfitted with security cameras. Two questions screamed through my brain. How could I get past these security goons? And, if I could, how would I get to Harrington?

At that moment, two black and purple clad FedEx delivery guys whisked past me, each stacked with an armful of jumbo boxes. They nodded to Security, who waved them through with barely a glance. I took that second to scoot close to them, the breadth of their packages providing cover. I hoped it would be enough to get me past the first floor of the building.

As the FedEx team closed in on the elevators, I slid away from them and ducked into the stairwell. FedEx provided me covert entry, but they couldn't shield me from Big Brother cameras in the cramped quarters of an elevator. Remembering how Todd's Special Ops team had shuttled me up the stairs of the Montagne without being spotted, I knew this would be my best bet for getting to Harrington.

I trudged up the stairs. Assuming Harrington had an ego as big as his building, I bet his personal office space sat on the top floor. When I reached the lucky thirteenth level, the stairway ended. I cranked the steel handle of the door I believed led into the Harrington's office, praying it wasn't locked. The handle didn't move. Damn. Bolted solid.

The next second, the door flew open. A dishwater blonde with over sprayed hair whipped past me, almost knocking me down.

"This freakin' building. Nowhere to smoke. Like working in a prison."

I felt she was rude, and in need of Smokers' Anonymous, but I wasn't about to confront her. She was my ticket to finding the answers I desperately needed.

I slipped inside the opened door. My eyes scoured the hallway for security cameras. None. I crept down the hall. The clicking of computer keyboards and people reciting, "Thank you for calling Harrington and Associates. Mr. Harrington is tied up at the moment, but if you'll…" told me I'd reached the outer offices of the esteemed Mr. H.

The hall took a sharp right. Poking my head around the corner, I screened for cameras. And again, spotted none. Just rows of workers rattling into their headsets—fingers playing across their keyboards.

It seemed Mr. Harrington had no compunction about spying on others, but didn't relish recording devices within his closed-off world. Or maybe he assumed his security team and technology weeded out the unwanted so well, he didn't need monitoring on his floor. Whatever the case, I was damned lucky he'd made this lapse. Or had he? Perhaps the thirteenth floor scrutinized one's comings and goings in a more subtle manner. Could there be hidden cameras?

I didn't have time to worry about it. If he and Stewart were in a meeting, it wouldn't go on indefinitely. But how to get past this endless arsenal of employees? I feared the closer I got to Harrington, the sharper the scrutiny may be.

I decided the best way to get to Harrington was to march down the hallway like I belonged. I strutted along like a super model on a runway. Cool, calm, confident. And it worked! Nobody gave me a moment's glance. Damn, I was good.

But my cocky balloon deflated when I took a closer look at Harrington's crew, and realized it wasn't my brazen demeanor allowing me access, but the fact the crew was too busy multi-tasking—texting, YouTube, Twitter—to detect my presence. At that moment, I loved technology.

Thank goodness Mr. Harrington's receptionist also loved techno, so I was able to scoot past her—right up to the door bearing the plated name: Mr. Charles Harrington, President. I knew I should be polite and knock, but at this point, manners ranked low on my list of priorities.

I shouldered through the door, finding a wide-mouthed Mr. Harrington seated behind the biggest mahogany desk I'd ever seen. The man seated across from him whipped his head around. It was Gold Tooth. What? This was Stewart? I knew Stewart was a Traveller, but I figured he'd have a hint of class.

How could such a scummy piece of inhumanity worm his way into the graces of Charles Harrington?

I slammed the door shut behind me. Head high, shoulders squared, I crossed the massive office.

Harrington practically shouted at me, "What the hell are you doing in here? You don't have an appointment."

"Me?" Pointing at Gold tooth, I countered, "What the hell is that slime ball doing here?"

Harrington folded his arms, rocked back in his seat. "This is Mr. Stewart. A business associate of mine." Then he mumbled, "Not that it's any of your business."

I proffered my hand to Stewart, then recalling Gold tooth's sweaty chest, thought better of it. Pulled it back. I didn't want any of him oozing onto my hand. "Nice to meet you, Stewart."

He nodded at me. "And you. You are?"

I took another step forward. "Oh, I think you know who I am. I'm Maggie Leman. Wife of the former president of Leman Land Development. The company you're running into the ground."

Stewart sprang from his seat, hand grasping his pocket. Reaching for a weapon? "You know nothin' what you're talkin' about."

Shooting a glance to Harrington, Stewart seethed, "I told you to stay wide. What's she doin' coming in here like she owns the place?"

Charles Harrington's face registered blank. "I have no idea how she got in here." Looking at his computer, he clicked a few buttons. "There's nothing on my security cameras. Lobby...first floor...twelfth..."

"What about the thirteenth? That's where's she's standin' right now."

"This is my private area."

"The ref got in. Must not be that private." Stewart plunged his fingers into the depth of his pocket. "She best get the fuck out of here. Now."

And then the office door flew open. Nicole Harrington swept into the room. "Daddy, I figured out how to—"

My head whipped around so fast my neck felt like my chiropractor had cracked it. "Nicole, what are you doing here?"

Her steel blue eyes bore into mine. "This is my father's office. I'm here to see Daddy. Question is, why are you here?"

CHAPTER FIFTY-FIVE

Though outnumbered three to one, I wouldn't let these high-end socialites and this low-life Traveller intimidate me. "Nicole, what do you think I'm here for? I'm here to discuss the Swing Green, Drive Green event. Since this tournament is a tribute to my recently departed Grant, I want to make certain all the arrangements are secure."

Nicole took a towering step toward me. "Are you crazy? My father has no time for such nonsense. He's a busy man. You think he plans all the events he sponsors?" Boring her eyes into mine, she added, "No. You're not crazy. You're here for some other reason." Then in a cop-like voice, she bellowed, "Just what are you doing here, Maggie Leman?"

Though her five-foot ten police presence rattled me, I couldn't let her know that. I returned her glare. "I told you, Detective. I'm here to discuss the details of the golf tournament. So if Daddy isn't working this event, who is? Whom do you suggest I talk to?"

Nicole swung her gaze to her father.

Mr. H. cleared his throat. "I have so many items on my calendar, it's difficult to say. But I believe my secretary tapped Diana Hutchinson to handle this one. Mrs. Leman, I suggest you contact her. You can find her at—"

"I know where to find Diana. And that's exactly what I plan to do. Have a lovely day."

I didn't dare take a moment to let the detective ask me any more questions and the fact that Diane may still be missing in action. I was out the door on a mission to locate this shady woman.

I did want to ensure Grant's tribute was handled properly. That he was awarded a proper tribute at the Swing Green golfing event. But there were more pressing problems I needed to quiz Diana about. Like what was up with her family, namely, Uncle Stewart? What was he doing clubbing it up in the hallowed Harrington high rise?

Entering Diana's office, I noticed a departure from the last time I'd been there. Absent was the throb of frenetic activity and Diana's cries to squelch news of golfers exhibiting bad behavior.

All I heard were the light tapping of keyboard fingers and soft voices. "Good morning…if there's anything the Newport Hills can do for you…"

I walked up to Miles, Diana's assistant. "Miles, right? Hi. I'm looking for Diana."

He eyed me like I was an intruder—not a long-standing member of the club. "May I ask who you are? And why are you interested in Diana's whereabouts?"

Whereabouts? Between the use of that term and his guarded behavior, now I really was interested in where she was.

"I'm Maggie Leman, and I'm here to talk to Diana about the details of the upcoming Swing Green event. I'm certain you can appreciate how important this tournament is to my late husband's legacy. I want to ensure all details are meticulously attended to."

"Mrs. Leman, how rude of me. I am sorry for the lapse. It's just that I'm so busy."

"Apology accepted. So where's Diana?"

Miles cleared his throat. "It appears Ms. Hutchinson has gone missing."

"Missing?"

He raised his hands in a signal of reassurance. "I don't mean by missing, anything bad has happened to her. We just don't know where she is. She hasn't shown up for work and isn't returning my texts. But from what I've heard, this disappearing behavior is not out of character."

"You don't have to tell me. I've been around Diana for

years. So who's handling the tournament now that Diana's fled the scene?"

"I am. Or trying to. To be honest, I'm overwhelmed."

I smiled at the young man. "Well, let me underwhelm you. I handled many large affairs during my marketing career. And the centerpiece of this event is me, posthumously accepting my late husband's award. Just tell me where you're at, and we'll take it from there."

Miles breathed a sigh of rescue. "Thank you, Mrs. Leman. I didn't know if I could pull all of this together."

Miles and I worked for hours. We secured and double-checked the details of this event—like consulting with the catering manager to ensure the awards banquet menu would meet the fussiest of food palettes, and talking to the head bartender to secure the most popular alcoholic beverages were on hand or better yet, in the members' hands.

When it came to organizing the dinner's seating chart, I hit a snag. So many club members changed spouses as often as they updated their wardrobes. How could I know whom to seat next to each other without causing a clashing of divorced couples? I needed to link up with the one person who had the skinniest of skinny on relationship switch-outs in Newport Beach—Regina.

I buzzed her cell.

"Mags, dear, it's been ages. How are you doing?"

Hearing my friend's confident, familiar voice washed me with a sense of calm.

But Regina's next comment, "I hear you took out a member of the Travellers," hit me like a tsunami.

"Regina, that happened less than 48 hours ago. How did you learn about this so soon? I wasn't charged. I'm certain it hasn't been reported in the media. Or has it?"

"No, relax. You know I have my ways."

"You had sex with one of the responding officers?"

Regina laughed. "No, although I hear there's some hot new recruits on Newport's force. Maggie, you're so stressed you forgot about my police scanner? After hearing about the incident, I wanted to call you, but I've been in court pounding away on a bitch of a case. Or should I say bastard, as that's what the soon-to-be ex is."

I smiled at Regina's weird sense of humor, and how her adversary would soon be washed away.

"And because you're being represented by Winston Cunningham, I knew the police wouldn't file charges. Smart move retaining him."

"Regina, how did you know I sought counsel? That wouldn't be relayed through your scanner."

"No, but even though Winston and I specialize in different aspects of the law, Newport Beach attorneys are a closely-bound group. Word gets around quickly."

"I wish you could represent me."

"Oh, Mags, I can understand that. But you have the best defense lawyer in town. If I ever murdered someone, he'd be the first person I'd call."

"That's very reassuring, Regina."

"Believe me, I've come close. But enough of this tawdry murder business. Let's talk about the tournament."

"You know about Swing Green? Regina, with your hectic schedule, you rarely hit the links."

"Darling, my golf moves may be a bit crusty, but I never pass up the opportunity to brush elbows with the NB elite. Fab time, moneyed business connections…"

The term connections triggered thoughts of the Travellers. My fingers scaled along Diana's laptop, tapping upon the tournament's guest list. Scrolling the entries, I noted familiar upper-crust names. But I also noticed duplications of dubious names I'd crossed in recent days. Three Johnstons, two Stewarts, one Keith…the list read like a Travellers' reunion.

My fingers froze. I breathed into the phone. "Regina, do you know who you're teeing off with?"

"Jax and a couple named Charles and Esther Keith."

"You don't know how lucky you are to have Jax."

"That goes without saying. I've gotten so used to his steeled body nuzzled close, I don't know what I'd do without him."

I cleared my clogged throat. Mumbled into my cell. "Better keep him spooned."

"And why is that my dear? Except for the fact he's a gorgeous hunk?"

"Because the tournament's roster is filled with Travellers' names. And you're teamed up with a couple of them."

Regina's voice caught for a second. "Yes. Thank God, I have Jax. But Maggie, from what my bodyguard has learned from certain undisclosed sources, it's you who needs protection. You are still packing, aren't you?"

CHAPTER FIFTY-SIX

Regina suggested I tote a gun to the golf tournament. I knew bringing a weapon onto the hallowed grounds of Newport Hills violated every sacred guideline of the club. But the Travellers didn't operate within conventional rules. And no longer would I. Plus, no one would know I was carrying a lethal weapon. They didn't have a metal detector in their lobby. It wasn't like I was entering a courthouse, or jail—at least not now.

Problem was, after I shot Cousin Johnnie, the police confiscated my Ruger. But I had another one tucked away. One only those closest to me knew about. And there was no money trace tying it to me. This was a weapon I hadn't fired in years, but I was well trained on a 9mm Berretta. My father snagged it from a street gang member during a drug bust gone bad. He'd given it to me as a gift for my sixteenth birthday. After my party and countless times after my dad drilled me on how to handle the weapon.

First, I had to get to it. I grabbed my keys and the one Carmen had slipped to me. I headed to First American Bank and signed into the safety deposit boxes. From one, I retrieved my weapon. Another, the duplicate set of papers that showed Stewart muscling into Grant's business. I wanted the docs as backup evidence…just in case the first set went missing. I was killing two birds with one trip to the bank. I only hoped I wouldn't be killing another one, meaning a Traveller. Shooting Johnnie was bad enough. I didn't relish taking another one out. But I worried even more I may be the next one to be out.

CHAPTER FIFTY-SEVEN

The next morning was the big day—the Swing Green, Drive Green event. Determined to display a confident persona, I dressed in my most chic golfing outfit—a Jamie Sadock Gunsmoke zippered polo, matched with a tighter than tight, neon green skort. I swept my mane into a ponytail, and fitted my club-logoed visor onto my forehead.

I tucked my acceptance speech into the voluminous Gucci bag I always toted when golfing. High-end country club, but sporty and spacious. Big enough to hold the items needed to transfer to my golfing bag: iPhone, lipstick…gun. I was now ready to hit the greens.

The entryway of Newport Hills teemed with club members wearing the trendiest golfing attire I'd seen since Grant and I had VIP passes to the Masters. I thought I'd dressed high-end. But the prices of these clothing lines consumed more green than most people spent on their entire spring wardrobe. Actually, an entire year's.

I made my way through the crowd, pressing toward the welcome table to pick up the sheet containing tee times and foursome matchups, and, my favorite—the freebie gift bags. As I strolled through the crowd, I met murmurs of condolences and congratulations about Grant's accomplishments. My emotions ran the scale from sadness, to pride in my husband, to anger and revenge. But I couldn't waste time thinking about my loss. I needed to find who was responsible.

As the golfers buzzed about, chatting about their golf swings and how they vowed to go green, I spied Nicole

Harrington entering the lobby. Duncan Reid and Bridget flanked the detective. What was she doing here? After Johnnie's demise, I assumed Bridget had skipped town like her cousin.

And because Bridget was at the scene of Cousin Johnnie's shooting, no, was an active cat fighter, normal police protocol would have Detective Harrington grilling this young woman straight off the grill about what transpired that fateful night

But Bridget sashayed alongside Nicole as if nothing were amiss. My guess was that Bridget slipped between the world of the Travellers and that of the silver-spooned. She didn't feel the need to pull a disappearing act like Diana did, or be interrogated by Nicole. But who knew. Maybe Nicole had taken care of her police business with Bridget prior to the tournament and considered the young woman to be in the clear.

I stood transfixed, analyzing the body language of Nicole's threesome. Nicole appeared, of course, cocky. As her party passed through the lobby, the detective smiled, chatting it up with Bridget. Dun looked like he was struggling to keep pace with the women, seemingly ignored by Nicole. Nicole knew Dun's gunshot wound made it impossible for him to strut like a rookie. Why was she leaving him in the wings while cozying up with Bridget?

I needed to find out what was up with this odd trio. I spotted a monumental guest who'd had a stellar career in the NFL before retiring to a life filled with daily rounds of golf and slipped beside him. Lucky for me, this man was too engaged in conversation with a female member who'd had one too many breast augmentations to notice my tight proximity. Even luckier, I kept running into people who could hide me undercover.

A waiter cruised by hefting a silver platter of champagne flutes. I snatched one from him. I needed fuel to douse my tension-fueled fire. Then Todd sauntered in, reigniting the flame.

Of course, Todd, always on testosterone autopilot, spotted

me through my massive body cover. He sauntered up. "Maggie, what are you doing in the shadows? You're the toast of the tourney."

I mouthed, "Todd, I'm trying to stay incognito."

Todd quizzed louder, "What, Maggie? I couldn't make that out."

I started to tell Todd to keep his tone down, when a familiar flash of blond hair told me my cover was blown. Nicole stared in my direction, eyes narrowed. She didn't waste any time making her way over to me. "Mrs. Leman. Oh, excuse me, we're teeing off together. Let's get back to a first name basis. Maggie, what are you doing tucked behind this monolithic man? You're the honored guest. You should be mingling among your guests."

I started to give an excuse that I didn't like crowds, but she didn't allow me the opportunity.

"Unless, there's some reason you don't want to be spotted."

Clenching my shouldered Gucci bag, I felt an almost irresistible urge to shut her down via inappropriate club manners. Meaning, pull out my Beretta and take her out. I tried to stay calm, but even with my countless yoga sessions, I couldn't help being sucked into her snippy bait. "Listen, I've had enough of—"

"Maggie," Dun said as he stepped in to join us, "Nick told me you're accepting Grant's Building a Greener Future Award. He'd be so proud of you. Especially with everything that's gone down."

Nick chimed in. "Yes. It's amazing she can pull this off."

I ignored Nicole's accusatory remark. "Thank you, Dun."

Then turning to Bridget, I held out my hand. "Nice to see you again. You're the real estate gal."

Nicole's intercession seemed a tad too quick. "Bridget's the Realtor for Harrington and Associates."

"I didn't realize your father was into real estate. I thought your family business was manufacturing."

"My father's into a lot of things."

Thinking of the dubious Stewart meeting and his beloved mistress, I almost blurted, "I bet he is." But I kept my mouth shut."

Nicole went on, "By the way, there's been a change in the tournament roster. The Keiths had to cancel, so Bridget and Dun will be rounding out that foursome, trailing our lead cart. Along with Regina Evans. Oh, and that muscled guy she's been hanging on, I mean around with lately. Who is that man, anyway?"

"He's Regina's administrative assistant."

Nicole smirked. "I bet he is."

As if on cue, Regina and Jax made their grand entrance. Both outfitted in club-ruled golfing attire, they weren't dressed to attract attention. They just did. Their perfect physiques coupled with sexually charged body language lowered the chatter of the crowd to murmurs as this couple slinked to my group.

Regina nodded silent hellos around, ending with Bridget. "I'm so happy to finally meet you, Bridget. I hear you're quite the up and coming Realtor in this area. Congratulations."

How did Regina know Bridget's mainstream name and identity? The young woman had virtually stayed in the Travellers' shadow since arriving in town. Was there anything going on in Newport Beach that Regina didn't know?

Regina glanced to Nicole then back to Bridget. "Oh my, look at you two. Your features so similar, you could be sisters...almost twins."

Todd chimed in. "You're right. They could be. And of course, both beautiful, as are you and Magpie."

Ignoring Todd's compliment, Nicole glowered at Regina.

Regina chatted on as if she didn't notice the catty stare. "Ms. Harrington, I don't see your father." Glancing around the room she said, "Has he arrived yet? I'd love to personally congratulate Charles for chairing this worthy cause. Going green is so important these days."

"My father's running a bit late. He's not feeling up to par today."

Regina pressed her fingers to her lips. "Oh dear, I hope it's nothing serious."

"No, probably just a touch of the flu. He'll be making his appearance. But he's sitting out the tournament."

My mind raced. Sitting it out? Charles looked fine when I'd seen him yesterday with Stewart.

Nicole's voice trailed on. "No need to worry. He found a golfing replacement. Mr. Stewart's right hand man will be rounding out the foursome. It will make for a tight crew."

Stewart! Right hand man! My champagne flute shattered to the floor.

CHAPTER FIFTY-EIGHT

The clamor in the room stopped. All eyes riveted to me.

"I'm so sorry." I dropped to my knees, wanting to wipe away the mess.

Todd moved in beside me, nudging me back to my feet. "It's okay, Maggie."

"No. I spilled my drink all over the floor!"

Two waiters swept upon the scene, clearing the mess.

Regina pressed her cheek into mine. "Todd's right. Don't give it a moment's worry." She glanced about. "Look, the crowd's already moved on."

Following her gaze, I realized she was right. The guests had returned to their normal club chatter, forgetting I'd dropped the flute.

Only Nicole seemed fixated on my *faux pas*. "Something bothering you, Maggie?"

I straightened my back. "No, I'm fine. Just a bit nervous about my speech." Slipping my hand into my bag, I stroked cold steel. "Yes, everything is fine."

"Good. Because as soon as my father arrives, I have an important announcement to make. We don't want anything interrupting that, do we, Dun?"

He sheepishly looked at Nicole. "No, we don't, darling."

Darling. So they were a couple. No wonder they were always palling about lately. Oh my God, what could their big news be?

No time to ponder about it. Not when I spied Charles Harrington lumbering into the room. I took a double take. Whoa. He was not looking his usual, vibrant, self. Was he sick like Nicole said? Or...I couldn't even go there.

And, he was closely followed by Stewart and a twenty-something-year-old man with raven hair so slick, it looked like it'd been styled with Crisco. Wait, I knew this man. He was the one who almost snapped my head off in the club's parking lot?

Nicole grabbed Dun's wrist and squeezed between the guests in the direction of her father. The way she pulled him along, Dun looked like a puppy in training.

A few minutes later, the chiming of silver upon glass, followed by a man's weak voice. "Excuse the interruption. My family and I have some news to share."

All eyes riveted to Charles Harrington. He clasped his arm around Nicole's shoulders, slightly leaning into her. His eyes looked hooded like he was tired or sick. That wasn't surprising, considering Nicole said he wasn't feeling well. What was surprising was how fast this ailment had come on. The club's marketing assistant, Miles, handed a cordless mike to Mr. Harrington. He passed it to Nicole.

She gave a tight smile. "On behalf of my family, I'd like to welcome all of you to Swing Green, Drive Green. We appreciate you taking the time, and money..." she paused a moment for the crowd to give its perfunctory twitter, "...to support this worthwhile cause. I don't have to tell you how important responsible environmental building is to our beautiful town. After the tournament, we'll be presenting The Building a Greener Future to someone who's made a profound contribution to this cause."

My right temple throbbed in anticipation of hearing Grant's name publicly announced.

Nicole continued. "But before we start today's festivities, I have some even bigger news to share."

What? Was I so nervous I missed Nicole's accolades to Grant? Or could Nicole be so rude to mention the award, but not who was receiving it? I looked to Regina. Her pursed lips confirmed I hadn't missed a thing. Nicole made no mention it was Grant receiving the award.

Nicole's voice trailed on, "On the behalf of my family, I'm proud to announce that Duncan Reid and I are going to be married." She nodded her head, signaling Dun to step beside her. He hobbled up, taking his allotted place. Nicole went on, never glancing at her soon-to-be-betrothed, but eyeing me. "And after I wrap up my police caseload, and by that, I mean bringing in the bad guys…" again the group gave a polite round of chuckles. "After that, I'll be retiring from the force and joining Harrington and Associates." The crowd erupted in applause, acting more excited about Nicole's career move than her impending marriage. And by the flash of her smile, so was she.

After the detective's big announcement, the crowd dispersed, making their way to their respective golf carts. I pulled Regina and Todd aside. In a low voice I asked, "What was that all about? Have you ever seen such an unemotional marriage announcement? Nicole didn't even look at Dun."

"I agree," murmured Regina. "I've met with hundreds of couples over the years. Studied their body language and how they respond to each other. That is not a loving couple. At least not on Nicole's side. I'd say with expert certainty that Nicole has ulterior motives for marrying Dun."

Todd added, "I agree. And here's a scintillating tidbit. Fairly recently, I was scheduled to meet with Mr. H. about Gitan. His assistant told me the meeting prior to mine was running late and to take a seat in his private waiting area. Mr. Harrington's office door was closed, but I could hear what sounded like a heated conversation going on behind it. I heard Mr. H. saying something like, 'I've told you I'd like to see him at the wedding, not in the wedding.' Then what sounded like a female voice, 'trying to help your family.' The words were muffled, but they seemed odd to me. Especially when Nicole Harrington came bursting out the door."

I shook my head. "I also overheard her saying something like that. What does all this mean?"

"Apparently Nicole needs Dun for something," Regina said. "It's obviously not money. He doesn't have any and the Harrington's have plenty. And I'd bet my law practice that it's not for love."

I asked, "If it's not those two biggies, why else would Nicole marry Dun?"

Regina pressed her eyebrows, as if she was examining her past caseloads, searching for an answer. "You know the saying, keep your friends close and your enemies closer."

"Yes, but Nicole and Dun aren't enemies."

"Maybe not, but I'd say for some strange reason she wants to keep her steel eyes on him. My gut tells me she's hiding something, or protecting someone. It has to be very important to her and perhaps to her family. So important she's willing to walk down the aisle for it. She needs Dun for something."

Miles tapped my shoulder. "Mrs. Leman, the tournament's about to begin. They're waiting for you in the lead cart."

"Thank you. I'll be right there."

I paused until Miles was out of earshot. "I don't have a good feeling about what's going on. Like the fact that Charles Harrington has suddenly taken ill. He looks terrible. Actually, he looks like you did, Todd, when Diana pumped you with Oxy." Thinking back to that evening, my voice cracked. "God, she gave you so much dope she almost killed you."

"But they underestimated me. Or should I say my tolerance level? But why would Nicole keep Charles out of the tournament?"

Regina gazed from Todd to me. "The substitute. Let me guess. He's one who does not follow the etiquette of the fairways, and on that does not play nice."

"Oh God." Regina added.

"My thought exactly."

Todd hugged my shoulder. "Magpie, we're playing the gentlemen's game of golf at the most prestigious enclave in Newport Beach, and Regina's professional bodyguard is trailing you. What could go wrong?"

Thinking about the tree-studded course that snaked along cliffs overlooking the ocean, I thought, a lot could go wrong, but I didn't want to jump on the conspiracy train.

"Okay, Big Guy. Regina's foursome is following mine. Where are you in the lineup?"

"Bringing up the caboose."

"You're the last group to go? You've been a member since this place opened. How could they disrespect you like that?"

"Relax, my lovely. I asked for the late start."

"Why?"

"If I'd had a robust night of socializing the prior to the tournament, I wanted to be sober enough to make it to the tee on time."

I shook my head, wanting to give Todd a smack on the head, but the tournament was starting, and I needed to pack my golf bag. Walking to the lower-tiered level of the club where the golf carts sat, I noted a club assistant approach me. "Mrs. Leman, I loaded your clubs onto your cart."

"Thank you." I slipped him a five-dollar bill. Now, how to switch my pistol from my Gucci bag to golf bag without being detected? Particularly by my golfing partners.

To my good fortune, a member of the local press, along with their cameraman, pulled Nicole aside to interview her. Stewart and his associate hovered in the outer confines of the club's cart garage, out of sighting range. Apparently the Travelling men shied away from the lens. That didn't surprise me. Remaining elusive was part of their family way, and public pictures popping up would certainly go against their creed.

This gave me my chance. I whisked around to the back of the cart and slipped my pistol into the side pocket of my Pings.

Now I was ready. The game was about to begin. I prayed it would be an innocent round of golf, but with the poisonous path my life had taken, I feared I might not be playing for charity but for my life.

CHAPTER FIFTY-NINE

I stepped up to first tee of the country club I'd belonged to for the last fourteen years. I stared down the rolling green fairway as if it were the first time I'd ever seen it. I could smell the familiar scent of sweet grass and eucalyptus trees, felt the waft of an ocean breeze. This beautiful setting should feel so familiar, but my queasy knees and leaden head made me feel I'd never stepped foot on this course before.

No time for nerves. I could feel all eyes of my foursome trained on me. Regina said certain people didn't like the questions I'd been asking around town. Questions I'd been asking about the golfers who made up this group. I was certain they wanted to see me hit the balls wayward. I'd bet they were silently chanting Mulligan under their breath. I focused on the ball, and on the hundreds, maybe thousands of dollars I'd poured into golf lessons. I didn't know the exact amount. Grant had always taken care of those things. My throat started to close. Focus, inhale, exhale, mind only on the task. Laser your eyes on the ball. As if in slow motion, I swiveled right, club smoothly swinging up, then down, meeting the ball. Following through, my gaze trailed the ball from the tee down the middle of the fairway—at two hundred twenty-five yards.

I nailed it. So elated with myself for withstanding first tee-off pressure, I wanted to high-five Nicole as she strutted up to her tee. But a slapping of palms would not only violate the silent rule on the greens, but I assumed the detective had no desire to pal it up with me. Plus, being a police officer, she might take this as a physical assault and bring me up on charges. I gave her a curt nod and then walked to the golf cart.

Stewart and his greased hair buddy were dipping their hands into the ice chest nestled in the back of the cart. Because of our early tee time, normally this container held only water, but they were pulling out sixteen-ounce cans of Schlitz.

When finalizing the event, Miles and I made certain hospitality tables dotted the course, offering a variety of high-end alcoholic beverages aimed at the connoisseur. Were the Travellers so classless as to bring their own beer, especially a boring lager, and start knocking them back at the first hole?

Nicole, distracted by the cracking open of the cans, stopped mid-swing. She shot an angry glance at Stewart and his buddy. They lowered their eyes, holding their cans in their laps like two schoolboys caught passing dirty notes.

I'd expected the Travellers to return Nicole's icy stare, but they did nothing. These men were criminals. They usually snubbed their noses at the law—not bowed down to them. Nicole was a cop, but she seemed to hold an odd, authoritative power over these con men. Did she hold a mysterious control card in her deck?

Her nasty glance passed along, Nicole looked ready. Like mine, hers sailed long and straight up the fairway.

Then Stewart and his cohort took their swings. Not pretty golf. Stewart hit a lame drive hooked right. His buddy's shot zinged into the eucalyptus trees, and he called for a Mulligan. Oh, God, this was going to be a long round.

The Travellers' golfing skills were so bad, Regina's trailing foursome had to hold their tee-offs. I'm certain that didn't set well with Regina's courtroom scheduling mode.

Thankfully, about four holes into our round, the Travellers settled into a decent golfing rhythm. Had they taken time off from a life of crime to take some golf lessons, and their teachers' instructions were kicking in? I suspected they were getting such a buzz from their morning beer that they were shedding their stiff golfing style for a more fluid swing. Whatever the reason, it seemed to work. Our foursome now moved along.

After teeing off at the sixth hole, I felt myself beginning to relax—even enjoying being out on the links. As we traveled down the fairway, I began to think that snugging my Beretta into my golf bag screamed paranoia.

I two-putted the hole and then took a moment to gaze about me, inhaling my surroundings. Our foursome sat high above the jagged coastline. My eyes trailed the rocky cliffs that ran along this stretch of the course. As waves crashed into nature's wall, water sprayed me.

Our cart buzzed onward toward the course's signature seventh hole. The machine slowed as we climbed higher along the coastal cliff. Then we made a sharp right, leading to a breathtaking green, plunked upon a small peninsula jutting over the ocean.

I'd played this hole countless times, never thinking how the flag and cup were placed strategically above a craggy sheer wall. Stunning, but one bad putt too close to the precipice coupled with a slip of the foot could prove deadly.

We stopped short of the green. I chipped onto it. My ball, following the path of gravity, rolled close to where manicured green met rocky cliff. Nicole leaned on her club not bothering to suppress the smirk on her face. I could almost hear her saying, "Oh, too bad your ball went downhill. Kind of like your new life." I squelched my urge to give her a good clubbing. Rudeness on our course was strictly forbidden, and violence was definitely frowned upon.

I didn't like sitting upon this ocean cliff, and I felt violent vibes from Nicole's bitchy manner. Then I heard more cracking of beer tabs. So Stewart and his buddy had opened more brews. I knew their downing of ale while giving each other peevy jabs would occupy them for the next few minutes.

I took this as my opportunity to set up my protection. Strutting back to the cart, I reached into my golf bag, grabbed my putter—and my gun. I stuffed my weapon into my right pocket. Clink. Damn! The steel Beretta struck the wooden tees stored inside. Why hadn't I the foresight to switch these tees to my left pocket?

My pulse raced. I willed myself to relax. The Travellers

couldn't have heard the slight noise above their golfing party.

My hands quivered, and I three-putted the hole. Mentally slapping myself for letting my uneasiness bungle my game, I reached down to retrieve my ball. Bam! Someone slammed me from behind. My face hit hard upon the bladed green.

I twisted around to confront my assailant, when I heard a guttural laugh. I peered up at Stewart, his gold tooth glinting off the sun.

"Oh, excuse me, Ma'am. Didn't mean to knock you. Guess the Schlitz is kickin' in. You need to move along so's I can get my shot in."

Shot! His hand came toward me. He was going to kill me!

I reached for my gun. Not fast enough. Stewart grabbed my right arm. I thrust it back, desperate to extract myself from his serpentine grasp. Then I realized he was unarmed.

"Hey, what's wrong with you? Just tryin' to help you up. Come on, we have a gentleman's game to play here."

Gentleman. He was far from that. And this encounter on the seventh hole was beyond strange. Had Stewart accidentally bumped me in his inebriated state or was that a warning? Seven was supposed to be a lucky number, but it didn't seem lucky today. But maybe it was. Stewart hadn't pulled a weapon. Eleven holes to go. I hoped my luck held out.

CHAPTER SIXTY

After surviving my club's signature seventh hole that hugged the jagged cliffs of the Pacific, the course snaked two more fairways along the coast, then made a U-turn, trailing north, back to the clubhouse—to safety. I couldn't wait for the game to end. This tournament, designed to benefit a worthy cause, now felt like a deadly game of chance.

As we doubled back, I noted how the cart path paralleled a sharp ravine that cut along the backside of the course. During the hundreds of times I'd played this course, I'd never noticed the sheer drop adjacent to the trail. Never gave it a moment's thought.

But today…everything was different. If Nicole cranked one angry steer of the wheel, we would careen down this deadly decline. My mind raced back to a tragic accident along this trail. A newly-divorced woman who'd received a fifty-one percent stake in her husband's thriving business was golfing with a couple of his partners. As she bent down to retrieve a wayward ball, she slipped into the ravine, cracking her skull against the jutting rocks. The ex-wife died upon impact. The thick foliage made it impossible for the police to determine if a second set of footprints had followed her to her ball's lie.

I forced myself to look across the fairway, away from this deadly drop. A thick grove of eucalyptus trees lined the opposite side of the course. The stand separated our leg of the U-turn course from the holes we'd played. But not by much distance. As we hit along the tenth fairway, I could hear sounds from the follow-up golfers though the trees. The crack of club upon ball, the whoosh of a ball zinging through the air, the cussing of an angry player who'd hit a hooked shot.

Climbing out of my cart to tee off on thirteen, I heard Todd's hearty and, I knew, intoxicated chuckle through the trees. Then a crunching of cleats upon dried foliage.

"Not another one. Seems my baby wants to play in the woods today."

Todd had vowed to tone down his lifestyle. By the slur of his tongue, apparently this didn't apply to golfing events. I knew Todd was buzzed, but at least he sounded congenial, as opposed to my Travellers who were getting more drunk and surly with each passing hole. Particularly Stewart.

Nicole, on the other hand, remained cold sober. Didn't imbibe in the alcohol and didn't initiate any clubby conversation with me. She practically grunted whenever I tried to open any chitchat as we cruised along the course.

But I noted on more than one hole after sinking her putt, she scuttled back toward the cart, exchanging glances, even utterances with Stewart. This chumminess between silver spoon and tin fork raised my suspicions with each rounded hole.

I also couldn't configure her relationship with Dun. I knew that police partners often got close. And the two remained friendly after Dun retired from the force. But her cold, sudden engagement announcement had plagued me since she'd uttered it just before tee-off.

After hitting our second shot along the thirteenth's par five, Nicole guided the cart back to the Traveller's short lie. They'd executed lame swings, landing their balls half the distance between Nicole's and mine. Waiting for the men to catch up, another awkward moment loomed between us two alpha females.

Until recent events, I'd never used that phrase to describe myself. I thought my years as a matriarch and yoga enthusiast had dowsed my competitive nature. But I now considered myself a member of this elite, female aggressive group— trapped on the fairway with another one.

And within a foursome I didn't trust. When Stewart

bumped me to the ground on lucky hole seven, he'd made the excuse it was a drunken mishap. I took it as a warning of something bad waiting to happen. I now slipped my hand into my pocket, fingering the weapon I hoped I wouldn't have to fire.

I turned to Nicole. "I'm so happy to hear about your engagement. It's lovely to hear you and Dun are a couple. I thought the two of you were just friends."

Nicole grunted. "Yes. We have been for years."

Years? Was she referring to the friends or couples part? How long had they been involved? Could it have been before Dun was shot? When he'd been blasted in the back when she called him to her house?

After the shooting, Dun vowed to pursue the Travellers. From what I'd garnered, it appeared Nicole was a bit lax in this pursuit. Even stranger, Nicole and her family now seemed to be quite tight with the clan.

Before the tourney, Regina recited the cliché, "Keep your friends close and your enemies closer." By marrying Dun, was Nicole proposing to do just that?

A thousand questions flashed through my brain. I had but a moment before the Travellers returned to the cart. Time to choose my words wisely.

"So you've been involved for years. I may have seen one too many police dramas on T.V., but I guess it's prevalent for partners of the opposite sex to fall into a relationship. And I'd bet this sexual drive ramps up even more when one's driven to protect his partner—at any cost."

A vein pulsated in Nicole's right temple.

"Particularly when the partner's life and her family's lives have been threatened. I know that's why Dun rushed to you the night he was shot. What I don't understand is when you received cryptic phone calls, you didn't have him fix that damn gate."

"That's none of your damn business."

"You're right. The fact Dun was a married man at the time isn't my business."

"And your tawdry past is none of my concern. What I'm wondering about are your ties to the Travellers, to the Harrington empire, and if these ties might explain why my husband was killed."

As if on cue, the mention of the Travellers seemed to send them sauntering back to the cart. They climbed in, and Nicole punched the accelerator. She weaved up the course like she was the one drunk.

I heard a, "What the fuck?" from the backseat of the cart. Nicole ignored it. She darted a sudden right. I nearly careened out of the cart. Grasping the edge of the glassless windshield, I barely kept myself from being tossed to the ground.

Nicole skidded on the breaks, and we slammed to a halt. My head snapped forward, then back. I felt whiplashed. Struggling to right my spinal cord and clear my brain, I slipped a gaze to my crazed driver.

Nicole clenched the steering wheel like she wanted to strangle it. She stared straight ahead, seemingly uncaring about my physical distress. Then a twitch of her head. Hard steel pressed against my spine.

A Scottish burr breathed in my ear. "Okay, bitch. This is it. End of the road. Or should I say, course? Get the fuck out."

"But we haven't finished our round."

"Don't get smart with me."

"I'm not trying to be."

"Then try cooperatin'. Do like I say."

This was it. The end of my fairytale lane. As I'd feared, Gold Tooth Stewart was going to kill me.

A sharp punch of metal gave me a spasm in my barb-wired back.

"I said, get out!"

I crawled out of the golf cart, sneaking a glance at my perpetrator. My God, it wasn't Stewart. The Scottish burr sounded like him, but it wasn't. It was his greasier-than-greased-hair accomplice. My mind ran a manic-paced brain scan. This man was younger than Stewart. His trigger reaction would be fast. But not a seasoned leader. Less quick with the brain. Making my only chance for survival—outsmart this young man. Or shoot him.

CHAPTER SIXTY-ONE

The slick-haired Traveller nudged me off the fairway toward the ravine. My mind raced. How would I get off this course alive? Even if I got the upper hand on this guy, Nicole and Stewart lurked in the wings. Such a familiar public place, but now a lonely deadly one. Grease boy pushed me a few more steps, precariously close to the rocky drop-off.

At that second, a ball soured over the eucalyptus stand separating the two legs of the course. What a shot! A lousy shot. The wayward ball bounded across the fairway, pinged off the hood of our cart, zinging toward greased hair and me.

"The fuck?" he yelled. His gun gyrated down my spine, released the pressure of steel.

I jabbed my left elbow hard into his ribs, whisked my right hand into my pocket, and grabbed my gun. I spun around, whipping it into his chest.

Our eyes locked. My finger trembled on the trigger. I willed myself not to fire. God, how I wanted to.

His pistol hung at his side. I yelled, "Place your gun on the ground."

He took a half step backward, but held onto his weapon.

I said, "Put it on the ground. I swear I'll shoot you. Like Cousin Johnnie."

With the mention of Johnnie, he laid down the gun.

"You idiot!" Nicole sprung from the cart, and came in my direction. No weapon in hand, but the raged look on her face told me she didn't need one. I hoped she didn't have one hidden.

Then a sharp crack that sounded like a gunshot zeroed in

on us. Nicole stopped.

A voice bellowed across the fairway. "Nicole. So, sorry. Hope I didn't scare you. Should have shouted fore." Todd stumbled out of the grove of eucalyptus trees. He waved a severed tree branch like a drunken peace offering. He must have snapped it, making the ominous gunshot sound, while following his wayward shot through the woods.

Nicole's head swept to Todd, to me, and back to Todd again. I could almost see a twisted silver spoon churning in her head. Then she reached behind her back and whipped out a gun. Aimed on Todd.

Too drunk, or too far away to see the silver glint, Todd kept walking. "I must be the worst golfer out here."

Nicole trained her gun tighter.

My heart pounded at the thought of Nicole gunning him down. No! I kicked Stewart's crony in the groin, aimed at Nicole, and fired. Missed. I strained to pull the trigger again. Adrenaline flooding my body, my hands felt like dough. With all the years of my father's training, when called to duty, I couldn't control my nerves to save my friend.

Nicole turned to me. She smiled, lips stretched tight as the grip on her gun. She took two long strides toward me. "Well, Maggie. Seems you've gotten yourself into a bit of trouble. Trying to kill a police officer. Looks like the death of your husband has driven you to the brink. Obsessed with me and my family. Seeing conspiracies where there are none. Too bad it has to end this way. Me, a cop, defending myself from a deranged widow."

Oh, God.

"Drop it, Nicole." A familiar voice rose above the slowing hum of an approaching golf cart.

She lowered her gun an inch. "Dun, I'm so glad you're here. Maggie's truly gone over the edge. She was going to shoot me. Look, she has a gun."

"I said, drop it."

"Darling, what are you talking about?"

Dun hobbled from the cart, closing in on Nicole. "I'm

talking about drop the darling bit. And the fucking gun."

Nicole's eyes widened. "I don't understand. Maggie tried to kill me. Look. Check the evidence. Her bullet's embedded near the green."

"Stop it. I know you've been using me."

"Dun, why would I do that?"

"To get me to stop investigating the Travellers. And learning about your ties to them. "

"Dun, you have no reason to believe—"

"I have every reason. Your half-sister, Bridget, has been very cooperative. Told me about your scheme to have Diana pretend to be her to lure club members into compromising situations. Members with extensive real estate holdings, like Grant Leman and Andrew Richardson. Drug them with Oxy, transfer properties, and then pose them to look like they were having an affair."

"Why would Diana pose them?"

"To inject the sleaze factor, to throw off the investigation."

"You're crazy. Like scrawny Diana could overpower those men, even if they were drugged."

"No, but that guy cowering over there could."

Nicole let out a guttural laugh. "That's ridiculous. He may be a con artist, but how could I get him to commit murder? And why would I do such a thing?"

"How? By paying him off. Why? To convince your father of your value to Harrington and Associates. Show how you could expand its presence in the realty market. Prices are down. Now's the time for the greedy to gobble up as many properties as they can. After your public divorce, your infidelity put a smear on the Harrington name. You were iced out. But if you could bring easy money into the company."

"We don't need money. We're the Harrington's. We're worth millions."

"Maybe. But foreign competition has put a huge dent in your family's manufacturing business. The core of the Harrington holdings. That's one reason your father was so concerned that the Gitan line was faltering. He knew he needed to revamp his business model to bring the family assets back to what they once were."

"You don't know anything about my father. He didn't even want you to marry me. But I convinced him you'd fit in."

"Let me tell you, Nicole, while you were prancing about talking to the media, Charles and I had a telling conversation. Amazing how Oxycodone makes a person run at the mouth. Seems your father didn't like how you were forcing yourself into the Harrington business while cozying up to the Travellers."

"Interesting theory. But how can you prove it?"

"By tracking your bank accounts, darling. Remember when we opened that joint account? Gave me easy access to your bribery spending habit. And this."

Dun pulled a tiny silver device from his left pocket. Dangled it in the air. "Recording devices don't lie. And I have all your lies and deceits recorded here. Thanks to Bridget wearing a wire. Conversations about your real estate schemes. Pushing married men into compromising situations. But what really seals your fate is the covert meetings you arranged with Diana and slick-hair when you gave him the order to kill your marks. Bet you didn't know Bridget slipped a bug into your Gitan, did you?"

"Bridget would never do such a thing. And I'm a cop. I would never contract a murder."

"Not what the wire says. You clearly stated you wanted the victims taken out, to avoid any chance of them remembering anything. Even if you had them hopped up on drugs."

"Dun, I love—"

"Can it."

"Fuck you. You're no longer a cop. Your investigation won't hold up in court. There's nothing you can do. "

"You're right. I'm no longer a law enforcement agent." Nudging his head toward a granite body rising from the cart, he said, "But Jax is. He's been working this investigation the whole time. While I've been working you."

"You son of—"

"And let me add how your favorite attorney, Regina, was more than happy to play you. Jax isn't her private bodyguard, and not her administrative assistant. He's an undercover member of the Santo Reno Police Department. Their team has been working with the Newport Beach force to clean up their town. And solving the country club murders is number one on their list."

"You bastard. You're nothing but a washed-up cripple."

Dun shook his head. "Take it from here, Jax."

Jax whipped out a pair of plastic zip cuffs. "You're under arrest."

Todd stumbled up to our group. "Hey, what's going on?"

I tucked my gun into my pocket and slipped my arm around my friend. "Todd, I'll explain everything to you. But first, let's have a little Sex on the Beach."

His eyebrows rose.

"I mean the drink. You, me, now. In the clubhouse."

"Anything you say, Magpie. Just promise me one thing."

"What's that?"

"You won't rule out some future sex on the beach. And I'm *not* talking about the drink—you, me, in my sleeping bag."

Thanks for reading my book. If you enjoyed it, won't you please take a moment to leave me a review at your favorite online-retailer?

Connect on Social Sites

Twitter: https://twitter.com/LeslieKohler
Facebook: https://www.facebook.com/lesliekohler
Linkedin: www.linkedin.com/in/theseminarcopywriter
Website: http://www.lesliekohler.com

Discover other titles by Leslie Kohler

Sins of the Border
Papa's Shoes, A Short Story
Shadow of Darkness, A Short Story

ABOUT THE AUTHOR

Leslie Kohler grew up in the small town of Loomis in northern California. After graduating high school, she moved to southern California's Newport Beach area where she attended the University of California at Irvine. She achieved a bachelor's degree in psychology, and acquired teaching certificates in both general education and special education. After fourteen years living in Newport Beach, she relocated to Arizona.

Leslie continued to teach until she become a stay-at-home mom to care for her two small children. This afforded her the opportunity to pursue her love of writing. Her professional work can be found in magazines and newspapers, such as: Highlights for Children, Skipping Stones, Listen, Positive Teens, the Arizona Republic, and her short story, *Shadow of Darkness*, appeared in Sisters In Crime Desert Sleuths 2011 Anthology, *SoWest, So Wild*.

Leslie went on to publish her first murder mystery, *Sins of the Border*, much of which is based upon her life. Her second mystery, *Disposable Lives*, gives a unique glimpse of Leslie's experiences with the Travellers, a secret society of modern day gypsy con artists.

Leslie currently works as a special education teacher in Phoenix, Arizona. She is also working on the next installment for the *"Lives"* series, *Uninsured Lives*, in which she recounts her real life encounters with a serial contract murderer.